Brian!

The Things We Tell Ourselves

VICTORIA NAMKUNG

Thanks for your support + friendship!

**STANDARD
TIME PRESS**

STANDARD TIME PRESS

Copyright © 2015 by Victoria Namkung

ISBN-13: 9780996328005
ISBN-10: 0996328009
First edition: July 2015

Printed in the United States of America

This is a work of fiction. All of the characters, organizations and events portrayed in this novel are either products of the author's imagination or are used fictitiously.

Library of Congress Control Number: 2015907774
Standard Time Press, Los Angeles, CA

For my mom, who loves a good book

JUNE 2001

1

People always ask me why I'm single. My answer? Because the only men I meet are gay publicists and George Clooney. My job is what I suspect many girls would dream of doing. I interview movie stars, iconic musicians and the world's top fashion designers for *InStyle* magazine. I've shared a drink on a Beverly Hills patio with a bearded Brad Pitt, lunched with the effervescent Cameron Diaz, seen Angelina and Billy Bob's blood vials in person and been rendered speechless by a petite but still scarily intimidating Madonna. Surreal? Yes. Exactly what I thought I'd be doing when I decided to become a journalist? Not in a million years. I know I am lucky to have this job, especially since it's my first real non-waitressing one. I'm well aware of the fact that I'm not picking lettuce on the side of the road.

Because I work for a respectable publication, part of what I do is make my subjects sound witty, intelligent or otherwise interesting. I'm not digging for dirt or out to embarrass anyone, so I turn a blind eye when I see a beloved actress coming out of the bathroom with coke under her nose, or notice a certain star's husband kissing that star's assistant in the phone banks at the Beverly Hilton.

Despite the occasional goody bag or comped dinner at the Chateau Marmont, it isn't all glamour, especially when you're up until 4 a.m. transcribing the twenty-eight interviews you did at the Golden Globes until you're seeing double, and starving because you're working while everyone else is eating. I've been pushed out of the way by competing reporters, groped by a member of a certain celebrity's entourage and sometimes have to chase down my payments like a collection agency representative.

People often say, "Oh, you're like Carrie Bradshaw, with your little laptop!" I want to slap these people.

As a kid, I wanted to be a newscaster covering stories of war, crime and political scandals. My dad, a tenured anthropology professor at University of California, San Diego, said I could be the next Connie Chung and would set up mock segments for me to record with his giant VHS camera. He thought it would be good for me to have a role model I could relate to. It didn't register with me that Connie Chung was Asian, like me; she was just on TV reading the news, as far as I was concerned. But unlike her, I have a mum who is white and from London.

In high school, where I was deputy editor of the student-run newspaper, I thought print journalism was where it was at. I loved interviewing people and having a field pass to go wherever I pleased during high school football games. Anytime there was an issue I felt passionate about—the right to opt out of a cat dissection during senior-year anatomy class; the fact that a neighboring school was calling members of our baseball team the N-word at games with no repercussions—I could do a story on it and start a conversation. It gave me enough power. I didn't care about being Connie Chung; I just wanted a byline.

I took a summer school journalism class after my junior year and learned the five Ws—who, what, when, where and why—and how to quote sources and write headlines and deks. After graduating high school, where I somehow found time to study even though I spent every free hour I had at the beach, I majored in English at the University of California at Irvine, since it was the closest thing to journalism I could find. During my sophomore year, I started writing stories for the school paper. Anytime a piece of mine was published, I'd grab a few issues and put them in my bedroom closet. By senior year the stack was so massive I started storing the copies in my childhood bedroom so they didn't take over the diminutive apartment I shared with my best friend, Rebecca.

Growing up in Carlsbad, a suburb of San Diego, I was never a huge fan of celebrities. I didn't have a favorite New Kid on the Block or scream for a teen heartthrob. Those boys were too manufactured, and frankly a bit too feminine, for me. Even Donnie Wahlberg, the tough New Kid who wore cross earrings and a leather jacket, seemed like some music executive's idea of a bad boy. And who wants to be with a guy who can dance better than you? My crushes tended to be on local pro surfers or my friend Jill's thirty-eight-year-old stepdad (I fully blame Drew Barrymore and Tom Skerritt in *Poison Ivy* for this).

I never collected autographs or stood in line to meet a celebrity, and now my days and nights are filled with people whose entire livelihood revolves around The Famous. Everyone is on someone's payroll, telling an actress she looks great in a hideous dress or jockeying for a position in the entourage/glam squad/whatever you want to call it. In L.A., fame and celebrity are so inherently tied to the economy and culture that everyone I meet is connected to the industry somehow, whether as a prop master, set designer, florist, makeup artist or an on-set accountant.

When I took a job as a research assistant at *InStyle*'s West Coast office after graduating college last year, I assumed I'd be chained to a desk fact-checking fashion credits, but after a few weeks they decided to send me out as a red carpet reporter. There was no boot camp or even a meeting to prep me. They just said to figure it out—and put on some lipstick.

I had initially applied to work at *Time*, but their only available position was as an unpaid intern, and you had to be receiving college credit in order to work for free. The receptionist who was kind enough to tell me this over the phone suggested I try *InStyle* or *People*, which were in the same building on Wilshire Boulevard, near my apartment. As much as I preferred current events to beauty tips, I figured I had to start somewhere, and since I wasn't in New York City, where most publications are based, I just went for it and they said yes.

My first celebrity interview was a big one. I was assigned to cover the premiere for the film *Traffic* at the Academy of Motion Picture Arts and Sciences. It was a formal cocktail party and screening, and I must have changed outfits sixteen times before heading a few miles east on Wilshire to Beverly Hills, then paying ten dollars to park in a concrete garage overflowing with Escalades and black town cars. I'm not shy but would hardly call myself an extrovert, and I was totally intimidated by the idea of questioning A-listers when the biggest interview I had conducted thus far was with my university's chancellor for the school paper. I didn't understand the logistics of how it was going to actually happen (where would I stand? Who would introduce me?) and kept testing my tape recorder to make sure it worked so I wouldn't have to write everything down on a notepad. I wanted to be able to make eye contact.

I was the youngest person in attendance. Don Cheadle couldn't have been nicer and told me his big night was eclipsed by the fact that his daughter had started kindergarten that morning. A stunning Catherine Zeta-Jones, wearing a red, sparkly Paco Rabanne halter top, smiled warmly at me as she answered a few softball questions about the film and her personal style. Was it really going to be this easy?

But I was there to get an interview with Michael Douglas. Not only was he a star in the film, he was also the biggest guy in the room. The crowd around him waiting to give their congratulations was at least three people deep, so the odds weren't looking too good for a newbie reporter who was twenty-two but looked closer to nineteen.

In these situations, a publicist from the studio, or one they hire for the night, is assigned to you to facilitate the process (and also to make sure you don't ask anything inappropriate or offend anyone). However, this after-party was filled to the brim with agents, managers, studio executives and other celebrities—also known as 600 people more important than me—and I was left to fend for myself. I managed to find out which of the many men surrounding Michael Douglas was his personal publicist, got his attention and asked if I could get a quick quote for the magazine. "Good luck," he said with a smile, over the noisy crowd.

No one was going to get my quote for me, so I got a little creative. And by creative, I mean aggressive. I'm not sure what came over me, as I tend to be mellow compared to my colleagues, but I pushed my way through the crowd and grabbed Mr. Douglas' forearm. I can still picture him turning around, almost in slow motion. It was as if he'd read my mind. As if he knew this was my first big celebrity interview and that he should be nice to me so I wouldn't be traumatized for life. He greeted me like a long-lost family member and stepped away from his group for a brief interview. My mum, who is a huge fan of his, would have died to witness this. Even though she has a non-Hollywood career as a CPA, I can always count on her for the latest celebrity dating gossip or a comment on Renée Zellweger's haircut.

I asked Mr. Douglas three or four of the questions, and he answered completely candidly and with a great sense of humor. I knew my editor would be thrilled, and I was pretty pleased with myself. I thanked him profusely and walked away a bit stunned.

The magazine started sending me to press junkets, awards shows, personal appearances and store openings on Rodeo Drive. There were a few other reporters who worked red carpet stuff exclusively, but I started getting the majority of the assignments. I stopped going into the office altogether and became a permanent freelancer. The money was better and I didn't have to share an office or a computer with the two annoying interns from USC. I was kind of hooked on the bright lights, fancy dresses and free food. It was a rush.

■ ■ ■

Just like in life, there's a hierarchy when it comes to the red carpet. The big entertainment shows like *Access Hollywood* and *E! News* always get the first positions. If you're with *USA Today*, you might get the first spot in line for the print publications, but if you're with a women's magazine, most of the time you're halfway down the carpet, and it can be a challenge. Fortunately, when you work for *InStyle*, almost every celebrity wants to talk to you, and his or her publicist will help to make it happen. Sometimes a star is delivered right to me, like a Christmas present, while neighboring reporters are ignored, and then I get lots of side eyes and loud sighs.

So you have the line of journalists, plenty of publicists dressed in all-black and wearing headsets, lots of security, professional autograph seekers and screaming fans. It can be distracting, and if you look down for a second or answer a phone call you can miss an interview. I've seen fights break out among assistants and event planners and watched crashers be escorted out by beefy security men. I've been evacuated due to a bomb threat. It's pretty intense and ridiculous at the same time. You'd think we were doing something important and dangerous, like covering the front lines of a war.

Most of the male reporters are gay, jaded or super competitive, or a combination of the three. The business attracts an odd bunch of people, and now I am one of them. Yes, a cameraman or sound guy will occasionally flirt with me or even ask to hang out after a premiere, but it doesn't interest me. The last thing I'm thinking about when I'm working is dating. I just want to get my interviews done so I can attempt to meet up with my friends at Renee's, our local bar, before they leave to wake up early for their real jobs.

Six months ago I ended things with my high school sweetheart. We were together almost five years, surviving college life at schools that were two hours away from each other, and spending summers practically living together. John was the epitome of a nice guy, with a mop of brown hair, always-tanned skin and the build of someone who'd spent his life in the ocean, but we had grown apart in many ways and wanted different things in life. His plan was to move back home to Carlsbad, surf all day and bartend at his parents' restaurant in La Jolla, and I wanted more than that.

After a year of being a regular on the red carpet scene, I know pretty much everyone, which is weird since I still feel a bit green. TV-show producers nod in my direction, the head security guy who is at every premiere in town always gives me a hug, and I have befriended a few girls from rival publications. They're the only ones with whom I can complain about my so-called dream job. I feel guilty saying anything negative to my friends, who are toiling away in assistant positions at agencies or entry-level sales jobs, working double the hours I do for half the pay.

Tonight, one of my PR acquaintances has invited me to an evening called Australians in Film. The industry association for Australian filmmakers and performers in the U.S. is screening newly single Nicole Kidman's latest movie, and there will be an opportunity to have a one-on-one with her afterward. Only a handful of journalists were invited, and my editor approved the story in a heartbeat— "a huge get," she said—and since I've never met Nicole

Kidman before, it will be something new. Since she is incredibly tall, I decide to wear my highest heels. I learned this trick after an awkward interview with Geena Davis, who towered over me and made me feel like a five-year-old playing dress-up next to her regal mother.

I try to get someone to go with me as I was given a rare plus-one invite, but no one can get out of work in time for the four o'clock event. Since I'm still relatively new to L.A., friend options are limited. There's Elizabeth, a cool girl who works at *InStyle* and gets me my event credentials (a hideous laminated badge that you wear around your neck), my funny neighbor Anil, and a few girls who moved here after college. I would probably not hang out with them on weekends if they didn't live in my West L.A. neighborhood, and they probably feel the same. So once again I get all dolled up, drive across town and am the youngest and least famous person in the room.

I walk into the theater lobby not recognizing a soul, and head in to get an aisle seat toward the back. As usual, it starts more than half an hour late because we are waiting for the director or producer or whoever it is that enjoys making an audience of several hundred busy people just sit there. I overhear a married couple lamenting the fact that they have to reserve their son's bar mitzvah date two years in advance. On the plus side, there are no movie trailers at these industry screenings, just a quick introduction by a rotund studio executive who praises Nicole, the filmmakers and financiers. Clapping. Clapping. More clapping. Finally the lights go down.

■ ■ ■

Immediately after the film, which is hauntingly good, I hit the lobby bar as at least 300 industry types pour out of the theater. The petite blonde Australian publicist sees me and motions for me to wait right where I am. *Okay*, I nod back. One thing I quickly learned doing this type of work is to make the most of free food and drink so that even if the interview is a bust or I am exhausted from standing around for hours, I will have had some success, even if it comes in the form of four stuffed mushrooms that I inhale within two minutes.

Contrary to my wishes and what seems fair, the magazine provides me no wardrobe budget ("You're not on camera," the assignment editor explained), so I tend to wear the same three black dresses over and over and switch up the accessories. I always feel pressure to look good since I represent a magazine that's associated with fashion. This is how I justified buying a pair of half-off Yves Saint Laurent heels after the holidays.

"Can I get a Ketel One and soda?" I ask the six-foot-tall, bronze bartender, who is clearly an actor because he is simply too gorgeous to be working an event for ten bucks an hour. This guy, *Camden*, he says, is better looking than the leading man in the film I just saw. That's the thing about L.A. No one is really just a bartender or waitress or Pilates teacher. Everyone's an aspiring filmmaker, screenwriter, actor or model, and they're all here to seek their fortune like it's 1849 and gold is running through the streets.

Go to any coffee shop at two in the afternoon and it will be completely packed. Listen closely and you'll hear about a busted development deal at FOX, an improv troupe that might get a pilot on Comedy Central, or how someone is "this close" to getting their SAG card. Whenever my parents visit me, they often ask if anyone actually works in L.A. or if they just talk about working. They worry that I'm not getting any quality intellectual conversations in.

In Carlsbad, there are surf-industry executives who could be mistaken for beach bums but are actually running global brands. If you meet one, he might talk about the day's waves or a new café that serves the best cornflake pancakes before anything business-related comes up. It's all very chill and down-to-earth. But when you meet someone new in the City of Angels, they immediately ask you what you do for a living. Not because they want to know more about what makes you tick, but because they want to know how you might be able to help them.

When I say I'm a writer, everyone immediately asks, "Features or television?" And as soon as they realize I can do nothing for their shitty screenplay or spec script, their eyes start darting off in directions past my head, and then they just walk away, as if I'd told an offensive joke and deserve to be shunned.

Model-handsome Camden puts the drink on the bar and flashes me an incredible smile that seems to house many more teeth than a regular human's. This guy is so attractive it is making me uncomfortable, so I thank him, pull out my BlackBerry, find a dollar and put it in the tip jar. As I'm squeezing a lime into my drink, a man approaches me from the other side of the room with a glass of white wine in his hand.

"Hi," he says, offering a warm smile.

I detect an Australian accent from just the one syllable. He has a regular number of teeth, from what I can tell. I don't recognize him as an agent or a manager so I just raise my eyebrows a bit, waiting for him to say something else.

"I saw you walk in the door and I thought, I have to meet her," he says. "Who *are* you?"

"Just a girl having a drink," I reply a bit coldly. I have one eye out for the publicist so I can do my big interview, pick up something for dinner and get home in time to watch *Six Feet Under*. I also notice that nobody is eating the miniature burgers, mac and cheese and whatever else is trendy in L.A. this month being passed around on silver trays.

"I'm Simon," he says, putting his hand out and letting it linger a bit too long as I grab it.

"Georgina."

He looks down at his shoes—nice, Italian, leather—as if he's deciding whether or not to continue trying to engage me. I'm not in the mood for networking or making new friends as I'm in total work mode and waiting for Nicole Kidman, who is across the room, talking to her assistant. She is easily one of the most beautiful women I have ever seen in person. Being in a room with her porcelain skin and giraffe-like neck is enough to make anyone feel like a hideous troll.

Simon looks considerably older than me, and pretty average in terms of height and build. He's nice-looking but isn't my type. I'm used to beach boys and guys who use a skateboard as their primary mode of transportation. Then again, I haven't been dating much of anybody these days as I never say no to work.

Simon says he's a foreign correspondent for an Australian network and is based in L.A. for now. "Once in a while I do stuff like this, but more often it's politics and national stories," he says, setting his wineglass on the bar. "I used to cover the White House, actually, before moving to Los Angeles."

"Really?" I ask, perking up.

"Yes, but that must seem boring compared to all this."

He tells me he also writes a popular column for the *Sydney Morning Herald*, where he interviews politico types. He has the kind of job I dream about. But I keep my cool admirably, acting as though I meet people in his line of work on a regular basis. All of a sudden I am finding Simon far more interesting—and attractive—than when he first appeared.

"I freelance for *InStyle*," I tell him, embarrassed. "I'm supposed to talk to Nicole Kidman, but they asked me to wait here for a bit."

"She just left," he says, smiling.

"Shit. Are you serious?"

"I have to do a quick thing, but please don't leave," he says, motioning to a cameraman I saw chain-smoking out front earlier. "There's so much more to talk about."

Now that I have nothing better to do, I drink my drink, check email and watch my new acquaintance tape an intro to his story on this event in front of the Australians in Film banner. He glances over to make sure I'm still there and gives me the sign to hang on for a minute. I don't know why, but I do. When the red light goes on, he's all energy and wide eyes and a bit cheesy, but this interlude gives me a moment to scan him. His thick auburn hair already has some flecks of gray, and he's wearing a French-cuff shirt with knotted navy cuff links, not something you see much of in a city where people have dressy and casual versions of flip-flops.

After finishing the intro, he parts ways with his cameraman and returns to the makeshift bar where I'm still standing. "Since you won't be meeting with Nicole, what do you say we go next door and share a bottle of wine instead?" he asks, placing his hand on top of mine, which gives me a bit of a jolt as I haven't been touched by a man in a few months. "We can talk shop. And it's really too early to go home, isn't it?"

"Nicole?" I raise my eyebrows. "You're on a first-name basis?"

"Well, yes," he says matter-of-factly.

Surprised by his unwavering confidence and intrigued by the invitation, I say okay. I don't love meeting new people and despise small talk since I have to do so much of it as a reporter, but when else am I going to have a chance to pick the brain of a former White House correspondent? Simon must be at least fifteen years older than me. His blue-green eyes are kind. He focuses intently on everything I say, as if I'm spouting genius-level gems of wisdom. Usually I wouldn't respond to being brazenly hit on, especially at work, but there's something charming about him. Something I immediately like. This is a first for me, like everything I've been doing in L.A. this last year.

Simon reaches across my body and puts a five-dollar bill in the tip jar, perhaps showing off for me or asserting his dominance over gorgeous Camden, and is in my personal space for the first time this evening.

"What are you wearing?" he asks. "You smell amazing."

"It's gardenia. My friend Emily makes perfume oils."

"Lovely."

"I have to eat something or I won't be able to drive home," I say as we walk to the neighboring hotel lobby. The jacaranda trees are in full bloom, turning the wide boulevard into a sea of lavender.

"Their moules-frites are amazing," he says.

We're led to a wooden two-top inside the hotel's French brasserie, where Simon insists I sit on the more comfortable striped banquette. "So, what type of wine do you like?" he asks, fingering the list as my eyes scan the room for anyone I could possibly know. Seeing as I have about five friends in all Los Angeles, I'm guessing it won't be an issue.

"Anything's fine," I say. "Something white?" The truth is, I know nothing about wine and don't plan to have more than a glass. I am feeling self-conscious because

Simon looks like my uncle, in his traditional blue blazer and brown leather loafers.

The waiter, whose impressive head of hair is fashioned into a slick pompadour, seems preoccupied and asks us twice if we want flat, sparkling or "L.A.'s finest." Simon picks a bottle of Chardonnay I have never heard of. "Actor, right?" I ask Simon after the pompadour disappears again. It's common to get bad service at trendy restaurants because the servers are mainly on the job for the flexibility of schedule or the chance to be discovered by an industry heavyweight. "I waitressed my way through school, and we took our jobs pretty seriously. I think most of the staff in this city would rather be at an audition."

"Maybe he can try acting like a waiter if he puts his mind to it," Simon says wryly, and I laugh.

"My favorite game to play is Weather Girl or Porn Star," I tell him. "I send my best friend headshots and she has to guess, but she always gets them wrong."

"That's very funny."

"L.A. is strange like that."

"It can be wonderful as well," he says. "I like how you never know where the day will take you."

"Have you been to that event before?"

"No I haven't, actually. I was there as a favor to an old Aussie pal. I hate doing fluff."

"That fluff is paying my rent," I reply a bit defensively.

He smiles. "I didn't mean anything by that. We all do what we have to do. If this is your first gig, it's certainly not a bad place to start."

"Trust me, it wasn't my dream job, but it can be fun sometimes."

"Would it be inappropriate if I asked you how old you were?"

"Yes, it would," I say, "and I'm twenty-two."

"You carry yourself with a maturity that belies your years. That's meant to be a compliment, by the way."

"How long have you lived here?" I ask. "In the States, I mean."

"Nearly a decade. I was first sent to Washington to head up our bureau there. I miss it a bit, but you can't beat the lifestyle here. It's actually very similar to Sydney. I live in the Palisades."

At this point I figure he is straight-up lying to me. No journalists, Australian or otherwise, live in fancy Pacific Palisades. He is trying to impress me or get me into bed, or both.

"And where are you from, Georgina?" he asks as the wine is poured.

"San Diego originally, and then I went to college in Orange County, but I have been living in West L.A. for about a year. I started as a research assistant at the magazine but am now on my own," I explain.

"But how does a young woman like yourself make enough money to live in Los Angeles? It's not exactly affordable."

"I get three hundred dollars a night," I explain, unsure of why I am telling a virtual stranger about my finances. "More for awards shows."

"Like a call girl," he says with a laugh. "Well, you'd make loads more than that."

"One of my neighbors thought I was one," I say, lightening up with the first glass of wine.

"How do you know?"

"I usually leave the house at night and don't come back for hours, and I'm always dressed up when she sees me in the hallway. She finally saw my byline one day and knocked on my door, with the magazine, and said she was so relieved that I was not a 'woman of the night.' I was actually flattered. I've been told the call girls in this town are as beautiful as the actresses."

"If you want to see one, just go to the bar at the Peninsula or Regent Beverly Wilshire on any given night," he says with a devilish smile. "Not that I would know."

"Of course not," I say, smiling, tucking my hair behind my ear. I'm holding my phone in my other hand, in case my editor calls to find out what's going on with Nicole Kidman. We often communicate right before and after an event, particularly if they are on deadline in New York. I dread explaining that there was no way I could get the interview. They have to pay me regardless of how many interviews I get or don't get, but this is the first time in at least fifty events that I will come back with nothing. I feel like a bit of a failure even though I know it isn't my fault.

We tell each other work stories, he more so than I, and he makes me laugh. "Your smile is what made me want to talk to you," he says, though considering the film was depressing as hell, I'm not sure when he had the chance to see me smiling. "I had to meet you afterwards. I can't think of the last time I crossed a room for someone. I assumed you were someone's date, but then I noticed you were on your own after the film."

"I'm on my own a lot at these things," I say as I pick at my mâche salad. "I usually try to avoid talking to anyone I'm not interviewing. Pushy agents and creepy managers aren't really my thing."

"So what does interest you?" he asks, lowering his voice an octave.

"Dating hasn't been a top priority for me lately because I work a lot."

"Well, I imagine you have no problems getting them. Dates, I mean," he says, smiling and holding eye contact. I can tell he is trying to suss out my situation. "Surely some of the male stars come on to you."

"Once in a while, but I have no interest in being the tenth girl some actor takes home that week," I say. "I have a work friend at *People* who got way too chummy with a group of actors from these WB shows. He started partying really hard and got caught up in the lifestyle and is now at Passages Malibu. He emailed a group of us and said 'Never let them become your friends.' I wrote that on a Post-It note and put it on my desk."

"Journalistic integrity is important, of course, but how could you blame anyone for wanting to get to know you better?" Simon leans in a bit. "I for one wouldn't mind knowing everything about you."

"There's nothing that exciting to share," I say, noticing Simon staring at my mouth as I speak.

"I don't believe that for a second. Go on. Tell me everything. What do you do for fun when you're not working?"

"I hang out with friends in Santa Monica when I can, but I work nights and they work days, so it can be a challenge."

"You're working a glamorous graveyard shift."

"Kind of." I laugh. "I rarely work Sundays, so I like going to the Getty Center."

"That isn't far from my house," he says with a big smile, as though he's plotting something.

"I love the view," I quickly continue. "Sometimes I don't even go in the museum—I just like sitting in the courtyard, being surrounded by the architecture. I take a book with me."

"I'd love to go with you sometime."

"We'll see," I tease. "Let's get through this meal first."

"Tell me something else."

"I go to matinees by myself once or twice a week, since I can. Do you notice how it's impossible to just turn up and try to see a movie in L.A. unless it's at an off time?"

"That's so true, isn't it? I try to get my hands on screeners so I can avoid the theaters."

"The first few times I went, I thought it was odd how everyone stayed to watch the entire end credits, clapping for certain people and not for others. I guess it's exciting to see your friend's name on the screen. Yet we don't clap for ER doctors or scientists, do we?"

"Well, that's Hollywood for you. Egos are everywhere."

"And what is with all the 'For Your Consideration' billboards and ads?" I continue, referring to the constant award campaigns, paid for by television shows and films, that make appeals to local voting Academy members. "It's like this city's pastime is congratulating itself."

"You're very funny." He winks at me.

"But there are things I love about living here."

"Such as?"

"You can get anything you want very easily. There are Mexican kosher restaurants and Persian ice cream shops. Strip clubs sit next to private schools. The options for things like good sushi and music venues are overwhelmingly good. And each neighborhood is so unusual. Where else would you find a Thai Town and Byzantine-Latino Quarter in the same city? I love driving down Pico Boulevard, from Santa Monica to Downtown, because you pass what feels like a hundred different countries. L.A. is so different from where I grew up."

"You're quite fascinating," he says.

I'm flattered but also a bit skeptical, since it could all be a big bag of bullshit. We have an easy banter, though, with no awkward silences. After the second glass of buttery Chardonnay and more chitchat, Simon's intentions become clearer.

"And you're gorgeous, you know," he says.

That is not something I hear every day. Yes, I think I am attractive, and even pretty on good days, but *gorgeous* is a word that only my mum seems to use about me. Living in Los Angeles, it's hard to feel that great about yourself when *Playboy* Playmates, models and actresses roam freely at the same parties, restaurants and bars as you do. My Pilates instructor is a Lakers Girl. I hear women who are size two (next year it will be zeroes, followed by double zeroes) complain about their bodies on a daily basis. It feels like a part-time job to not fall into a vicious cycle of self-loathing, extreme dieting and permanent body dysmorphia.

I love visiting Rebecca, my best friend, in San Francisco because the second I step off the plane in the Southwest Airlines terminal I instantly feel about three times more attractive. It isn't that Bay Area girls aren't beautiful, many of them are, but they aren't as concerned with their appearance as they are in L.A. It's easier to meet a female tech entrepreneur in San Francisco than a *Maxim* model, whereas here it's the opposite. Rebecca is beautiful, with icy blue eyes and naturally highlighted blonde hair that women in L.A. pay hundreds of dollars every eight weeks to try to replicate.

"That's very sweet, Simon, thank you," I say, looking at my dinner napkin and gripping my phone tightly as the back of my neck begins to perspire. "But when are we going to address *that*?"

A few moments ago I'd noticed a wedding band while Simon was gesturing. I'm not that surprised. He's older, worldly, sophisticated and accomplished. I remind myself that I am out in the wild, not in college, where everyone you interact with is at a similar station in life. When you're twenty-two and looking to date guys around your age, watching out for rings just isn't in your wheelhouse.

"Ah, yes," he says, looking at his band. "I was trying to figure out the best way to bring that up."

"I'm all ears," I say, realizing that my willingness to entertain whatever story he's about to tell already makes me partially complicit in his deceit. After all, if I were outraged, I would have already left the table.

"I was married about nineteen years ago, in Sydney." I calculate that I was three years old when he took his vows. Then I tell myself to push that image aside. He continues. "We've been living abroad almost all of that time and have two children, ages ten and six. Things haven't been good for many years. I was patient, especially when the children were much younger, always assuming the relationship would be better as they grew up. But things are actually worse. I'm a bit at a loss as to what to do."

"What about divorce?"

"I don't think I could."

"Are you religious?"

"God, no." He laughs. "But our families are quite intertwined, and I don't want to put the children through it—at least not when they are this young."

"Well, some might say that happily divorced parents are better than ones who stay together unhappily."

"That's the thing," he says. "We don't argue. We're like best friends, or more like brother and sister, I suppose. We get on well, but there is zero passion. We haven't had sex in over a year. I've tried everything I can think of, but

I believe that ship has sailed and it's not coming back for me."

"I'm sorry to hear that," I say, legitimately stunned, unable to imagine why a woman would withhold like that unless it was for medical reasons or out of pure repulsion. "So because of this, you go around town taking girls out for moules-frites?"

"No, darling. I have never done anything like this. I saw you and simply had to meet you. I didn't have a plan beyond saying hello."

I don't know if I can believe him.

"Let's change the subject," he says, pouring the rest of the wine. "Georgina's an unusual name for an American girl."

"It is. My mother is from London originally," I explain. "She met my dad as a student at Cal and never went back."

"Cal?"

"Berkeley."

"Ah, I see."

"So I'm Korean and English."

"That boring old combo?"

We laugh and I finish my wine, feeling careless and flirtatious for the first time in I don't know how long.

Simon moves closer toward me across the table and says, "I realize this is incredibly forward, but I simply have to make love to you."

It is simultaneously the most inappropriate and the most exciting statement I have ever heard. I always hated the phrase *make love*, especially when it is clear that any encounter with Simon tonight would be far from love. I don't say anything but look him right in the eye. Our waiter is heading toward us but decides to check on the neighboring table after noticing that we are engaged in some sort of sexualized staring contest. I feel butterflies in my stomach, like when I was in high school and a guy I liked would smile at me and I would dine on that for a week. I'm aware of my rapidly increasing heartbeat and fidget in my seat. The restaurant feels ten degrees warmer.

I say nothing; I just hold his gaze, forming the earliest stage of a smile, and wonder what would happen if I said yes. I want to say yes. Simon gets up from the table and disappears for a solid five minutes. I look out the window and realize that I'm more than buzzed and it's still light outside.

When Simon returns he finishes his final glass of wine in a large gulp, then crosses to my side of the table, sitting next to me on the banquette. "I've just booked a room upstairs, and I do hope you'll join me," he says, placing his hand on my thigh, which makes me jump a bit.

"What do you mean?" I ask, genuinely surprised. I knew he wanted to sleep with me, but I didn't realize he meant right this second, here in this hotel.

"I was debating staying over anyway because I've got an early meeting at CNN across the street tomorrow, and you just gave me all the more reason to want to stay." He says this as if it's a normal way of spending a second hour with someone you just met.

"I don't know. I mean, my car is next door, and"—
I'm lying now—"I'm supposed to meet a friend." Then I
wonder aloud, "Can you really check into a hotel without
luggage? Doesn't that look incredibly odd?"

"I think we can manage. We've both been drinking,
so it's not like we can drive home right now, and traffic is
awful at this time," he says, kissing me on the cheek, and
I can't fight him on that point. "It would take at least an
hour to get back to the Westside. Let's just go upstairs. We
can watch a movie while we sober up."

Even at twenty-two, I know this is a lie. Every first
make-out session I've had from age twelve until now started with "watching a movie." I have slept with one man in
my entire life and am desperately curious about being with
someone else, but no opportunities have really presented
themselves, thanks to my crazy schedule of working nights
and my current lack of enthusiasm for out-of-work ac-
tors/musicians/screenwriters/fill-in-the-blank. I know it's
wrong, but my gut is telling me to go upstairs, to do something dangerous for once, so I smile. There's something
about him and I am already enthralled by whatever it is.

"Okay," I say.

Simon takes my hand and rubs his thumb across the
top of mine. I feel more sexual excitement from this small
gesture than I have in months. It's all so unexpected and
spontaneous and I feel increasingly nervous as I realize I
am really doing this. Simon gives our waiter the international sign for the check, looking in his eagerness like a kid
waiting to open his presents on Christmas morning.

■ ■ ■

It's 7:30 in the evening on a Wednesday, and the only time I have ever been in a hotel with a man. We walk down a long hallway with Simon's hand on the small of my back, directing me to the bank of elevators where a German family with three cameras among them is already waiting. Do they think we are a couple? Do they know we met only ninety minutes ago?

L.A. is filled with young women dating older men, and it usually creeps me out. Is that how we look to everyone right now? But it's not like he's fifty, so I tell myself to stop worrying about it. I often complain to Rebecca that I don't relate to guys our age anymore, but I certainly never thought about sleeping with an older, married man. Simon presses the number twelve and holds my hand, which feels small inside his.

The second we get into the sparsely decorated, modern room and the door closes behind us, he kisses me. It is electric. He knows what he's doing. It's the right tongue-to-lip ratio and I can feel every part of my body coming alive, tiptoeing out of hibernation. He feels familiar and foreign at the same time, and I simultaneously can't believe I am doing this while feeling proud of myself for it.

I know he wants it badly, which gets me even more excited. I feel his erection pressing on my thigh while we kiss. By some miracle I have on my best black lace Chantelle bra.

"How old are you?" I ask him between kisses, an attempt to give myself a moment to think about what is happening before it's too late.

"Forty-two," he says, his face now slightly flushed but smiling. "Do I look it?"

"No," I lie.

This is going to be my first one-night stand and the only time I have ever gone anywhere with a total stranger. Girls my age do this kind of thing all the time, don't they? Right as I'm justifying the behavior in my mind, it occurs to me that no one in the world knows I'm here with him. I don't know Simon's last name and he doesn't know mine. We have no friends in common except maybe the PR gal from the event, and she didn't see us leave together. But there is something about him that I immediately trust, for no reason, really.

It feels so good. Thanks to the cocktail at the screening, the wine and no real dinner (unless you count lettuce and the stuffed mushrooms), I am much more uninhibited than usual. Obviously, since I've ended up in a fancy hotel room with a man nearly twice my age.

"Your skin is incredible," he says as he begins kissing my neck and collarbone. He has soft hands and prickly stubble on his face. I'm the right amount of lightheaded. For the first time in my life I actually feel the blood coursing through my body. Is that even possible, or is it the nerve endings he's awakening? I'm immediately wet but still enjoying the foreplay, something I haven't had much of in years.

Toward the end of our relationship, John and I had soulless quickies that felt more like stress release than sex.

I remember once asking John to "just fuck me like you don't know me." He was so disturbed that I would say something so vulgar that he refused to sleep with me for a few weeks. I didn't know why I said it at the time. I think I was so checked out from the relationship that I just wanted to feel something, anything, different.

Simon sits on the buttery leather-covered bench at the edge of the bed while I remain standing. He turns me around and unzips my knee-length dress, which could pass for Dolce & Gabbana in the right lighting, though I suspect it's of no importance to him. What matters is that he's about to see a twenty-two-year-old get naked for him. Under regular circumstances I would never stand in my bra and thong in a fully lit room in front of a man, but right now I don't care. From the look on his face, I might as well be a Victoria's Secret model. I feel freedom in knowing I'm probably never going to see him again. I'm now just in it for me.

It will be a great story for Rebecca, who's dumbfounded by the fact that I've been celibate for six months in Los Angeles, save for a couple drunken kisses at bars with boys who didn't make enough of an impression to go further. She is always reminding me that this is the time when I should be going crazy, but I'm not someone who goes crazy. I'm the designated driver. I pay all my bills a week before their due date. My apartment is always clean. I make my Christmas cards by hand and never forget a birthday.

I reach for my left heel to take it off, and Simon stops me. "Leave them on," he says.

"If you say so," I say with a soft smile. "Do you have a thing for heels, Simon?" I have never met anyone with a legitimate fetish, so I'm almost hopeful he will say yes.

"I have a thing for *you*," he says, his hands on my waist. "Can't you tell?"

I turn to face him and climb on his lap. He looks at me like he's dying of thirst and I'm in possession of the only Evian on the planet. I feel like I could ask him for anything in this moment and he would say yes. I study his face for a few seconds. His eyes are light, with flecks of brown. He has a rounded nose, square jaw and straight teeth.

He devours my décolletage before delicately removing my bra, looking quite pleased with what he sees. "What on earth did I do right to deserve this?" he asks, gently taking my left breast into his mouth.

After thirty seconds he starts unbuckling his belt, and I move over to the head of the bed, which is dressed with plush sateen Frette linens. I watch as he grabs a condom from his wallet, wondering why a forty-two-year-old foreign correspondent is carrying Trojans around like a teenager. I like the idea that I am about to have sex with a man who has interviewed our president. The biggest person I interviewed this week was Damon Wayans.

The sex is intense but over in a couple of minutes. Simon immediately apologizes, wearing a silly grin. I'm not upset. If what he told me earlier is true— that he hasn't had sex for a year—it's more than understandable. I'm in a similar boat but don't say so. We lie on the fluffy white king-size bed; I'm staring at the ceiling, and he's staring at me. Bryan Ferry's cover of "Sweet and Lovely" is playing out of the hotel CD player that must have been on the whole time.

"I have never done anything like this," I say, a bit shocked with what has transpired over the last three hours.

"You don't have to make excuses," he says, still winded. "Trust me, there are no judgments on my end."

Apparently he doesn't believe me, but I don't care if he does. I get up, put a bathrobe on and take a pack of Marlboro Lights from my bag. I'm stepping out onto the narrow terrace, which faces the lights of Beverly Hills, when he comes up behind me.

"Those things will kill you, sweetie," he says, putting the pack down on the table.

I'm not really a smoker, but I've taken to the habit when I'm home alone after an event, which seems to be most evenings. We go back to the bed and I wonder how long I should stay here before I can go without being rude. Simon asks me more questions about my life, where I live, if I'm seeing anyone and what I want to do after the red carpet. I tell him I would love to be a foreign correspondent like he is, living abroad and interviewing people who do more important things than make movies.

"Why not start now?" he asks.

"I just finished university last year, and I think it would kill my parents if I moved too far away."

Simon looks confused. "But they aren't financially supporting you anymore, right?"

"No, but they paid for most of my college, and I'm their only child."

"Sweetie, I think you should do what you want. Life is too short."

I silently wonder why he hasn't taken his own advice when it comes to his marriage.

■ ■ ■

My parents can be overprotective at times, always asking if I have enough cash and complaining loudly anytime I have to work an event that goes later than ten o'clock. I always tell them not to worry. My habitat is the velvet ropes of the red carpet, not the yellow caution tape of a murder scene.

I suppose I can't blame them entirely. When I was a senior in high school, my three best friends had a horrible car accident. Driving on the Pacific Coast Highway, all of them wearing seat belts and probably listening to Nirvana, they were hit head-on by a drunk driver on the way to school and died instantly in a fire. It just so happened that I decided to get a ride with someone else that day. Simple as that. The accident devastated the whole community and was all over the news for a week. I lost my little piece of the world in a fleeting moment. They lost everything. From that day on, no matter whom I ran into, well-meaning people asked how I was holding up, their eyes turned down and their foreheads creased. They pitied me. An emergency grief counselor made herself available to me. Friends and family checked up on me endlessly, and I hated it.

The funeral was worse than the day it happened because I wasn't in shock anymore and could process the severity and senselessness of it all. There were so many people there that a full-blown PA system had to be installed for the hundreds of people who couldn't fit into the church. Reporters tried to get interviews with me, and people who'd never even met my lifelong friends were wailing as though they had lost their own son or daughter. I was heartbroken and confused and guilty that I survived because I decided to get in my friend Emily's car instead of riding with Brenda, Ryan and Christina. I was one of the girls who lived, who got to hug her parents tight, attend prom a few months later and go off to college. The accident was the end of an idyllic childhood. I now knew that people died for no good reason.

■ ■ ■

As Simon tells me how he originally wanted to have a political career instead of just covering politics, I realize that even people with cool-seeming jobs are sometimes settling for something else. I hadn't envisioned my life revolving around getting a funny quote from Mel Gibson or having to find out what Sandra Bullock was wearing to her movie premiere. In college I was a serious student, preferring to read academic journals instead of gossip magazines, and talking Marxist theory with professors. I wrote op-ed pieces against Nike's use of sweatshops in Asia and racist portrayals in cinema.

My professors encouraged me to pursue academia and eventually teach at a university, but I felt a pull toward journalism, where I thought I could still make a difference even if I wasn't holding a picket sign. John, however, was vocal in wanting me to move back to San Diego—so I could do what, I have no idea.

During the school week, I was all about maintaining my 3.89 GPA, sneaking into film-studies classes so I could watch *Breathless* and *Belle de Jour*, and learning everything I could about creative writing and journalism. On weekends I was like any other normal college student—I just didn't wear hemp necklaces or chug beer. I couldn't wait to finish school and move on to a more glamorous and exciting life in the big city, where you could find anything and everything you ever wanted and things you didn't even know you wanted.

■ ■ ■

Simon tells me a bit about being a foreign correspondent in New York and Washington, then moving into lighter fare in L.A. after switching networks. He wrote a book on Australian politics a few years ago that did quite well. I dream of writing a book one day, but I'm still too young. There's serious backlash at the moment against twenty-somethings writing their memoirs, and what would I have to say, anyway?

He takes a quick work call, and when he returns to bed he starts kissing me. I'm impressed that he's up for it again so soon and understand I won't be leaving just yet. Simon spends a generous amount of time exploring every inch of my body. Just seeing the top of his head between my legs is bringing me to the brink of an orgasm. It all feels so good, but much of the pleasure I'm experiencing is cerebral. This whole scenario is just plain naughty, any way you slice it. And much to my surprise, I'm completely into it. In one night, I've managed to go from the good girl to the woman who is sleeping with a married man in a random hotel room.

His confidence and experience are what excite me most. The accent creates its own form of arousal. He tells me what he likes, what he wants, what he wants to do to me. He can't seem to get enough. We have sex in every position that I am aware of, almost like we're in a race to try them all. As Simon lights up every erogenous zone on my body, I think about how natural it feels to be with him.

Before John, I was only with boys, like David, who transferred to our school in eighth grade. He asked me to "go" with him one Friday afternoon while we were standing by our row of blue lockers. I was stunned, as I had no idea he even liked me, and said "okay" while staring down at my Converse sneakers. David was a year older and already six foot two at age fourteen. His deep blue eyes were framed with thick brown lashes, and his smile always looked mischievous. A star basketball player, he was already being recruited by local private high schools.

Since both of my parents worked and I was often left to fend for myself until dinnertime, David would walk me home after school, and we would spend the next two hours making out like it was the only thing on earth that truly mattered. Our hormones were raging, but David never wanted to go further than kissing, due to his strict Christian upbringing and polite manners. After months of heavy-duty make-out fests with lots of rubbing and clothed grinding, where he'd sometimes tell me afterward that he worried I was going to hell since I hadn't accepted Jesus as my savior, I wanted more. I'm not sure I even knew what more really meant, but I was willing to find out. David looked at me like I was crazy for suggesting it. In that moment, at age 13, I realized I was being seen as the aggressor and backed off immediately. I got his message, that it *wasn't* okay, loud and clear. I never tried to push beyond kissing after that. Things began to fizzle as we finished the school year and David went off to a fancy prep school with a state-ranked basketball team while I went to our local public high school.

A couple years later, I heard that David got a girl from a rival high school pregnant while at Christian summer sleepaway camp. One of his friends told me that the girl looked a bit like me "but had no tits," which was supposed to make me feel better.

Already I can tell that Simon is the type of man who wouldn't say no to any sexual want I may have. He would never deny himself pleasure, and he's clearly getting off on making sure I'm more than satisfied. When the second round is over, he looks completely spent and absolutely thrilled with himself. "I have to get in better shape," he says, breathless and patting his stomach, which is fairly flat but certainly not ripped.

At 10:30 I say I should go. There's no way I'm spending the night. I have nothing with me, my car's still in the Grant Parking lot next door, undoubtedly racking up a small fortune, and we have nothing else to talk about. He doesn't fight me about leaving but asks, "When can I see you again?" I'm getting dressed and fixing my hair, which now looks like I have been doing exactly what I have been doing. "I want to take you to a proper dinner."

"Seriously?"

"If you think I'd leave you alone after tonight, you're crazy."

I'd assumed this was a one-night deal, having read so many women's magazines that say men love the chase, but tell him I'll email him if he likes. I'm not quite sure what to make of all this, or if I want him having my phone number. It's not like I can introduce him to my friends or family down the line. We're not going to hit the Viper Room at midnight on a Monday to check out a new band. He wouldn't think it's fun to sit in the bustling courtyard at Renee's and drink vodka sodas all night while girls teeter around in their heels, shouting "Woooo!"

I'm not comfortable with the age difference outside this hotel room, so where could it possibly go? I have to force myself not to think about the fact that he was already twenty years old when I was born.

He hands me his card, and there it is: Simon Grant. He works in Century City and has a 310 number like I do. He kisses me goodbye, and I walk out of the room and down the long hallway as if I've done it a million times.

2

I'm working more and more evenings, which makes it hard to have a social life of any kind, let alone a dating one. I was told that summers are slower but I'm working nearly every night, sometimes hitting one event after another. I think about emailing Simon after coming home late from a black-tie dinner two days after our rendezvous, but I decide against it. Anytime I catch myself thinking about it, thinking about him, I get the same feeling. It's like those couple seconds on a roller coaster right as it's about to go down and your stomach drops. The scenes from that night replay crystal clear in my head in the oddest of places: on a reporter-filled shuttle bus heading to an awards show, during my dental checkup, selecting fruit at Trader Joe's. Anytime I think of him, I immediately feel alive.

Finally, when I can't contain the desire any longer, I open my white iBook and type a one-line email to him.

From: Georgina Park
To: Simon Grant
Date: June 26, 2001 at 11:25 PM
Subject: Hi

Hi. Last week was a surprise, wasn't it?

From: Simon Grant
To: Georgina Park
Date: June 26, 2001 at 11:31 PM
Subject: Re: Hi

I've been trying to find you. I realised after the other night that I didn't even have your bloody last name. I even went to a newsstand to try to find it in your magazine. Now I have your name and your email, but I need more than that. I can't stop thinking about you.
☺ ☺ ☺

I picture him at home on his laptop, probably working late researching a story, his eyes eager to read the next message. I can't invite him over now. It's nearly midnight, and I have to get up early to pick up press credentials for the MTV

Movie Awards. I don't want to initiate our next meeting, so I just write back.

> *From: Georgina Park*
> *To: Simon Grant*
> *Date: June 26, 2001 at 11:45 PM*
> *Subject: Re: re: Hi*
>
> > *I think about you, too.*

> *From: Simon Grant*
> *To: Georgina Park*
> *Date: June 26, 2001 at 11:48 PM*
> *Subject: Re: re: re: Hi*
>
> > *I know a bloke at Time Inc. and asked him if he knew any of the InStyle reporters. I tried describing you. He asked me what celebrity you look like, but I couldn't come up with anything. As my efforts were proving futile, I gave up. I didn't want him finding you and then wanting you for himself.*

Famous Asian women run through my head: Lucy Liu, Michelle Yeoh, Tia Carrere. Yeah, I look like none of them. While I can pass for Asian, I have atypical features, like an angular nose, inherited from my mother's side, and big, light brown eyes framed by the coveted double-fold crease, the most popular cosmetic procedure in South Korea and other parts of East Asia. As a young girl I was called "exotic" or "Eurasian." I've had more than one mixed-race couple carefully look me over to see what *their* kids might look like.

I'm often asked the tactless "What *are* you?" from Vietnamese nail salon workers and drunken white guys in bars. When I say Korean and English, it just opens the door for more questions. If I'm really not in the mood or it's coming from an offensive place, I say, "I don't know, I was adopted." That ends the conversation immediately.

■ ■ ■

Simon begins instant-messaging me on AOL the next day. Anytime I'm online it seems he is, too. I wonder when he actually gets his work done. I imagine him in some gleaming high-rise in Century City with valet parking, a state-of-the-art gym and an in-house five-star restaurant, while I'm in my one-bedroom in West L.A., which gets very little natural light—a crime in California, where the sun is golden and can make almost anyone look good in the magic hour right before sunset. My building is behind the dingy Odyssey Video, where you can rent ten adult movies for ten dollars. I mean, doesn't one movie do the trick? Thanks to the rise of Internet porn, this shop will close in the near future.

Between transcribing interviews, filing stories and emailing invoices, I watch his messages continue to pop up every day.

SG: When can I see your gorgeous face?

My days are pretty free. I sleep in until nine or ten, eat a bowl of cereal, watch the news, do some work, maybe go to the gym if I'm super motivated, then get ready for work.

SG: Whatever you're doing right now can't be as fun as being in a hotel room with me.

Sometimes the event is just down the street and I can be back home within two hours; other times I spend ninety minutes in the car and then work an awards show for four hours where I'm either outside in harsh sun or in a freezing cold warehouse-type room backstage, a good mile from where I parked. On those nights I'm too exhausted to eat dinner or squeal to anyone that I just met Justin Timberlake.

SG: I promise to make it worth your while.

With each message I lose composure. I have to see him again even though I keep telling myself it's wrong. He has a hold on me that I can't explain to myself. It's like he turned on a switch that's now stuck in one position.

SG: I can get away for a few hours tomorrow.

I have to transcribe some interviews from earlier tonight, submit them by 9 a.m. and then allow myself some time to get ready for his visit. This is crazy, but I guess no one would know. All my neighbors have regular work schedules, and out of the six units in my building, I'm always the only one who's home.

GP: Okay. Come over at 11 a.m. Here's the address.

This is the first time I've ever arranged for morning sex.

SG: I'll be there!!!!

■ ■ ■

It feels weird to be getting dressed this summer morning since I know I'll be getting undressed within minutes of Simon's arrival. But as it's only our second time together, I don't feel like I know him well enough to just answer the door in my short pink robe—though that's ridiculous, considering he's already seen and touched every square inch of me. I settle on an easy-to-remove crinkled silk Jigsaw slip dress I found in London a few years ago.

It hits me that Simon will be the first man who isn't just a friend to step inside this place, my very first grown-up apartment that I'm not sharing with roommates, where I pay all the bills and get to decorate however I choose. I become very aware of my secondhand Pottery Barn sofa, miniscule dining room and bad brown carpet. It's a far cry from the hotel room we were in, with its chrome fixtures and sleek furnishings.

Do I look like a college student still? I want to come off mysterious and worldly. I have a few cool pieces of art from college friends and a pretty tapestry that Rebecca brought me from Morocco, but that's about it. I remove a family portrait that's sitting in my bedroom. My parents don't need to see this, and I don't want Simon to see them.

All of a sudden *I* can't remember what he looks like, even though I spent hours with him the other night, and feel a mild panic setting in, but a few minutes before eleven there's a knock on my door, and there's no going back now. Simon steps inside, wearing the grin of a man who knows what's ahead of him. It feels weird seeing him here, and I feel a little less sure of myself this time, dead sober as I am. I say hello and wonder if this is a mistake.

But here he is. The threshold is crossed. He doesn't check out the apartment or ask about my displayed souvenirs from my summer trip to Italy. He grabs me by the waist and pulls me toward him. I smell a hint of aftershave as he kisses me and feel myself getting excited.

"You're shorter than I remember," he says, smiling and setting down a bag from Wally's, a wine shop between his office and my apartment.

I'm five foot six but was probably closer to five nine when we first met, thanks to the heels. Since he's about five foot ten at best, I wonder if this pleases him. My ex John and my high school boyfriends were all conventionally attractive, tall and athletic. I didn't realize that age sixteen was probably the last time I would see washboard abs anywhere near me. I probably should have appreciated that more, but hindsight is always 20/20.

"But I remember your freckles," Simon continues, his finger grazing the smattering of light brown dots above my cheeks and nose. "I've thought about them. And a few other things, of course."

"Can I get you anything?" I ask, even though all I have is water from the Brita and English Breakfast tea.

"Yes. You."

He starts kissing me passionately and leads me to my bedroom as if he's been there before. He looks older than I remember, especially here, among my twenty-two-year-old's stuff. He's wearing a navy gingham Brooks Brothers button-down shirt with khaki pants and wire-rimmed glasses that make him look professorial. I decide in this moment that he's an old forty-two.

In L.A. there are fortysomethings still pursuing stand-up comedy or music or acting, and they don't want to grow up. Their hair could start going gray or they may get lines around their eyes, but they still date five girls at once, eat tacos for dinner and dress like they're twenty-five. Simon is not one of those men. He has a refined elegance about him.

"Do you like Serge Gainsbourg?" I motion to the stereo on my dresser that's playing "La Chanson de Prévert."

"I'm not very familiar," he says. "But keep it on."

"Why are you dressed so nicely?" I ask as he starts unbuttoning his shirt.

"What do you mean? I'm going to work later today, what would you expect me to wear?" I'm too embarrassed to say that most guys I know just wear T-shirts with surf-brand logos or witty sayings.

I wonder how we can possibly replicate the intensity of the other night in the hotel room. This concern quickly disappears as Simon takes over, kissing my neck, his freshly shaved skin rubbing against my face, telling me how he's thought of this moment a hundred times since we were in that hotel room. I'm not sure if it's the age difference or the fact that I'm not his wife, or a mixture of both, but Simon makes me feel like I possess some magical prowess.

"You are so goddamn sexy," he says before disappearing under my slip dress.

He's as eager as they come, but his age and experience allow him to take his time, like he wants to build as much tension as possible, and my body responds accordingly. I return the favor, enjoying the feeling of turning him on so much that he is gasping until the last second, when I lead his erection inside me. He looks happier than someone who just won the lottery.

■ ■ ■

That afternoon I decide to call my best friend to confess.

Rebecca and I met as freshman year assigned roommates and were fast friends from the start, bonding over our mutual hatred of Phish and frat bros. We didn't much care for the three other girls in our suite but spent nearly every day and night together. Although we are as close as friends can be, we're quite different. Rebecca wouldn't be caught doing anything as frivolous as watching MTV or reading *InStyle* ("I only buy it to see your name," she says) and will choose comfort over fashion any day. It's puffy North Face jackets, sensible footwear and cozy flannel pajamas for her. Once in a while I'd catch country music playing in her car, even though she was raised in Manhattan and attended the famed Spence School.

But we get along like a house on fire. Maybe it's because she has a British mother as well, or that neither of us has sisters, or that we both felt a bit like outsiders at a college where most people spent their weekends getting shitfaced and/or lower-back tattoos. Rebecca doesn't comment on my growing collection of vintage leather jackets or the fact that I'll happily spend a night's salary on a new perfume, and I don't suggest that she change the shoulder-length haircut she's had since high school, or start listening to punk rock. We are who we are and there is always 100 percent acceptance—something I've never experienced with anyone else on earth. It's an unconditional love you don't usually find with insecure, competitive twentysomething girls. She is my cheerleader and I am hers.

"Bec?"

"Hang on a minute," she says. I hear her reprimanding some poor guy in her office for forgetting to drop off important negatives. She's been working as an in-house photographer at a startup that's supposed to revolutionize the food-delivery world, but she really wants to be shooting architecture and interior design projects. "Okay, I'm here. What's up?"

"I'm not sure quite how to explain this," I say in a low voice, even though I'm all alone, "but I'm sleeping with a forty-two-year-old man I just met last week."

"You're shitting me!"

"Let's keep it down over there," I say, though I am beaming. "I don't need your whole office to know."

"You have to be kidding!"

"I am not kidding," I say. "And please don't tell anyone."

"Who am I going to tell? I'm so proud of you, G."

"We don't really have anything in common except work, and not even really that, but the chemistry is off the charts," I tell her. "Like, better than any night I ever had with John in five years."

"So what? Obviously the last thing you need right now is a serious relationship. You should be out having fun. Sowing your wild oats. You have a lot of time to make up for."

Easy for her to say. She's dating a snowboarding instructor from Tahoe who looks like an Abercrombie & Fitch model and adores her. I don't think Rebecca has ever been single. As soon as one relationship is over, in rush the guys waiting in the wings, all posing as friends until they have their golden opportunity to vie for a chance.

"We had sex three times today," I say, almost whispering. I feel like I've finished an intense Pilates class. With Simon, I'm using muscles that have been dormant for too long. "I know that's too much info, but I just feel like I have to tell somebody because I can't believe it myself. Is that normal?"

"This is so great," she continues, like a proud mother. "You made my day."

"His name is Simon Grant. In case I turn up missing, maybe you should write that down," I say, half joking. "He's Australian and apparently a big-time reporter over there."

"I love Australians."

"I know, who doesn't? I think his accent is half of it."

"Totally."

"He has chest hair. I mean not a lot, but he's, like, a man," I say. "He brought a bottle of champagne over this morning, and we had mimosas in bed. I don't know what I am doing. This is crazy."

"This is actually perfect for you," she says. "Wasn't ambition and the maturity issue partly why you and John broke up? So why wouldn't this be great?"

"Did you hear the part about him being forty-two? He's closer in age to my dad than he is to me. You don't think that is strange?"

"It's not really a father-figure issue unless he's thirty years older than you, so don't worry about that," Rebecca says, as though we were all given a manual at birth on how wide an age gap there can be before it turns creepy. "Who cares, Georgina?"

"Everyone in my world would, except you."

"Then don't tell anyone," she says. "Just have fun. As long as you're being safe, I don't see the problem. You are being safe, right?"

"Yes, of course." Even with John, I never had unprotected sex. He said he didn't want to know what it was like or else he'd be afraid he wouldn't ever want use a condom again.

"Then I don't see what the problem is," Rebecca concludes.

"I've never just hooked up with somebody. I don't know the rules."

"Rule one is it's nobody's business," she says loudly. "God, you've got to lighten up. You're the oldest twenty-two-year-old on the planet, Georgina."

"I can't really see him in my world. It's not like we're going to roll up to a dive bar together to play darts. He's a bit fancy. He wears sport coats and is on TV. I mean, he drives a BMW," I say.

"So do you!" she exclaims. She's correct: I drive a used 3 Series that I got dirt cheap from an old neighbor after graduating from UC Irvine. "Just get out of your head and enjoy yourself. I'm sure he can teach you a thing or two about a thing or two."

I laugh and say goodbye. Rebecca is right. Why not just have some fun?

■ ■ ■

Two days later, Simon and I meet up again at my place at around 11 p.m. I had to work late covering a gala for St. Jude Medical Center. As they showed heartbreaking videos of sick children, guests played on their Sidekicks and complained about the bread basket.

"You look like a million bucks," he says, pulling back for a head-to-toe view. "Just lovely."

"Thank you. You always look nice," I say. "But do you ever wear jeans?"

He laughs and I notice he's holding something behind his back. "I've brought something extra special for you," he says. I recognize the smell immediately.

"Thank God!" I exclaim, snatching the In-N-Out bag from his hand. "I only made it through the wilted-salad course because I got to interview Tom Hanks and Rita Wilson together, but I could only do it backstage during dinner."

"Is he as nice as they say?"

"Yes, exactly what you would imagine. He teased me because I used two tape recorders. He said I was very thorough for an entertainment journalist."

"I know you think this is all stupid, the celebrities and fashion people," Simon says, "but this is great training ground. You seem very comfortable talking to them. Whatever you do next, you'll be ready to interview anyone."

"It gets a bit better each day," I admit. "The biggest stars have been the easiest ones to deal with because they are total pros. The only person I've ever gotten attitude from is Jake Busey."

"Who?"

"Exactly."

I kick off my strappy purple Stella McCartney heels, which I got for $75 at a private press sale (this perk being enough to keep me in this world for at least another year or two) and grab my goody bag to look for the mini bottles of Effen Vodka while Simon tells me about the $20,000 annual wardrobe budget his network provides for him. Of course I'm jealous, but I'm not doing too shabbily these days, with fancy robes, Kiehl's hair products, Louis Vuitton wallets and Chanel makeup all gifted to me during events in $10 million Malibu mansions and tented backyards in Beverly Park. It's excessive —I'm already being paid well for my work—but I'll happily take it. Sometimes I'll give swag to my mum or Rebecca, but usually I keep it in a drawer and peek at all goodies from time to time as if they're badges of honor.

"Do you know that I saw Spielberg waiting in line for a goody bag?"

"How tacky."

"Doesn't he have enough cash to buy and sell us all?"

Most of these events are for charity, but an absurd amount of money is spent on calligraphy and sixty-eight-point stock invitations, catering (usually The Patina Group, Along Came Mary or Wolfgang Puck), A-list entertainment and top-notch security, event planners and publicists, not to mention comping thousand-dollar-a-seat tables of approved reporters like me. Sometimes the celebrities themselves are paid to be there, much like they are to guest-DJ at some Vegas nightclub or sit front row at fashion week.

Still in the evening's finery, and barefoot, I take a big bite of the burger and grab a few fries before making us both dirty martinis in non-martini glasses with the jar of green olives I have in my sad, almost empty fridge. We take a few sips, but for the sake of not wasting any precious time, I bring him into my bedroom, where I unzip the black silk DKNY dress I stole from my mum after she deemed it too sexy for a CPA.

"What about the food?" he asks.

"I'll finish it later."

Feeling more comfortable with Simon and emboldened by the way he sees me, I take the lead this time, undressing him and teasing him until I can't wait any longer. I wonder why I feel so free when I'm with him. Is it because we have no mutual friends? Is it because he's mature and I know he won't go blabbing about it to anyone? Is it because we have some sort of sexual connection that might not exist with others? I don't know the answer. All I know is I am having fun for the first time in ages.

After our "lovemaking," as he refers to it, and between sips of my drink, I tell him I'm pitching my first story to the *Los Angeles Times*. "I want to write different kinds of stories," I say as he nuzzles my neck. "I feel like if I get published there, then I will consider myself a journalist."

"You're one now," he says, gently kissing my cheek.

"I don't think asking Debra Messing about her favorite lipstick is real journalism. I made a deal with myself that if I'm in the *Times* by age twenty-three, then I will continue being a writer."

"And if you don't?"

"I always thought I might become a teacher."

"I know someone there, at the Metro desk. Do you want me to call in a favor?"

"God, no. I want to do it on my own. I want the Sunday magazine."

"It's really competitive, you know, but I'm sure you'll be fantastic," he says. "I'd be happy to read your query before you send it off."

I smile and thank him, but I've already sent the pitch, about an undiscovered local artist I admire, off to the managing editor and am just going to hope for the best. Simon and I are having a nice time together, but I'm not fully myself around him. He's essentially a stranger, and we haven't spent the majority of our time together talking. He has yet to hear me laugh uncontrollably, enjoy a meal I cooked for him or see me around my friends or family. I don't know his birthday or what sports he played as a boy growing up in Brisbane.

That's part of what making our meetings so addictive; whatever we're doing together just lives inside the walls of my apartment, and the past and the future seem sort of meaningless and irrelevant.

As we bask in the afterglow, he picks up my copy of *A Heartbreaking Work of Staggering Genius* from my nightstand. "Any good?"

"It's incredible," I say. "Amazing in every way. I may have a bit of a crush on Dave Eggers."

"Trying to make me jealous?"

Simon strokes my face with the back of his hand as I tell him about the book. I'm uncomfortable with his caress because it is so intimate, more personal than any of the sex we're having. It feels too good, and my body tenses up in self-protection. "You have the softest skin I have ever felt," he says, rubbing the outer edge of my thigh.

"Thank you," I say, not making eye contact.

"I'm sure all the blokes tell you that."

"There are no blokes," I say, cutting him off. "I think I'd better get some sleep. I have a long day tomorrow that involves Lance Bass from 'N Sync. Please try not to be too envious."

"I don't like sharing you with a boy-bander," he sighs in mock outrage.

"He seems gay to me, so I wouldn't worry about that."

I stay in bed and watch as Simon gets dressed and grabs his wallet and phone from my white Ikea dresser. He is finally going home after a day that started at six o'clock this morning, with him chasing some story downtown.

He says, "I meant to tell you earlier: I've got to go away for a week on assignment."

"Oh? Where to?"

"Back to D.C. Our prime minister is meeting with President Bush on Friday."

I sit up, wild with envy. "Are you interviewing them?"

"The chances are looking good, but I won't know for sure until that day."

"I can't wait to hear about it."

"I have a decent rapport with John Howard, but Bush is such an idiot I'll be acting my arse off."

"I'm not a fan, but he's still our president."

"He's not mine." He laughs. "But when I return, I want to take you for that real dinner."

"Okay," I say, wondering why going out to dinner is so important to a man who is already getting what comes after dinner for free. "I will be around."

We've only seen each other three times, but I start feeling something for him. It's beyond the sex and the champagne and the excitement of having a secret. It's probably the oxytocin, a chemical form of bonding that happens to even the most independent of women. Then I remind myself that this is going nowhere. It's just sex. I'm not looking for a relationship. And even if I was, he's completely unavailable.

Simon kisses me goodbye, lingering a bit. I can tell he doesn't want to leave as he interlaces his hand with mine. I quickly move mine away when I feel his wedding band. It feels like a bucket of water has been splashed on me.

"Can I ask you something?"

"Anything, darling."

"How are you able to be here?" I ask.

"I work all the time, all over the place," he says. "She doesn't question my whereabouts. Don't think she cares where I am, really."

"You're not worried that you're going to get caught?" I ask, more concerned for myself than for him.

"No. And you shouldn't worry about that. Sometimes I wonder if this is how Clare wants it," he says, revealing her name for the first time. "She doesn't want to sleep with me and can't provide an explanation as to why."

"I know," I say. "But I just feel bad. If you didn't have kids, maybe I wouldn't feel like this."

"Do you want to see their photo?" he asks, and before I can say no he opens his wallet and flashes an adorable snapshot of a boy and little girl. "That's Michael, he's in fourth grade, and there's Hannah, she's just finishing first."

"They're beautiful," I say, wishing I could unsee their sweet, innocent faces.

Simon kisses me goodbye and goes home to his sleeping family while I go to bed alone, wondering how this is all going to play out.

3

Rebecca is the only person in my entire world who knows about Simon, because she is the only person I truly trust with information like this. But I failed to tell her the most important part: that Simon is married. He is not separated. He is not angling for a divorce. He is married. Plain and simple.

But I continue to see him anyway, and what bothers me most is that I'm not losing any sleep over it. At different points in the day I ask myself why I'm having an affair with a married man. I am not a seductress; I'm a red carpet reporter who has only slept with one other man on earth and lives on leftover Zankou chicken. But these secret meetings have become a full-blown addiction, and like any good junkie, I compartmentalize and justify my behavior.

Some things I like to tell myself:

He's married—I'm not.

His wife obviously doesn't love him or she'd have sex with him.

If it weren't me, he'd be with someone else.
Just one more time and then I'll stop. For real.

When I don't see him, it's like having an itch I can't scratch. I now crave Simon not just for the sex, which is still as exciting as it can be, but for the way he makes me feel. Knowing that he needs me, is risking a marriage in order to see me, makes me feel power I've never experienced before. I've heard girls my age say they can't even get a guy they've slept with to call them back. Even though Simon and I are doing something that society says is wrong, I'm happy.

And the physical connection is unparalleled. I always want more, and he can't get enough. Many times he asks to plan the next visit before our heart rates have returned to normal. I feel free when it's over and he walks out the door and I continue with my day as a Very Nice Girl who occasionally volunteers at a soup kitchen and gives money to homeless vets on Wilshire Boulevard.

I can't tell anyone the truth about Simon. My parents would be ashamed. They didn't raise me to ruin someone's marriage. The friends of mine who still believe in true love and the fairy tales we've all been told certainly wouldn't comprehend the situation. *I* don't even understand how I'm willingly participating in it.

When I really try to analyze how this could have happened, how I arrived in that hotel room, I come up with nothing. I've lived a fairly charmed life. I have a loving father. I was never touched inappropriately. I lost my virginity at a sensible 18 years of age to John, whom I trusted and adored. I would be heartbroken if someone cheated on me.

I try to remember that, but it doesn't work. It isn't enough to keep me away from Simon, and it seems nothing can keep him from me. Neither of us tries to stop the train. It isn't helping that we live only four miles from each other, practically neighbors in a city so expansive it sometimes feels like a small state.

While Simon is away for the week, we instant-message each other every single day, sometimes for hours at a time. We learn things about each other that we don't have time to discuss when we're in each other's arms. We often reminisce about the previous encounter or talk about the next one.

SG: I have a surprise for you.

GP: You're coming home early and on your way over?

SG: Don't I wish? Can you be free next weekend?

GP: I think so… Why?

SG: I'm doing a story in Orange County. Your old stomping grounds. It requires an overnight stay. I want you to come with me.

GP: Seriously?

SG: Yes. Can you imagine?

GP: I know a great place to stay. Both nights?

SG: Yes. I only need to be there one, but I will figure something out so we have the whole weekend.

GP: I'm excited. I miss you.

SG: Me too, darling. I cannot wait to see you.

I never imagined this would be a possibility. I'm thrilled by the thought of spending uninterrupted hours together in a different city, but also slightly nervous, as this is unchartered territory. We've never done anything mundane together, like pop into a drugstore, go to a movie or fill up at a gas station, and I'm not sure we need to start. And while we've now seen each other a handful of times, we've never gone to bed or woken up together.

We've been seeing each other in the mornings and afternoons, and our time is so limited that we have to make use of every minute. Every second, really. Our encounters feel like a challenge to see how many orgasms we can have collectively in an hour. Going on a real vacation together will be quite a change, and I'm curious to see if it will be even better.

■ ■ ■

I love waking up in August. My bedroom is the only place in my apartment where there's good light, and on summer mornings I lie in bed and work on my laptop for about an hour while the sun's rays stream through the venetian blinds. I make a mental note to ask the landlord if I can remove them and put up a simple curtain.

Before shutting my computer off, I set up my first ever vacation email auto-response. Even though it's a long weekend, I know I'll be receiving messages from editors and publicists, and I don't want them calling my cell phone if I can help it.

> *Hi there,*
> *I am taking a much-needed three-day week-end, but will get right back to you upon my return.*
> *Cheers,*
> *Georgina*

TRL plays in the background as I quickly pack a small bag while singing along to 112's "Peaches & Cream." I decide to call Rebecca so at least one person will know where I am.

"Hey, it's me."

"Finally coming up for air, I see."

"That's why I'm calling. Simon is taking me to Laguna Beach for the weekend. We're staying at that B&B. I just wanted you to know." Rebecca knows the B&B I'm talking about; we would always go to the used bookstore next door to it when we were in school.

"So I see you've gotten past the age thing."

"I guess. This will be the most time we've ever spent together, so I'll let you know how it goes."

"Don't forget the condoms. You can never have enough. And go to Las Brisas and sit outside," she says of the popular restaurant with sweeping views of the Pacific and its beautiful coastline. "It's romantic."

After we decided to move off campus, Rebecca and I lived together in Newport Beach for two years, but we only went to nearby fancy Las Brisas when her or my parents were in town and buying. You were more likely to find us on the peninsula, getting giant burritos or riding our beach cruisers to parties where dinner consisted of keg beer and cold pizza. I smile giddily at the thought of returning to some of my old haunts with a sophisticated man on my arm.

■ ■ ■

Today is our first drive together, my first time seeing him behind the wheel. He's not driving the dark blue BMW he usually brings to my place. Instead, he pulls up in a gray early-'90s Honda Accord, with a mess of papers and some trash strewn about the backseat. His wife's car, I assume, but try to push it out of my mind. It seems odd that he wouldn't clean up a bit since we're taking a 60-mile trip, but I don't say anything.

"Look at you," he says with a smile, eyeing my cleavage.

I'm wearing a pink and white striped Roxy cotton dress and already have a tan thanks to a four-hour stint working the Teen Choice Awards yesterday in eighty-six-degree heat. "Hi," I say, giving him a quick kiss.

It feels strange to enter his world, even if it is just one of his cars, and even more strange to be out together in broad daylight. I realize in this moment that I never say his name, except to Rebecca, and he never says mine. We've never had to introduce each other to anyone.

This is also the first time I've seen casual Simon. He usually looks so conservative, as news correspondents do, and I've often wished I could see him in a basic J.Crew button-down and jeans. Today he's wearing soccer-style shorts and a short-sleeve rugby shirt. He looks younger and seems thrilled to be getting out of town and having me all to himself for the weekend. It's our first official sleepover, a milestone I imagine only virgins and mistresses get excited about.

I'm not quite sure what the plan is for this trip. He has a story to do tomorrow, which is the entire excuse for the getaway, but apart from that, we will be together for nearly three days. As we get on the 405 South, he tells me there are CDs in the glove compartment if I want to put one on. I find an old Michael Jackson, a Linda Ronstadt and a Puff Daddy album that's two years old. I'm confused by the selection.

"They're Clare's," he says. "She needed the nice car this weekend."

"How about 97.1?" I ask, ignoring the mention of her.

"What's that, then?"

"Howard Stern."

"You have to be kidding me."

"I love him."

"I never would have guessed in a million years."

"He's not what you think," I plead. "Just for a few minutes."

We catch the tail end of the show and are just in time to hear Robin Quivers' news. I smile anytime I catch Simon laugh. I am secretly proud that I have just introduced a refined man with a broadcaster's haircut to the King of All Media. Robin mentions a story about a right-wing politician who has just been busted with a call girl. "If you have to pay for it, you don't deserve it," Simon says with conviction. I'm surprised to hear him say so and raise an eyebrow from behind my sunglasses. I obviously don't know him as well as I thought (I mean, we've probably spent ten hours together in total so far), because he seems like the type of guy who has such a voracious sexual appetite that he might have to get a professional involved once in a while.

After the seventy-five-minute drive, which concludes with the most beautiful strip of the Pacific Coast Highway and a rocky coastline, we arrive in charming Laguna Beach, an artsy beachside town. Since I lived in the area for four years, I know my way around the village, and I enjoy showing Simon the restaurants where I waitressed throughout college and pointing out my favorite gallery.

We pull up at the hotel, which I picked for its high hedges, hidden pathways and beautiful gardens. The room is under my name, so Simon mills about just outside the French doors while I check in. I recognize the girl behind the desk immediately—we went to college together. We never knew each other but were in the same art history class in the Social Science Lecture Hall, along with with 200 other students. I pretend not to recognize her, and she doesn't say anything to me other than "A complimentary breakfast is served from seven to ten in the main house." I wonder what this girl is thinking, since the last time she saw me around campus I was with a long-haired, twenty-one-year-old John.

The room is old-fashioned for my taste; it looks like something out of the English countryside. But there are beautiful wood floors, a private patio and a four-poster bed. It's early in the afternoon, so I figure we can grab a bite, walk around downtown and maybe even go to the beach if there's time. I put my duffel bag in one of the closets of our one-bedroom suite, and within seconds I feel Simon behind me. Apparently he isn't interested in taking in the sights.

We spend the next two hours in bed, even freer than we are at my apartment since there are no time constraints or jobs to return to, and I find that I genuinely enjoy spending time with Simon. We don't run out of things to talk about even though we've been together all day.

He surprises me by producing a joint. "Where did *you* get *that*?"

"One of our PAs gave it to me," he says proudly. "I haven't smoked in years."

"Have you tried California weed?" I ask. "Because it's pretty strong. My cousin was here from London last summer and smoked a bit at a party. We thought we'd have to take her to the hospital."

"It's something called The Chronic."

"Oh my God, you are screwed," I tease. "I know you lived through the sixties, but pot has come a long way since then."

"I can handle it," he says, lighting up. "Don't you worry."

"I thought you didn't like smoking," I remind him as I kiss his neck.

"This is different," he says, inhaling like a natural. "Here."

"Are you having a midlife crisis?" I ask him, propping my head up with my hand and taking the joint with the other. "I mean, first the young girl, and now you're smoking pot?"

"That's it." He places the joint in the ashtray, pins me down on the bed and starts tickling my sides. Laughing uncontrollably, I beg him to stop before someone hears us and comes knocking, or we set fire to the whole place and end up under arrest. We each have a few puffs and talk and laugh about everything and nothing. It's the most fun I've ever had as an adult. Simon has a goofy smile plastered on his face, and I feel more uninhibited than ever.

By six we're starving, so I suggest dinner at Las Brisas, knowing Rebecca will be pleased. We get dressed, he in a pair of gray slacks and a tailored checkered Thomas Pink shirt, I in a navy and white striped bateau top and silk knee-length skirt, since I've been going through a serious French New Wave phase of late. We decide to walk there and score a table on the breezy patio, which is filled with plenty of tourists who know nothing about us or the moral crimes we are in the midst of committing. It's good to be away from home, away from work, away from celebrities and publicists and my tape recorder. It's the only occasion where we've been outside of my apartment since that first night. It feels natural.

Over Corralejo Blanco margaritas and Mexican shrimp ceviche, Simon tells me stories about his career, from covering the horrific Oklahoma bombing to Princess Diana's tragic death in Paris. Even though he has many years of experience on me, what I am doing is a joke compared to the work he has done. But I'm less self-conscious than when we sat at that brasserie together that first night. When I look around, I see that no one is looking at us. People perceive as a normal couple, so I relax.

As Simon tells me a bit about a cameraman who he suspects has a cocaine problem, I think about how strange it is that he wears his white gold wedding band even when we are alone together. Maybe it's too difficult to remember to take it off each time, or he's afraid of leaving it somewhere, which would arouse suspicion in his wife. Maybe he figures there's no point in removing it, as we both know he is married. But at some point, a server or an innkeeper is going to mistake me for his wife. The thought makes my skin crawl with guilt.

"Obviously I wanted to come here so we could spend real time together, outside of your apartment," he says after perusing the dinner menu. "And today has been incredible. The best day, actually. But there's also something I need to tell you."

She knows.

He finally feels guilty.

He's ending it.

"Just say it," I say, feeling my body tense up. "It's okay."

"I'm being transferred back to Sydney. In eight weeks."

Just then the waiter comes by to tell us about the specials. I'm thankful to have a minute to handle the bomb that's gone off at our two-top. The news is a complete shock, like when you first plunge into the ocean and your heart freezes from the cold. But it's also a relief. The more we see each other, the more I wonder how it will end. No good can come from this affair. I remind myself to breathe and act normally. I'm disappointed but say that I understand. He tells me about his new gig—a big promotion to executive producer of the country's top newscast, where he'll manage seventy-five reporters—and says he's been in America long enough. It's not his home, after all. He's happy to go but says he will miss me terribly and continues to apologize for the timing. I'm already thinking about the last time I'll see him and how we will say our final goodbye.

"So I need to see you as much as humanly possible in the next two months," he says, grabbing my hand across the table. "I hope I haven't ruined the weekend. I wanted to tell you as soon as I knew it was for sure."

"Not at all," I say, even though it feels like a punch in the stomach.

■ ■ ■

Knowing there's an expiration date on whatever this is gives me an out, at least. It will be over before a single tear is shed or someone's feelings become too strong. I feel slightly giddy inside, knowing I will keep this secret for the rest of my life and no one, not even Rebecca, will ever find out. When I'm old, I can tell myself it was something impulsive I did in my early twenties and get a little rush of adrenaline remembering that first night and the many encounters that followed.

I never do anything wild. I'm allowed this one thing.

We head back to our cottage, where a bottle of wine that Simon brought is waiting for us. He steps out to the patio to open it. He does it with such ease; I love watching him. Even when I was waitressing, I could never manage to uncork bottles like that. From the room I watch him pour two glasses of Pinot Noir. There's a cool breeze blowing off the ocean. I shut the door and tell him I'll join him in a minute.

I take my bag into the bathroom. I run a brush through my windswept hair, powder my forehead and nose and dab a tiny bit of perfume oil behind my ears. When I return to him, I'm wearing a short, schoolgirl-type skirt, a white eyelet-and-lace push-up bra and four-inch black patent leather heels. My brown hair falls past my bronzed shoulders, just above the ample cleavage the bra is helpfully creating.

I got this getup at Trashy Lingerie on La Cienega. If you've ever seen a Playmate celebrating Halloween in the pages of *People* magazine, you've seen their work. I covered an event at their boutique the other day, and after it was over I decided to do a little shopping in anticipation of the weekend trip. I picked this outfit because Simon once told me he wouldn't be into me if I were a "giggly schoolgirl."

It was the first time I'd ever looked for something like this. In high school and college, boys are quite satisfied by the sight of a flesh-toned bra strap. John would always want to get right to the main act, and the times I did attempt to wear a cute nightie, he either ripped it or soiled it by accident.

Although Simon and I are far from needing to spice things up in the bedroom, I thought it would be fun to surprise him. Doesn't every man have a schoolgirl fantasy? He has never asked me to wear anything specific, but the saleswoman at Trashy Lingerie made it clear that "men are visual creatures." I spent at least half an hour wondering what he would think was extra hot. Most of the items were so comical (Little Bo Peep costumes, natch) that I couldn't even consider them. Plus, I had to think of what would look best on me, which takes precedence over what he would prefer. He doesn't have any fetishes, like leather or stockings, that I know of. He seems to be into anything that leads to me being naked.

I remember asking Simon early on if our age difference is what appeals to him the most. It certainly had become a turn-on for me because of the naughtiness factor. But he swore it isn't about that. "People don't sleep with people they don't like," he'd said. "If we didn't have an intellectual connection, I wouldn't be here."

Rebecca would disagree. She sometimes has hate sex, claiming that sleeping with someone you don't like or respect ensures that you won't accidentally start feeling something for them. I'll have to try that out sometime, now that I know my current partner is moving 7,500 miles away from my bedroom. Since I seem to dislike almost every man I meet, it shouldn't be very hard.

With Simon I sometimes find myself wanting to play the role of the girl coming of age with her mentor-slash-lover, who teaches her things about sex and life, but then we get into a ninety-minute conversation over IM about immigration policy, and I realize I might not be that girl. It isn't possible for me to play dumb for a man.

Simon watches as I walk out to the patio with my glass in one hand and a condom from his bag in the other. "Are you trying to kill me?" he says, pretending to clutch his heart.

"See, you do like schoolgirls," I tease.

He's lying on a teak lounger under the few stars that are visible in the sky. I laugh, feeling buzzed from the wine. I sit on his lap, facing him.

"I want to remember you like this forever," he says, running his fingers from my collarbone to my chest.

"Too bad you don't have a camera," I say, smiling and kissing his ear, which always gets him instantly hard, "or else you could."

"What possessed you to do this? I'm not complaining, by the way."

"I just thought since we were on vacation, I should do something out of the ordinary."

"Nothing you do is ordinary."

He lets out a long sigh as my hands start exploring. I lean forward and we kiss for a minute. Again I wonder if I'm one of many girls he's had in the past, and guess that I'm most certainly not the last. I don't really care. I unbuckle his leather belt with my left hand, steadying myself with my right. He looks thrilled by this gesture, and I'm so caught up in my uncharacteristic boldness that I forget we're outside. He motions for me to be quiet, and I mimic his motion back to him, since he's usually the one who makes noise. I hear waves lapping sand.

As I slide myself onto him, I think back to when I lost my virginity and how it took a couple months to ever get on top with John. It seemed like a very experienced thing to do, so I avoided it at first. I didn't want him to think I knew what I was doing. I wanted to seem innocent and inexperienced, which I actually was.

Even though I prefer Simon on top, every once in a while I like to be the one in control because it seems to take him to another place. I've heard things about powerful men liking to be dominated. He's never asked to be spanked or humiliated in any way, though, and I'm kind of relieved.

The encounter is fast and furious, and when it's complete we head inside to the cozy room, where I change out of my outfit and wash my face. We watch CNN from the plush king-size bed, but I'm not really paying attention. Simon is a total news junkie, able to watch for hours at a time, but I'm getting tired and accidentally fall asleep without saying goodnight. When I wake up, at around 4:30 in the morning, I see that he is spooning me from chest to ankle, his left arm wrapped around my waist. Somehow it feels like the most rebellious thing we have done so far.

4

It's a postcard-perfect, seventy-four-degree Laguna Beach day with blue skies, puffy white clouds and muscular guys playing basketball on the Main Beach Park courts. Simon showers and puts on a navy suit for the story he's doing, about a local sailing competition. Why this event interests Australians on the other side of the world is beyond me. He notices the lace-trimmed peach silk chemise I slept in last night and makes a passing comment about his wife only wearing flannel pajamas. We rarely talk about her, but it's obvious from the few things he does say that things aren't going well at home.

"Even in the summer?" I ask.

He laughs and kisses my forehead, then goes out to find a newspaper. He returns with a large cup of English Breakfast tea he fetched from the dining room, and a coffee in a to-go cup for himself. The tea is too hot to drink and reminds me of how my mum always says it's a proper cup of tea only if it's served scorching hot. Simon and I sit and chat for about twenty minutes before he has to leave. It's one of the longest conversations we've have ever had in person. Since our meetings have time constraints, we always do the majority of our talking online, making the most of in-person encounters. It feels a bit strange just sitting around together in the morning.

As I blow on my tea, I notice that Simon is staring at me with a forlorn look on his clean-shaven face. He looks boyish like this. I tease him: "Is everything okay? You look a bit upset. Is it because they don't have Vegemite?"

"I was just thinking that this is what life should be, you know?" he says before getting up to kiss me goodbye. "I'll be back in a few hours."

I say nothing. I know it can't be like this for much longer.

After he departs to meet his cameraman, I go on a walk, eat a bagel and hang by the pool for an hour, reading a worn paperback copy of *Permanent Midnight* that I found on a used-book table at the Mar Vista Branch Library. I've never experimented with anything besides pot, but my favorite genre of books seems to be the druggie novel. In literature, I've always loved the bad boys.

■ ■ ■

I'm relaxing in our room when Simon returns, earlier than expected and visibly stressed. He isn't wearing his jacket and has his crisp white shirt rolled up at the sleeves, with an extra button undone at the neck. I think it's the sexiest he's ever looked and am about to tell him so when I notice that something is definitely wrong.

"Is everything okay?" I ask, setting my book down.

"Yeah, the shoot went fine," he says, reading the screen on his phone. "But something has come up and I have to go back tonight."

I immediately suspect it isn't work, as I know Simon would do anything to stay here as long as possible. "Okay," I say, "Do we need to leave right now?"

"Yes, darling," he says, dejected. "I'm so sorry."

"I understand," I say quietly.

He knows he can't really make it up to me, so he doesn't say that he will.

A wife would balk at this sort of thing, nagging:

You promised me a romantic weekend away.

You're always working.

Put the bags down, we aren't going anywhere.

The girl sleeping with a married man doesn't say a word. I am entitled to nothing and don't expect anything. We start packing things up, and I cancel our dinner reservation at my favorite restaurant. While Simon loads the car I check out of the hotel, confirming that the $382 charge for our stay is correct. The hotel apologizes that they cannot refund us for this evening, as we are within the twenty-four-hour cancellation period. I say I understand and return the oversize brass key.

The car ride home is considerably quieter than the one down. Simon is preoccupied, so I just look out at the coastline and wonder what will happen next in this short-lived, dysfunctional relationship of ours.

"I feel like the least I can do is pay for the hotel," he says as we drive through Newport Coast on our way back to the freeway.

"Don't worry about it, it's fine," I say, though it is quite a bit of money for me. "It's not like you're my sugar daddy."

I say this playfully, but he doesn't laugh or smile. Rebecca often teases me about the age difference and how others would see me as a gold digger if things ever got serious, seeing as he outearns me ten times over, but I'm always quick to bring up the fact that he doesn't buy me gifts and certainly isn't giving me cash. What we have is simply a mutual exchange between equals based on sexual chemistry.

Simon continues to be quiet, which drives me a bit mental since he's usually so chatty and upbeat. Around Long Beach I ask him if everything is okay.

"I didn't want to burden you with this or make you feel uncomfortable, but Clare's favorite uncle has passed away," he says.

"I'm so sorry to hear that. Were you close?"

"I only met him once—at our wedding. But Clare adores him, so she's gutted. I think she is going to take the kids and go to Sydney for a week or two. We have to figure it out."

"I'm sure it's hard for her, being so far away from home."

"Yes," he says. "Fourteen hours and the worst jet lag known to man."

"I remember." My parents took me to Sydney when I was fourteen and my dad was presenting at an academic conference there. "I slept through our first night's dinner and was like a zombie at the zoo, until I saw the wombats. They were my favorite thing about the trip."

"But the real issue, I suppose, is that I think I'm falling in love with you," he says quietly.

I am stunned. The wind has been knocked out of me, and I'm at a complete loss for words. I never wanted Simon to leave his wife, never thought of us being together in a real way. He doesn't know enough about me to be falling in love. *This* isn't the real me. He has experienced the most fun, sexy and spontaneous sliver of who I am. He's had a good piece of the pie.

He hasn't been around when I'm stressed out over deadlines or spending hours on the patio of the Cat & Fiddle pub in Hollywood with friends, wasting the day away. He knows nothing of substance about my life. I don't think I've even told him what my parents do for a living. I'm positive he's simply falling in love with the way I make him feel: younger, more carefree, more alive. A welcome distraction from the humdrum of home life and the reality of things like Costco runs and DMV renewals. I probably remind him of himself as a hungry aspiring journalist.

"That wasn't my intention," I say.

"It's fucked up, isn't it?" he says with a half smile. "So much for no strings attached."

As we exit onto Wilshire Boulevard, I realize that this is the first day we've been together that we haven't had sex. He drops me off, and I say maybe we should take a couple weeks off from trying to get together. It's not what I want but what I think sounds responsible. It's the grown-up thing to do. Surprisingly, he agrees, which stings a bit, but it's probably for the best. I give him a kiss goodbye and tell him I hope everything will be okay.

■ ■ ■

It's Saturday night and I'm home alone, which feels strange. I call my friend Elizabeth, who's an editorial assistant and fact checker at *InStyle*. We've been meaning to get together since we live in the same neighborhood, and now that I'm suddenly available I hope she is too. I don't feel like staying home tonight after the last whirlwind twenty-four hours. Luckily for me she is free, and asks if I want to meet her at Q's, a sports bar usually filled with UCLA students that's walking distance from my place.

I put on a pair of jeans, low heels and a pink cotton tank top from Anthropologie. I love when it's warm enough in L.A. to go out without a sweater or jacket. Isn't that the reason we're all paying a small fortune to live in crappy apartments? I quickly sweep some bronzer on my cheeks and notice the tan lines peeking out of my top from earlier today, but oh well, it will be dark inside. I grab my ID, a twenty-dollar bill and pink-tinted lip balm.

As soon as I walk in, I order a dirty martini with three olives because it will hit me much faster than my usual vodka soda. I can't believe I'm at this billiard club instead of having a romantic dinner on the water's edge at Splashes. Elizabeth joins me a minute later and we catch up on petty office gossip and the guy she's seeing, a graphic designer for Fox who also plays bass in a hardcore punk band, naturally. Since Elizabeth and I work for the same magazine, I don't mention Simon or Laguna Beach. A few minutes in, two guys wearing plaid button-downs make moves to approach us. I give Elizabeth a look that says *Please, let's not*, but her body language says otherwise.

The Notorious B.I.G. is blasting through the stereo system as introductions are made. Greg is six foot two and looks like a former linebacker but surprises us by saying he works in IT. Paul is—shocker—an aspiring screenwriter who works part-time as a video editor. We indulge them in some light banter, and I wonder about Elizabeth's almost boyfriend, who's supposed to meet us later in the evening. Maybe she's trying to make him jealous since he won't officially commit to her. We have the requisite conversation about how we know each other and where we work. "That's nice that your sister is a fan of the magazine," I hear Elizabeth say to Paul, the shorter of the two.

I'm now on my second martini, contemplating an exit as soon as the punk-rock designer shows up, when Greg asks if I'd like to go to the upstairs patio for a smoke. I'm no longer buying packs, but I'm not turning down a Marlboro Light when I'm two drinks in. And I'm avoiding the fact that my married Australian lover thinks he's in love with me but will be leaving the country in eight short weeks.

Greg is sweet and seems genuinely interested in talking about my work. He's not classically handsome but teddy-bear-cute, and his formidable size makes me feel dainty. Elizabeth gives me a big smile that says *Go ahead*, and so we do.

"I know nothing about computers, so I'm sorry I can't ask you more about your job," I say once we're upstairs.

"But isn't it your job to ask questions?" he asks, pulling out a lighter.

"Well, yes. I guess I just mean I wouldn't understand the answers."

He mentions things like HTML coding and C++ and I'm proved right, but I smile and nod as though it's absolutely fascinating. I smile and nod for a living. I have mastered the art of making anyone feel interesting.

"You have an incredible smile," he says.

"Thank you," I say, blushing and smiling even bigger.

"And cute freckles," he says, looking at them affectionately. "Were you at the beach today? You look tan."

"Yes, for a bit."

He lights my cigarette, and we look out at the cars speeding by and the hordes of young women stumbling onto the crosswalk. Greg is the first guy I've spoken to in ages who isn't a celebrity, a colleague or Simon. He tells me a familiar story: After going to college in the Midwest, he moved to L.A. to pursue a career in film production, but quickly realized that eighteen-hour days and PA work were not for him. He still works in the industry, at a popular entertainment company, but in the more nine-to-five world of technology.

"But I think it's cool that you write," he says. "You must meet so many interesting people."

"Sometimes." I don't mention that on Wednesday I'll be in a hotel room at Shutters on the Beach with Nicolas Cage as part of a press junket.

"Do you have a website for your work where I can read your articles?"

"No. I don't know how to do that."

"I could help you," he says, waving a puff of smoke away from my face. "I wouldn't mind at all."

Realizing he's probably the nicest guy I've encountered during my entire time in L.A., I tell myself not to let Simon stop me from meeting someone who could be good for me. Before heading back downstairs, Greg and I exchange email addresses and phone numbers. This is the sort of guy I should be dating. He's easy to talk to, genuine and polite. He would maybe even pull out my chair and open the car door. He would be a nice Christmas party date. He might not make my stomach do gymnastics at the mere sound of his voice, but we could hold hands in public like normal people.

■ ■ ■

More than a week passes. Simon is just a few miles away from my place while his wife and kids are a world away, but I don't initiate contact. I wonder if he is thinking about me at all. Finally there's a chance for us to be alone in this city of millions, but we are working, eating, sleeping and drinking separately.

I try to occupy my time so I don't obsess on it too much, and while I'm taking a long walk on the bluffs in Santa Monica, among a sea of palm trees and homeless people, I get a call from Simon.

"I know we said we should cool things off a bit, but I can't," he says. "The time we do have left is limited, so let's make the most of it."

"Okay," I say calmly, even though my insides are practically bursting. I didn't anticipate how much I would miss him.

"I know we've had a couple meals here and there, but I want to take you on a real dinner date, to L'Orangerie."

"Simon, honestly, we can just order in, or I can cook you one of the five things I know how to make," I say, worried about running into anyone he may know if we go to a fancy place like that. Doing anything in public always makes me uncomfortable, because we aren't protected by the walls of my apartment. I remember walking him to his car once and bumping into my neighbor, a high-strung attorney who was never at home during the day until *that* particular day. Simon shook her hand and introduced himself like he was my boyfriend, and I thought he was crazy for being so brazen.

"I won't take no for an answer," he says. "How about tomorrow night?"

"If it's after eight I can do it. I have to work until around seven thirty."

"Perfect. I'll make the reservation."

"I'll meet you there because I'll be coming from Hollywood." It makes no sense to backtrack to the Westside only to dine in West Hollywood. "The magazine wants me to sit in on a photo shoot."

"I wanted to pick you up, like a real date," he says, "but I get it."

"I'll see you soon. And I'm glad you called."

"Me too, darling."

■ ■ ■

I've been to countless ballrooms, private estates and famous theaters for work, but L'Orangerie instantly takes my breath away with its grand entryway and fruit trees lining the exterior. It is the most beautiful establishment I've ever set foot in. Airy and open, with fresh flowers and glowing candles everywhere, the French restaurant is an L.A. icon, and I never would have seen it if not for Simon.

The maître d' greets me immediately, but before I can say anything, my Australian walks in seconds behind me, kissing me on the lips—a bold gesture for a married man, I think to myself. We are seated in a magical dining room that reminds me of a greenhouse, with its glass roof and flower-covered trellises. Harvey Weinstein is holding court at a nearby table. Simon is handsome in a full black suit, crisp white shirt, tie, the works. It's the definition of elegant. We celebrate our reunion with a glass of champagne and catch up on the past week.

"How was the photo shoot?" he asks me.

"It was fine, but I got stuck hanging out most of the afternoon with a member of the entourage who had a teacup Maltese in her purse," I say. "She was feeding it Niçoise salad and bottled water from catering."

"For fuck's sake."

"And there were some delays because the actress wouldn't come out of the bathroom for fifteen minutes."

"Why?"

"She thought her thighs looked fat."

"I won't even ask who you're referring to."

"The most fascinating part of the day was talking to the gay guys in this star's glam squad. You know they get something like five thousand dollars a day? And the magazine pays for it. I had no idea."

"Unreal."

"I will never feel bad about expensing *InStyle* for parking fees."

"Well, I'm glad you're here now," he says, reaching for my hand.

Simon encourages me to try foie gras for the first time, and it's the most decadent thing I've ever tasted. I've never felt more grown-up. As we're sharing a plate of roasted figs for dessert, he surprises me once again.

"I want you to stay at my place tonight."

"Is that a good idea?"

"Yes. I want you to see my home," he says. "Just this once."

"All right. I just want to stop by my place to pick up a few things."

A small army of disheveled paparazzi are assembled on La Cienega Boulevard as we leave the restaurant, dejected that we are nobodies. "Matt Damon and Ben Affleck are inside with some director," whispers the cute valet attendant, who is most definitely an actor, as I get in the car.

We drive to my place separately so I can later follow Simon to his. My mind races because I know this is crossing yet another line, but I dismiss the thoughts as quickly as possible and listen to "Loveline," which is just starting on KROQ. I prefer to listen to other people's romantic entanglements rather than focus on my own.

■ ■ ■

As we wind up what seems like a never-ending hill, I don't know what to expect. Simon has never talked much about his house, only occasionally mentioning that he likes to cook and that his network pays the rent, which must be around $10,000 a month. It's a nice four-bedroom Craftsman with a stunning view of the hillside, and even deer sometimes, he says, loosening his tie. He doesn't give me an extended tour and I don't want one. I feel a little uneasy about what I might see. We stick to the living room at first, listening to The Mamas & the Papas (I catch myself before commenting that my parents love this particular album) and drinking rosé on a white shabby-chic sofa.

"I grew up on this music because of my older brother," he says. "He listened to all the Laurel Canyon bands: Zappa, The Byrds, The Doors."

"I love The Doors," I say, joining him on the carpeted floor like we're teenagers. "Have you heard their Hollywood Bowl album? From 1968?"

He smiles. "You always surprise me. I haven't heard it since I was a kid."

"I'll bring it to you next time."

"Do you have a favorite Doors song?"

"'Moonlight Drive,'" I say. "Jim Morrison wrote it in Venice. Some people say it's about suicide, but it just reminds me of growing up at the beach."

Simon gives me a puzzled grin. "How do you know all this?" he asks, switching out The Mamas & The Papas for The Doors' *Strange Days*.

"I read everything I can when I like someone or something. I'll even read the book you wrote, if you give it to me," I say, rubbing his leg. "What about you?"

"I like them all, but if pressed to pick a favorite, it would have to be 'Love Her Madly.'" I smile, wondering if he's trying to tell me something. "I don't think I ever told you, but I've always wanted to live in California, particularly Los Angeles, because of that music," he says. "So many people have come here to chase a dream, whatever it may be. I didn't know how I would get here, but I'm so pleased that I did."

"California's influence around the world is sort of staggering. It's a beautiful, unusual place, for sure."

"And I never would have met you if I didn't come here," he says, kissing my shoulder. "When I got the assignment to move to L.A., I was set on finding a place in the canyon, but Clare thought the Palisades was more family-friendly, so I agreed."

Since it's already eleven, I start yawning, and Simon suggests that we retire to the bedroom. Even though this is the ultimate violation so far, sleeping in *her* bed, I somehow block it out as Simon removes every article of clothing from my body before he has even taken off his glasses. I am only focused on this one thing.

"Is this expensive?" I ask, grabbing his striped tie and turning it over to see the label—Paul Smith—before taking it off his neck.

"Why?" he asks innocently.

"Because I wouldn't want to ruin it if it is," I say with a mischievous grin.

"What exactly did you have in mind?" he inquires, unbuttoning his shirt.

"Have you ever tied someone up before?" I ask, scooting farther up the bed.

"No," he says, taking the tie from me, "but I think I can get the hang of it."

Everything feels heightened as my wrists are tied to the bedpost and Simon begins kissing me on the neck.

My body responds accordingly as he works his way down slowly, bringing me to the edge of an orgasm in a matter of minutes.

"Not yet," he says, teasing, before leaving the room for a minute. I see him silhouetted in the doorway for a moment before he joins me again on the bed.

"I just wanted to walk in the room and see you like that," he explains, "so I could burn the image into my mind."

He enters me slowly, working his way up to a faster pace as I hear Jim Morrison's voice wailing in the other room. My wrists eventually slide out but it doesn't matter because we are in a full-blown frenzy of desire. When it's over we fall right asleep, his tie still hanging from the wood post.

When I wake up with the sun at 6 a.m., the reality of the situation has finally hit me, and it's sobering. I go the bathroom, wash my face quickly with cold water because I don't want to wait the extra thirty seconds for warm water, and tell Simon to go back to sleep and that I'll speak to him later. I feel like a fugitive fleeing the scene of a crime as I get in my car and head back down the long hill, back to my one-bedroom apartment and real life.

5

I answer my phone when I see the caller ID. "Bec?"

"Are you watching the news?"

It's 7:15 in the morning, but I'm not yet awake since I was working late last night at a charity event at the Beverly Hilton. Why anyone holds a fundraising gala on a Monday night is beyond me.

"No, you just woke me up," I say groggily, detecting urgency in Rebecca's voice. "What's wrong?"

"Turn on the TV," she says, starting to sob.

The images on the screen are too shocking to believe. It looks like a big-budget action movie with plenty of CGI. A plane has hit the World Trade Center. It gets worse with each passing minute. Tears start streaming down my face.

After watching hours of coverage and talking to my parents several times on the phone, I turn off the television and consider having a drink at three in the afternoon.

I eventually log on to my computer and see a lot of messages on email and AIM relating to the disaster. My college friend Paula has a friend of a friend who works at Cantor Fitzgerald. A work acquaintance has sent out a poem asking people to pray for the victims. A few messages down, I see an email from Simon.

> *From: Simon Grant*
> *To: Georgina Park*
> *Date: September 11, 2001 at 4:35 PM*
> *Subject: New York*
>
> *I've gone to New York to cover the attack. Missing you already.*

■ ■ ■

In the aftermath of September 11, it seems as if everything has changed. People are scared, there's now a scroll beneath most channels, including non-news networks like E!, and I have no work to speak of. It would be considered bad taste to throw lavish premieres or arrange for a peppy awards show right now. Everything is very serious. I have more time off than I know what to do with, and in addition to worrying about the state of the world, I'm petrified that something is going to happen to Simon while he is getting the story.

I donate my O negative blood at a Red Cross event near my apartment and contribute a hundred dollars to the rescue effort, but I feel fairly helpless from three thousand miles away. I read a brochure from the national bone marrow registry and consider joining. "We desperately need people with your unusual background," a nurse tells me.

I try filling my days with museum exhibits at Bergamot Station and LACMA and take morning walks along Ocean Avenue in Santa Monica. The view of the water from the bluffs is calm and still. Sometimes the fog is so heavy down here that you wouldn't even know you're looking at the Pacific Ocean, but today it's a perfect shade of cerulean blue. But I feel pretty empty. The attack, and the fear that future ones will happen in cities like Los Angeles, is all anyone can talk about. My parents are terrified for me.

"Georgina, we would feel more comfortable if you just came home for a while," Mum tells me one Sunday.

"I have nothing to do at home."

"But you have nothing going on *there*, and it's so dangerous," she pleads. "You live a little too close to the Federal Building for me to sleep properly."

I compromise by spending four days with them in Carlsbad, which does feel safer, for whatever reason. But even in San Diego, where the military presence is huge thanks to Camp Pendleton and several naval bases, all people can do is worry, speculate and grieve. I spend the first night at home combing through some of my parents' old records: Patti Smith's *Horses*, Jimi Hendrix's *Electric Ladyland*, Joni Mitchell's *Blue* and Neil Young's *After the*

Gold Rush. After dinner, which includes Yorkshire pudding, my favorite English dish, we watch the news coverage, and it's upsetting and confusing. I never mention that someone I know is there, probably covered in human dust and debris and doing permanent damage to his respiratory system, all in the name of journalism. I've never felt like less of a journalist than now.

The next morning I meet my childhood friend Emily at Tamarack, the spot where we used to surf throughout high school and during college breaks. I still keep my yellow longboard in my bedroom at my parents' place. I haven't wanted to surf much since leaving Carlsbad, even though I always feel better after I do. There's magic in the salt water, but I haven't felt like getting wet since I moved to Los Angeles.

"Hey, you," Emily says, her eyes lighting up. "It's been too long."

We hug and she hands me some of her wax. It feels good to sit on the cool gray sand, which immediately affixes itself to my legs in a light layer. I put on a worn Billabong rash guard that I found at the bottom of my dresser and start to feel good for the first time since all of the devastation. Emily fills me in on the esthetician school she's attending and gives me all the gossip on our high school friends who are still living in the area. A handful are already married and having babies, which I'm surprised to hear. I can barely take care of a bromeliad.

"People ask me about you all the time," Emily tells me.

"Really?" I feel a bit defensive. "Why?"

"Um, maybe because you have the coolest job of any-one?" she says with wide eyes. "And you never come home anymore. You're too busy living the glamorous life in L.A. with the rich and famous."

"I heard that Paul Rogers is working at a think tank in D.C.," I say. "You don't think that's more exciting than standing on a red carpet?"

"No, Georgina. I don't."

Emily is the only person I'm regularly in touch with from high school. After the first couple years of college, I drifted apart from even my closest friends. It was often too painful to be surrounded by them because all I could think about were the three who had died. My three. When I'm in Orange County or Los Angeles there are no reminders of them, but here at home the memories are at every turn. Emily's family lives right by my parents, so it's easy to see her when I'm home for the holidays. She went through ex-actly what I did, so I've always felt a bond with her.

Our faces are completely bare of makeup, and our hair will get progressively wavier out here in the salt spray. "Let's go out," I say, motioning to the waves, which are a bit small, but at least no one else is around.

The water is cold and a shock to my system for the first few seconds, but then the ocean starts feeling more famil-iar. I dip my board under the first wave, letting the Pacific wash over me, and am transported to my childhood, when my friends and I would spend hours on the beach until our parents would force us to come home for dinner. This is where I had my first kiss while playing Spin the Bottle, and the place I would come to when I was in full teen angst mode and mad at my parents over something stupid.

My arms are instantly tired as I paddle out, which is no surprise, as I haven't been using these muscles at all lately. I'll be sore tomorrow. As we wait for a set, Emily tells me about her boyfriend, who works at a nearby taco shop and skates semiprofessionally, then asks if I'm seeing anyone.

"I am, actually," I say, not wanting to lie but not willing to tell the entire truth, even to her. "He's a journalist."

"You're stoked," she says.

I laugh to myself. If she only knew.

■ ■ ■

Simon has been in New York for weeks now, and tells me in a brief email that he is busy and exhausted. I try not to think about him, but really, how is that even possible? He's pretty much all I think about until I succeed in occupying myself for an hour or two with some petty but useful task, like organizing my closet by color. Because nothing is going on with celebrity events, my only beat as a reporter, I start back at the *InStyle* offices twenty hours a week, which is all they can give me, and wonder what I am going to do if the entertainment industry continues its nosedive during this war on terror and the rampant patriotism that's enveloping everything around us. It feels absurd to be fact-checking stories on jewelry designers and rounding up the best quotes from romance movies. I remind myself that

I'm lucky to be making money, which I desperately need, and to have twenty hours that distract me from obsessing about New York, a certain correspondent's safety and the future of the world.

I call Rebecca on my way home from work to see how she is doing, but she wants to talk about Simon. "What is going on with him?" she asks. "Is he still there?"

"Yes he is, and I need to prepare myself for the feeling, since he'll be going back to Australia within the next few weeks. It's hard because I am so bored at night. I'm used to working evenings."

"Georgina."

"What?"

"How do you know he's really in New York?"

"He told me he is, so I assume he's telling the truth," I answer, wondering why she would question that a correspondent would cover such a newsworthy event. "He's never lied to me before."

As soon as I say it, I realize the ridiculousness of this statement. Simon never lies to me, but he's lying to everyone else in his world. Every time he goes back to the office with a satisfied grin, or goes home and has to shower immediately to remove all traces of my perfume, it's a lie. And a big one at that. Of course he could be lying to me. It just never crossed my mind. Simon's broadcasts don't air in the U.S. and there's no place online where I can watch his reporting, so I have no real way of knowing what he does when he's not in my arms or under my skirt.

"It just seems odd that he's suddenly moving back to Australia, and now he's not even in town to pack up his life?"

"Another thing to blame the terrorists for," I say, attempting a joke as I pull up to my parking space.

"Are you even going to get to say goodbye?"

"Yes, of course. Actually, he's calling my home phone now—do you mind if I take it?"

"Go for it," she says.

"I don't mean to be one of those girls, but it might be important."

"G, go!"

"Okay, okay. Bye."

Simon sounds winded. "I'm back, and I have to see you. Are you home?"

"Yes."

"I'm on my way."

I immediately change out of my jeans and white V-neck T-shirt and put on a pale gray linen dress I got at a vintage store on La Brea last week. I quickly sweep some powder on my face and open a bottle of Malbec that I scored at an event.

The reunion is intense. He mauls me like a dog going after a piece of raw meat. We don't speak about September 11 or the last couple of weeks. I can tell he hasn't been sleeping well, and his conservatively short haircut has grown out a bit, revealing a thicker texture. He's rougher with me, handling my flesh with force. There are no warm kisses or long embraces, and he bites my neck so hard that I'm positive there'll be a mark tomorrow. He hasn't even said hello.

While we've certainly had our primal moments, sex with Simon is fun and gentle. His main focus is usually on pleasing me, and he likes to be affectionate before, during and after. He's more of a romantic than I am (one time I hurt his feelings a bit after telling him I could only cuddle for a few minutes without feeling claustrophobic) and always a perfect gentleman.

Not this time. After getting me undressed, he unzips his pants without taking them off and turns me against the wall. I get a rush from this out-of-the-ordinary dominant streak. I've been spending so many of my days thinking, questioning, worrying and doing. It's nice to not have to think about anything else right now.

He remains silent, but I hear him messing with a condom wrapper and am relieved that he's always sensible enough to remember. The only thing worse than sleeping with a married man is being pregnant with a married man's baby. Seconds later he pushes himself inside me, taking out what feels like a year's worth of pent-up aggression on my body, and within a couple of minutes it's over with a loud groan. For the first time, he doesn't worry about my pleasure but instead immediately runs to the bathroom, as if to get rid of the evidence. "I'm sorry I can't stay," he says when he returns.

"What do you mean? You can't go yet. We always have at least an hour."

"I could only get away for a bit with all that's going on. I have no choice, Georgina."

"You have to be kidding," I say, putting on my clothes and looking at the floor. "Then why even come over?"

"I'll be online tonight if you want to chat about things," he says with an exhausted sigh. "I'm sorry. I figured it was better than nothing."

He did, did he?

"What about New York?" I ask. "I've been so worried about you. Are you okay?"

"I am," he replies. "It was a nightmare. I feel like I've aged ten years. I'll tell you about it later."

"Why can't you tell me right now, while you're standing right in front of me?"

"I just can't, Georgina," he says, frustrated. "You're not the only one I've been away from."

"Nothing I can say will trump that, so go ahead," I retort, feeling a pout come over my face.

"I beg you to understand," he says. "I have to be with my family tonight."

"I've never stopped you from that. So I won't start now."

It finally hits me that this is a completely ludicrous arrangement, and so very convenient for him. After all, he is in control of when and where we meet. He can say no to me, but I never say no to him. I can always make it work because I am twenty-two, work part-time and have no one to answer to. Tears are welling in my eyes, but I'm determined to never cry in front of him. I'm not going to be a stereotype of some lovesick mistress-in-training. Simon doesn't ask me anything; he just gives me a quick kiss goodbye, says he's sorry, again, and disappears into the night.

It's the first time in our entire relationship that I feel used.

Over the next few weeks Simon is hardly able to get away, between work demands and having to pack up a 3,500-square-foot home for an international move, but I see him two more times and it's back to how it was before New York. He writes me a lot, saying he thinks about me constantly, but I'm already preparing myself for never seeing him again. When we IM, I tell him my work is still slow and that I'm worried about money, my career and the future of the world. He says I will be fine.

I keep telling myself the same thing.

6

This is the week Simon is leaving. I'm now working full-time in the offices at *InStyle* as a researcher, but I miss reporting, and part of me even wishes I were going to events. I was hired at $36,000 a year, which is significantly less than if I was doing red carpet gigs full-time, but I'll gladly take it during these uncertain times. Plus, there's health care. I'm not used to being in an office this much, and I could do without the mandatory birthday lunches and petty office dramas. I prefer being out on my own. Maybe it's an only-child thing, but I am just not a group person.

I haven't heard from Simon in a couple of days, but I know his departure is imminent. He promises we will have a real goodbye. I'm thinking about him when an IM pops up on my screen.

SG: Can you meet now?

GP: Yes, but just for an hour. I'm at the office on Wilshire.

SG: Well, I'm glad they haven't sacked you, with what's going on.

It's a few minutes before noon, and my editor is out on a schmoozefest with the city's top celebrity publicist, so the timing is actually more than okay. I often go home during lunch so I don't have to spend money at the Westside lunch spots everyone at work frequents, and also so I can have an hour to myself. It gets exhausting having to share an office with a bunch of women.

GP: *Is this it?*
SG: *I'm afraid so, darling.*
GP: *I'll be there in ten minutes.*

I grab my purse from the lower file cabinet and take the elevator down sixteen floors to the oppressive parking garage. I feel my heart racing. It's moments like these when being a neat freak pays off. I don't have to worry about unexpected company because my apartment is always clean.

He's there before I arrive and follows me to the front door with his hand on the small of my back, just like he did the first night we met. The gesture brings on immediate nostalgia, even though he's still here.

"Hi," I say, giving him a quick peck. "I can't believe you're going." It's only been a few months but it feels like longer, after the hours we've spent writing long emails and sending thousands of instant messages.

"We're all packed," he says. "It's surreal. I'm really going to miss California."

We catch up a bit, sitting in my tiny living room, and he teasingly asks whom I'm going to find to replace him. I laugh, playing along, but know in my heart that I'll never do anything like this again. I don't ever want to be with someone's husband. This was an unexpected one-night stand that turned into something more than I was prepared for. As much as I'll miss Simon, I'm also grateful that he's leaving before things get messy.

"I should ask you the same thing," I say, knowing it would be a challenge for Simon to return to a sexless marriage after the shenanigans we've been up to these last few months.

"There is no replacement for you," he says earnestly. "So I wouldn't even bother trying."

"That's sweet, but I need to know something."

"Ask me anything, darling."

"Before me, have there been others? Affairs, I mean." I ask because this is probably the last time we will talk, and I might as well know the answer.

"No, never," he says, furrowing his brow and looking me right in the eyes. "I told you that the first night we met."

"I won't be upset," I say, and I think I mean it. "I just want to know."

"I would never lie to you. It was just you. It *is* just you."

I'm not looking to feel special, but I believe him all the same. "Okay."

"Attraction is attraction, and when I saw you that day at the screening, I was determined to talk to you. The fact that you turned out to be smart, sexy and willing was more than I had hoped for," he says. "I have never done anything like that in my life."

"I never thought I'd see you after that night."

"But you couldn't stay away," he says, touching my knee and looking smug.

"No girl grows up dreaming of carrying on an affair with a married man," I say curtly, which makes his smirk disappear in an instant. It's the only time I've said the word *married* out loud in reference to him.

"Don't be so hard on yourself," he says. "I'm the one who's married, not you."

"I know," I say, looking down and fumbling with my keys. "I just never imagined myself in this situation."

"When you told me you were twenty-two, I had second thoughts," he explains. "But it was too late, I was smitten."

"I kept telling myself not to think about the age difference, but it's hard to ignore entirely."

"Every time was better than the last, which I didn't think was possible," he says, brushing my long bangs out of my face. "Didn't you think so?"

"Yes," I say quietly. "Absolutely. I feel like a different person when I'm with you."

"I honestly thought it would just be that one time in the hotel. I never planned for all of this. I didn't want to complicate things for either of us."

I have no idea why, but we don't have sex, even though it's our last chance. We talk, sitting side by side on my sofa, and hold hands. It's the most comfortable I've ever been with him, but after about forty minutes I say that I should go. But I have one last question. "Why did you trust me to keep your secret? What if I'd gone crazy?"

"Darling, you're too smart for that."

"Didn't you read the Kenneth Starr report? Monica Lewinsky was threatening the president of the United States. Girls go crazy all the time."

"Oh my God." He rolls his eyes. "You are not one of those girls."

"Did I tell you I saw her at a Motorola party in Hollywood? People were screaming at her like she was the devil. I heard a paparazzi guy tell her to get on her knees. It was sick."

We move on to the Chandra Levy case, which is still unsolved and bothers me every time I hear about it. Simon covered it extensively and is convinced that Gary Condit has nothing to do with Levy's disappearance. I am not so sure.

"Thank God you aren't a congressman," I say, teasing him. "With all those young, adoring girls around, who knows what kind of mess you would be in?"

"If they were anything like you, I'd be in serious trouble. But women just aren't like you, Georgina. You'll figure that out one day."

I kiss him for a few seconds, but I feel like I'm going to cry, so I pull back and play with the hem on my shirtdress. I didn't think I would be this sad to say goodbye.

"I would have dressed nicer if I knew this was the last time I would ever see you," I say.

"You have never been more lovely."

He smiles and gets up, while I stay seated on the couch. I take his hand and kiss it. He rubs my cheek one final time.

"I will never forget what this feels like," he says.

And with that, it's over.

7

There were a few weeks of missing Simon after he moved back to Sydney, but no tears or dramatic declarations of love. I was determined to move on. There was no other option. When an ocean and an entire day are between you, things just end naturally. That I didn't possess a single photo of us together made it much easier. Once he was gone he was gone, as far as I was concerned. I had no gifts, handwritten love letters, tchotchkes or mutual friends to serve as reminders. No awkward run-ins at holiday parties or favorite neighborhood restaurants.

I had my job and I had Greg, whom I began seeing here and there, to distract me for the first few months, and it worked. The entertainment industry was back in full swing, and so was I. There were more American flag pins being worn on the red carpet, but overall it was safe again to ask questions like "How will you be spending

Thanksgiving?" and "What was your biggest fashion regret?" Eventually I stopped thinking about Simon on a
regular basis, except for the times I'd meet an Australian
actor at an event or see a billboard with a shot of Bondi
Beach.

Once in a while we would IM, but I started signing on
less and less, since he was the only one I knew still using
AOL Messenger.

SG: Do you have any regrets?

GP: Just that we didn't have more time.

*SG: My biggest regret is that I was married. And how I treated
you the night after I returned from New York. I wasn't myself. I was
under so much stress. I think I was in shock from what I saw.*

GP: I know. It was out of character for you.

SG: I'm just relieved you agreed to see me after my behavior.

GP: Did you ever tell anyone about us?

SG: I haven't breathed a word. You?

GP: Just Rebecca, but she doesn't know the whole story.

SG: So, what are you wearing?

Life felt very much like it did pre-Simon, except I was now
a woman with real sexual experience and a secret that I
enjoyed keeping to myself. Work had become a bit more
frustrating in a post-9/11 world. Anytime I'd turn up to
an event, it meant a search of my car, bomb-sniffing dogs
and photo ID badges. Ad revenues were down, and payments seemed to arrive later and later. I started looking
for other opportunities, but anytime I found something
more meaningful, the pay would be half what I earned

with *InStyle*. I gave myself an internal deadline of a year to find something else and began freelancing for other publications, including the *Los Angeles Times*. My first story ran in December 2002. I was so excited about my debut that I got up at five in the morning and went to the local newsstand, only to see that they misspelled my first name. The circulation for that issue was two million. Greg was nice enough to Photoshop the correct spelling in so I could at least have it for my portfolio.

In early 2003, Simon unexpectedly had to return to L.A. for work. Since I was still single—and bored—I agreed to a reunion. We started emailing each other more and more the few weeks leading up to the visit, and I could tell right away that things were going to be exactly the same, if not better. Distance and time had done nothing to curb his desire, or mine. I had a little more experience under my belt, and I knew that I could spend a night with him without doing any permanent damage to my emotional wellbeing. I'd done it before, after all, and emerged unscathed.

Simon was staying at the Century Plaza with some high-level business associates for one evening only before heading to New York for a big meeting. I drove over there around nine on a Tuesday night, after his three-hour dinner meeting. It all felt very fitting, given our first encounter. His room was just a few doors down from the elevator on the eleventh floor.

As he kept me waiting on the other side of the door, my heart started racing. Was I at the right room? Was he still with a colleague? I was on the verge of turning around to call him from down the hall when the door opened.

"Well, this was certainly worth the fourteen-hour flight," he said. "Get in here, gorgeous."

Seeing Simon again sent a jolt of electricity straight through me, just like the night we first met. L.A.'s lights twinkled behind him as we had a long, warm hug and he took off the only coat I owned, a vintage '60s leopard print with oversize gold buttons. Everything felt familiar, from his scent to the texture of his stubble, and I liked being enveloped by him again after fifteen months apart.

"I've never seen you so covered up," he remarked, hanging my coat in the closet. "To be perfectly honest, most of my memories of you aren't fully clothed."

"It's freezing," I said of the uncharacteristic forty-two-degree weather that January night. "Anything under sixty-four degrees and the entire city freaks out, myself included."

"You look beautiful," he said. "I'm much grayer."

We caught up briefly, but I could tell he was dying to get to the main event. I was, too. I hadn't had sex in months. I'd been working most nights and wasn't in the mood to try online dating, as a few of my friends had suggested. I also had a newfound obsessive fear of contracting HPV. ("Everyone has it," Rebecca explained one day, like she was telling me about the weather. "And there's no test for guys, so yeah.") It was nice to have a reason to buy some new lingerie and say no to working a gala that night. There were plenty of eager interns and assistants just waiting for me to give up my spot, so I rarely turned down assignments, but that night I had to, for my own sanity. It would get me through another dry spell.

After kissing me for a minute, Simon pulled back. "Are you seeing anyone at the moment?"

"No," I said, unable to figure out if he'd be jealous or turned on if I had said yes.

"I'm surprised. I figured you'd be out there breaking hearts all over town."

"I went on a date a few weeks ago with a *Variety* editor," I admitted, leaving out the part where we shared a passionless kiss that made me wonder if Simon was the yardstick that every future man I am ever with is going to be measured against. "He was boring, awkward and rude to the waitress, which I didn't appreciate as a former server."

"I don't see you with someone like that," he said.

"No, you see me with someone twenty years older than me, who is completely unavailable and living on another continent, right?" I asked with a smile as I turned the radio by the bed to KCRW.

Zero 7's "Polaris" played in the background as we kissed again. "You know I wish things were different," he said, approaching me from behind and placing his hands on my hips. "It hasn't been easy being apart from you. That reminds me, I brought you something."

I was curious; we'd never bought each other gifts before. He pulled a small wombat stuffed animal out of his briefcase and placed it in my hand. That it was in there while he was having his meeting delighted me.

"That is so sweet," I said, placing it on the nightstand. "I love it."

Since I was in that hotel room that night for one reason only, I stood up and took off the red long-sleeved wool dress I was wearing, revealing a black bra/panty/garter/thigh-high situation I had proudly assembled earlier. It was very Bettie Page, if Bettie Page had been a mixed-race Asian girl with wavy brown hair and freckles. I could have worn anything, or nothing, and Simon would be happy, but this made him speechless for a rare moment.

"I am not going to last long with you looking like that," he said quietly, pulling me toward him. "What are you trying to do to me, darling?"

"I missed you, too," I said, smiling.

"I have never wanted you more than right this instant."

"More than that first night?" I asked, raising my left eyebrow a touch and toying with the waistband of his boxer briefs.

"I have to take a photo of you." He pulled out his phone.

"Are you crazy?"

"I won't get your face in it. I promise."

"I don't think so," I said, taking a sip of my gin and tonic.

"You look so incredible, and I just want to remember you like this."

"Fine." I gave him my best pinup pose, half-joking, and the flash went off.

"You look stunning." he said, motioning at the screen.

"I don't want to see it. It's embarrassing."

"Come here," he said, grabbing my waist. "You have no idea how much I've missed this."

There is something about hotel sex that is so much hotter than one-bedroom-apartment sex. Add in a married lover in town to help broker a multimillion-dollar deal to sell his network to a U.S. company, and you don't really need foreplay. We inhaled each other as if we both knew it was really the last time. I had no plans to be in Australia anytime soon, and he probably wouldn't return to Los Angeles once this deal was done.

The bed went unused as he turned the lights down and led me to face the window. I could just make out his reflection in the glass as he pushed my lace thong to the side and entered me slowly. The city view was insane, with a million lights dotting the horizon, but I could only focus on how good it felt to have him inside me and hear his breath rapidly increasing while Thievery Corporation played in the background. I quickly fogged up the window with my panting. After a few minutes, he had another idea.

"I need to see you," he said. "Sit on the desk."

We had never made use of office furniture before, so I obliged and wrapped my legs and feet, still in heels as he liked, around him.

"I think about you all the time, you know," he told me right before I came.

■ ■ ■

The king-size bed was massive and so soft, with all its fluffy pillows and a down-filled duvet. I climbed inside, euphoric, and my breathing returned to normal as I stared at the recessed ceiling. It felt like he'd hit the reset button and brought me right back to the summer of 2001. Simon grabbed some almonds from the minibar while I quickly downed an entire bottle of water.

After a few minutes of enjoying the afterglow, he had another idea. "Take a picture with me. We don't have any of us," he said, taking his phone from the nightstand.

"Is that really a good idea? In bed, of all places?"

"Of course it is. I don't want to forget this."

"I just think it's irresponsible to have evidence since you're still married. I'm trying to protect you."

"Live a little, Georgina," he said. "I will guard them with my life, I promise."

"Seeing as you were just vigorously pounding me from behind in front of all of Los Angeles, I wouldn't say I'm that uptight," I retorted, scooting closer. "Okay, fine, go ahead."

I sat up next to Simon while he stretched his arms and pressed the camera icon on his flip phone. I put my head closer to his and we took a few G-rated headshots together. He said he would email them to me.

"No, it's okay," I said. "You keep them."

I would never be that young, attractive or carefree again in my life, but the thought of someone finding those photos on my computer one day didn't appeal to me. I never wanted to have to explain anything about our relationship to anyone, and I liked the idea of out of sight, out of mind. I always joke with Rebecca that if anything ever happened to me, she would have to come in and do the digital and physical clearing out of everything incriminating in my apartment: old diaries, IM chats with Simon that I saved, condoms and my vibrator. The thought of my family having to go through that stuff makes me sick to my stomach.

"I may need to look at them on occasion, you know, to remind myself," he said as he kissed my face and nuzzled my neck, causing me to let out an uncharacteristic giggle.

"That tickles!"

"I love seeing you laugh. You need to laugh more. You're still young, unlike me, and you play it so cool all the time."

"I am not playing it cool; I just don't think you're that funny."

"Is that right?" he asked as he climbed on top of me, pinning me to the bed with his hands on my wrists.

"Please stop! Simon! I'm serious," I screamed as he grabbed at my waist, which tickled even more. "Someone's going to think you're murdering me!"

"Okay, but only because you're so gorgeous."

"If you want to see me laugh, then just make me laugh," I said as I pulled the soft sheets over me.

"I'd rather make you come again."

As we were lying there, intertwined and facing each other, I thought this was the happiest I had ever felt. Contrary to what readers of *Us Weekly* may think, being around celebrities all the time isn't that great. I'm always alone, even in a crowd. People are nice to me only because I'm doing something for them or for their client, and the conversations at awards shows and fashion parties leave a lot to be desired intellectually. Famous people and I have nothing in common on any level, and I'd like to do something more meaningful in the world than ask Jennifer Aniston about her favorite perfume.

I work hard, often until two in the morning, transcribing interviews until my eyes scream in pain and my wrists ache. I go to bed alone each night and spend most hours of the day by myself, too. I suppose I designed it that way by choosing to work as a freelancer and working nights instead of days. I don't expect anyone to feel sorry for me. It is what it is.

As I recovered from the tickling, I started stroking the cold, soft back of Simon's arm, something I had been doing since we first met. It was nice to know I was spending the night and we were in no rush.

"You know, being here with you and being in bed with you again—this is what it feels like to be alive," he said. "Everything else I do is just stalling, waiting and hoping for this feeling again."

A lump formed in my throat the instant he said it. It was exactly what I felt in that moment but never said to him or anyone else. I wondered if Simon might be the only person on earth with whom I could have this connection. If so, how depressing. In the year he had been gone, there was no one else, aside from Greg, who held my interest past a date or two. The two guys I'd slept with in that period had no real clue what they were doing, and I regretted the act immediately, on both counts.

In that bed, in that hotel I would drive past a hundred times after he returned to Australia again, was the first time I thought I loved Simon. But because I couldn't say how I felt, I just kissed him, put my head on his chest and changed the subject. "Remember that club we went to?"

"Oh my God, how on earth could I forget?"

Simon suggested that we go to a sex club a few months after we started seeing each other. Well, it wasn't a sex club per se. I mean, no one was having actual sex. But it was a freaky scene nonetheless. The club was essentially a warehouse near LAX with a rather sad makeshift dungeon and different themed rooms where you could "explore your fantasies," as the website encouraged. There were about fifty people there on a Saturday night, but the place had to be at least 10,000 square feet, so it all felt pretty barren.

"How did you even know about that place?" I asked, sitting back up.

"I saw something about it online and thought it would be fun to check out. I always wondered what went on at those things. Obviously I wasn't going to bring Clare, and I figured you might give it a go."

"Remember that guy in the silver bodysuit?"

We both started laughing, thinking of this poor fellow who must have been into some form of S&M that required him to wear latex from head to toe. We couldn't see his face underneath the suit. I have no idea how he was even breathing. We watched him for nearly an hour, and he never talked to anyone or did anything except stand in the middle of the main room, where a rockabilly girl was singing jazz standards a bit off-key.

"He looked quite sad with his shoulder bag, didn't he?" Simon remarked.

"Like, did he change into that at home and then drive over to Inglewood that way? Or was it just on up to his neck and then he zipped up the last bit before walking in the door? That scene was so fucked up. If it was supposed to get me excited, it did the exact opposite."

"Well, you were up for it, which I loved," he said. "You were always ready for anything."

I agreed to go with Simon because it would be an adventure, and who else would I go with to this type of place? It was something I never would have done before meeting him—or after. I didn't know what to expect or what to wear. My short black dress and heels were wildly out of place, as most women opted for fishnet tops, pleather and nurse costumes.

"I have a natural curiosity that will probably get me in trouble one day," I said. "I guess that's why I became a writer. I want to know everything."

"And you know how to keep a secret, which is key for any good journalist—or lover."

"Remember we talked to another couple who seemed somewhat normal? That blond guy and his wife."

"Right. I imagine they had two kids at home and got the sitter so they could spice things up, and then they saw that insane scene and probably wanted to run home."

"It was amazing how everyone was acting like they were just at some regular bar. Like, 'Yeah I have a collar on, my owner has got my breasts tied up with this special rope from Japan, and some clothespins are cutting off the blood supply to my nipples, but I'm still going to sip on my drink and make small talk.'"

"I just remember we got on the 405 as fast as we could," he said. "I don't know what I was thinking, wanting to go there. I guess I figured it would be hot, but what's hot is just being here with you."

I flipped on the television and we watch half an episode of *Seinfeld*, laughing in all the same places, before changing the channel to CNN. "Do you think there is going to be an invasion of Iraq?" I asked him.

"Absolutely. Bush wants to please George H.W. more than he cares about the implications for the rest of us. The U.K. and Australia are sure to join the efforts."

"A war is only going to strengthen the terrorists' resolve, don't you think?"

"Most definitely. And it will change the world for generations to come."

"I have a friend at Reuters." I told him of my college classmate Seth, who is the only other hard-hitting journalist I know. "I always want to hear about his stories because they are so different from mine, but he's jealous of my career."

"Why, does he want to be in closer proximity to the Angelinas of the world?"

"Well, I'm sure he wouldn't mind." I smiled. "But he always points out that I am better paid, safe, and have a chance at a normal life if I want one. I guess he feels like he can't have a relationship or keep many friends since he's always on the move, typically in Africa and the Middle East. And I agree with him. I don't want to be alone forever."

"Being a foreign correspondent can be exhausting," Simon said. "My home life has certainly suffered, no question. I was abroad when my father died. I wouldn't meet nieces and nephews until they were already walking and talking."

"I think I have a glamorized view of what that type of work actually is. Just like people have a glamorized view of what it is I do."

"The grass is always greener, darling."

"My dream would be to have a regular column, where I could write about a variety of interesting subjects and people, but get to stay here and have a personal life. That way I could feel like I'm contributing to a larger conversation, outside Hollywood."

"You'll get there."

■ ■ ■

At some point in the middle of the night, we had a long and passionate session in the bed, this time for what felt like hours. My lips felt numb from kissing him, and my legs began to tremble. As Simon got rid of the condom, I saw that the sun was coming up. We watched it together in matching plush hotel robes, like we were an old married couple with nothing to hide. I hadn't seen the sun rise since I was seventeen and stayed up all night on the beach on the last day of high school. Since Brenda, Ryan and Christina didn't get to graduate, we did a special ceremony for them, paddling out on our surfboards to place leis in the water in their honor. I remember thinking how surreal it was to be crying salty tears into the already salty ocean.

"How are you even awake?" I asked. "Jet lag is going to be a nightmare."

"It was worth it, darling."

"What are you going to do now?"

"I haven't been in a newsroom for the last few months, and with the sale I'll have more responsibility," he said of his new role as a television executive at Australia's largest broadcasting company. "I miss it already. There's nothing like the adrenaline rush of a big news day."

"I wouldn't know. Right now I'm working on a round-up of gifts that celebrities give each other as congratulations presents when they win the Oscar."

"You're too smart for all that crap," he said. "Maybe you should move to Sydney and work at the *Morning Herald*. I could help you get a visa."

He was dead serious, but I rolled my eyes. "You know, I lived in London for a year when I was nineteen," I said.

"You never told me that."

"You never asked."

"Well, I suppose there's a lot we still don't know about each other," Simon said quietly.

"Aside from the gray skies I loved it, but I had to finish college and see my family, and there was my boyfriend at the time, so I came back," I said. "I had a cute flat right near Portobello Road and family in the area, so I wasn't too homesick."

"Any romances?"

"No, I was a good girl, totally devoted to my boyfriend, but I had opportunities."

"Of course you did, darling."

I tell Simon about how I worked in a local pub for a few months to make some extra cash while attending University College London for my junior year. "Being American, and from California specifically, made me stand out wherever I went. Especially at work. There was an English bartender named Phillip who flirted with me incessantly, and I loved every minute of it. He was determined, but I never so much as kissed him."

"Poor fellow," Simon said with fake empathy.

"He was incredibly charming with his quick, dry wit, and he had a mop of wavy brown hair, like Hugh Grant."

"Is that your type?"

"I prefer a different Mr. Grant," I said with a coquettish grin. "Anyway, Phillip was only a few years older than I was but had left school around sixteen. He lived in a flat with four of his mates who were always getting piss drunk and shouting about football. I had no interest in either activity, but I liked his confidence and his talent for making me laugh constantly during my four-hour shifts. He would often volunteer to walk me home, even though I lived just a Tube stop away, and we'd sometimes share a cigarette on the way."

"You were torturing this poor bloke," Simon said.

"Not intentionally. Toward the end of my time there I found myself thinking of him quite a bit, and by the last week of work he was begging me for 'just a snog,' but I refused, even though I could feel the tension building between us with each shift. I would tell myself that I couldn't cheat on John, even if he never found out about it. And he would never cheat on me. Of that I was completely certain."

"He probably still thinks about you," Simon offered, "wondering what it would have been like if he were lucky enough to get close to you."

"It wasn't like *that*," I said. "I don't think he was in love with me."

"Georgina, it doesn't take long to fall for you."

"He was quite mopey when I left," I recollected. "I'm sure if I had stayed longer, something would have happened. There are only so many times you can walk away from a person when that spark is there."

"Tell me about it." He smiled.

"I don't find it easily. I can only think of a handful of people I've ever really connected with over the years. Obviously you're at the top of that list."

"Which is why I want you to come to Sydney."

"I can't move there," I told Simon. "Even if I did, it wouldn't be for us."

"Ouch."

"I don't mean it like that. I just mean that you can't promise me anything, and I don't know how we would manage to see each other in a city where almost every adult there knows your name."

"You flatter me," he said.

"I'm not trying to. It's just a fact. How many years have you been on television there?"

"Nearly twenty years."

"I can't imagine being even more discreet than we had to be in L.A."

"What if we didn't have to be? What if we could come out and not be so secretive?"

"I don't see how that's possible. Maybe the reason we have this chemistry is *because* of the secret. It's not a real relationship."

"Of course it is," he said. "Don't tell me there isn't a connection here, Georgina."

"I care about you, of course, but my whole life is here. I think we'd have to be in a relationship that's out in the open locally before I could move across the world," I said. "And how would we explain how we met?"

"I think things between us would be even better if our relationship was out in the open. There's so much we haven't done together."

"Because you are married," I added. I hated to bring it up, especially while we were lying in bed naked.

"What if I told you I was filing for divorce?"

8

GP: *I'm sorry I didn't know what to say last week. I was a bit in shock. I didn't know divorce was ever an option.*

SG: *Things haven't been good for many years. I kept hoping that the relationship would improve, but it didn't. The marriage was doomed from the beginning.*

GP: *Why? Weren't you in love then?*

SG: *Of course. Then. We met at university. I was 21 and she was 20. We both wanted to work in television and eventually she was my producer.*

GP: *You never mentioned this to me. I assumed she was a house-wife. Wow. I'm stunned.*

SG: *It was great when we were boyfriend and girlfriend, and I was happy to marry at the time. Now I realise we were both too young. Twenty-three. Can you imagine? We hardly knew who we were at that age.*

GP: *No. I can't.*

SG: *We started moving around for my career, and she wasn't happy once we arrived in the States. I knew it, but I persuaded her to give it a go. She quickly began hating me for it.*

GP: *Is that why you moved back in 2001?*

SG: *Well, I think I was ready to go back and see family, take the promotion and, yes, perhaps attempt to save the marriage, but things didn't change with the move.*

GP: *So it's not just about geography. Do you think she envied your career?*

SG: *Perhaps. She's had her own success, though. She's now producing a news program here. I think she just felt very alone in the States, L.A. in particular. I wasn't around a lot and we had two young kids.*

SG: *Are you still there, darling?*

GP: *Yes, sorry, I had to take a call. I'm back.*

SG: *Good. Honestly, I think we were simply too young to make such a commitment. It worked at first, but things have been broken for ages.*

GP: *Do you remember, when you left, you said that I was the only girl you were with, aside from her? Is that really true?*

SG: *Of course. I have never lied to you. You know that. I mean, I slept with a few women in my uni days, before Clare, but you are the only other woman I've been with since then.*

GP: *It didn't seem like it was your first time. Having an affair, I mean.*

SG: *I was so nervous that first night. You have no idea.*

GP: *Then you deserve a Golden Globe.*

SG: I bought a three-pack of Trojans in the gift shop when I went to book the room. I don't think I had bought condoms since I was at school.

GP: I was wondering about that. Well, I'm glad you did.

SG: Like I said, I hadn't been with anyone besides Clare since I was twenty-one.

GP: Is that why you went after a 22-year-old? ☺ To pick up where you left off?

SG: Very funny. I actually thought you were older. You carry yourself with confidence and maturity. The age difference disappeared for me in an instant. I always saw you as my equal.

GP: But I wasn't. I was fresh out of college, and you were the second person I had ever slept with. I may be mature for my age, but you have far more life experience on every level.

SG: I guess so, but don't sell yourself short, Georgina. You are remarkable. Perfect, actually.

GP: I'm blushing.

SG: I told you on that Laguna Beach trip that I was falling in love with you. That was true. It was quite painful to say goodbye. I was gutted.

GP: Well, I'm glad you came back, even if it was just for one night. I wish it could have been for longer.

SG: Me too. I never thought I'd see you again, so it was a treat and a lovely reminder of our time together. You know when I went to cover 9/11 and didn't know if the world was ending, I realised that I should have married you. What I thought was just a fun fling for both of us was something more serious.

GP: *As flattering as that is, I would have had to meet you in another time and place. I mean, I can't be married at 23. I'm not Mormon. I have so much I want and need to do. And you might be forgetting that you have not actually been available.*

SG: *You could do those things here, and with me. But I know what you mean. I often wonder why we couldn't have met five years later, when I was single and you were ready for something more serious. Who knows, maybe the taboo nature of it all is what you were interested in. I don't think you ever wanted to be with me; you just wanted to sleep with me. And I was so desperate for a sex life. I found one, and much more than that, thanks to you. I figured that our affair would help me keep my family together, because I don't think I could have lasted much longer without a physical relationship.*

GP: *At first I enjoyed doing something so far out of my typical behavior. I've always been a model daughter, student, reporter, etc. But then I grew to truly enjoy being around you. Sometimes I wonder what would have happened if I never went to the screening. Would you have approached a different girl? Would she have slapped your face upon finding out you were married? Would you have had to go to some chat room for married men seeking affairs?*

SG: *I never thought about it, darling. It wasn't a plan. You know I never strayed before, but there's only so much I could take. At that time I felt genuinely isolated by her lack of affection. Still do.*

GP: *Does she treat you badly?*

SG: *No, but we're essentially just roommates. I can't think of the last time we had sex. I haven't felt desired by her since our first year of marriage. Eons ago. The few times in a year when we do make love, it's missionary only, and she often jumps if I even touch her.*

GP: *That's sad, Simon. It's not right.*

SG: I haven't had a blow job in over a year. To her, sex is a chore. It's as though she's dead from the waist down. All of her affection and love is given to the children, and I'm not sure there's much left over for me. For a long time I didn't mind, because she's a wonderful mother, but a person can only take so much. My sex life these days consists of a lot of time in front of the computer with a box of tissues.

GP: That was too much information, but I understand. It's a waste, right? Two people under one roof, and they would rather masturbate than be with each other?

SG: I doubt she does. She has always been a bit uptight when it comes to sex, or even her own body.

GP: How could YOU marry someone who's uptight in bed? I think she needs her hormones tested. This doesn't sound right. I thought women hit their sexual prime in their 30s and 40s?

SG: I didn't know any different. It was better in the beginning. We sort of grew up together in the marriage, and for many years I was fine with it. But then I wanted to try different things. After so many years, you evolve. I want an imaginative sex life. I haven't felt wanted by her since the early days. And the children made it more challenging. I thought they would bring us closer together, but that hasn't been the case, unfortunately.

GP: And she judged you for wanting sex or to try new things? Or simply just said no?

SG: Both. That's part of what was and is so exciting about being with you. Not just the sex, which is exhilarating, but that you are so open. I like that you initiate new things and come up with surprises and outfits. God, the outfits.

GP: The other night was particularly memorable. I'm not sure I can ever look at a hotel desk again without getting a bit flushed.

SG: I like experimenting and being someone else for a change. It was like being a character.

GP: But see, that's what I was alluding to the other night. I'm not even sure if we truly know each other. If you were essentially being a character, or showing just one side of you, then there are obviously other sides or "characters" that I don't know, and vice versa. You're seeing an hour or two of life with me. Maybe it's the best hour or two of your day, or your year even, but it's not the day-to-day life of what a real relationship would entail.

SG: I just don't think life with you could be boring, Georgina.

GP: I'm sure you could get sick of me if we actually spent more than 24 hours together.

SG: You always have something interesting to say. I can confide anything in you. In some ways you know me better than anyone. We connect on many levels.

GP: Well, it may take 48 hours then.

SG: And sexually, I'd go as far as saying we are soul mates, wouldn't you?

GP: We are very compatible in the bedroom, yes. I feel more alive when we are in the same room than when we aren't.

SG: Maybe people like us aren't made for marriage.

GP: Perhaps. But you've lasted longer than most. Are you serious about splitting up?

SG: Yes. I think she wants it, too, but just doesn't want to have to admit it. We're essentially living like siblings. We get on well, the families are close with one another, but the passion and romance are long gone. However, she doesn't like to fail at anything, and it's complicated with the kids. Unraveling it all—the house, friends, figuring out custody—will be a challenge.

Seeing the word *kids* typed out makes me feel disgusted with myself. It's hard enough to ignore the fact that Simon is married, but knowing he has children, whom he adores, is what usually upsets me in the moments when I question my behavior, when I worry what my karmic retribution will be ("That's not how karma works," Simon says) and how I can be so drawn to someone who's doing something I don't approve of. We rarely speak of them. I've only seen one photograph, and even that felt inappropriate.

GP: She doesn't know about me, right?

SG: God no. I have never said a word to anyone, and I don't plan to. I have no problem keeping secrets. It's part of my job.

GP: I just don't want to become part of any divorce proceedings. I don't want her to ever know my name.

SG: You're not the reason we're splitting up, so don't lose even a minute of your life thinking that. This would have happened eventually, with or without you.

GP: You don't think she ever noticed that you would come home at a strange time or that you weren't initiating sex anymore?

SG: If I actually felt guilty maybe she would notice something, but I honestly feel like I'm entitled to a sex life. I'm not dead. I needed to feel something; it had been so long.

GP: I get it. I just don't ever want anyone to know.

SG: I will protect you at all costs.

GP: I appreciate that. In my mind, there are levels of being unfaithful. There's the "I got drunk and I just kissed someone at a bar and it was wrong and I will never do anything like that again." There are other people who are having full-blown emotional affairs at work or wherever, but they never even touch each other, so it's not officially considered cheating. Then there are people who have sex, maybe once, maybe twice, with almost nameless, faceless people. Which is worse?

SG: Maybe all of these people are just trapped in unhappy relationships and need to know that they are still alive and desired. Maybe they need to know that they can still make someone smile. Or orgasm. ☺

GP: Then there are people who not only have sex and share meals, but they chat often and genuinely enjoy each other's company. They respect each other. Some would say that they might be in love. They used to get off on the danger of it all, but it ends up becoming a real thing where birthdays are celebrated and tears are sometimes shed. The affair continues for years, maybe even a lifetime. I don't want to be one of those people, Simon. That's so many layers of deception. It's just wrong.

SG: What do you mean? I've never heard you bothered by me being married. I figured you liked some element of it.

GP: Let me shed some light on the topic then. I do not "like" the fact that you are married. Ninety-nine times out of a hundred, I would have said no way. You weren't the first married man to ever hit on me. But there was something, like a magnetic pull, going on between us once we went to that restaurant. Pheromones, chemistry, whatever you want to call it. It was the last thing on earth I was expecting that night. I saw your wedding band early into the meal and debated just making up an excuse and getting out of there. Then we talked at dinner about your being unhappy for quite some time. I couldn't comprehend it. You were cute, funny, smart and powerful. Isn't that what excites most women?

SG: Sweet of you to say.

GP: *Still, it's not something I ever aspired to do. And if I were Clare, it would be bad enough that you were fucking someone half your age, but that you're discussing intimate details of your marriage with her, too? That would put anyone over the edge. I just feel bad about it, even though I appreciate knowing more about how you found your way to me.*

SG: *Well, it's ending, and no one will know about us. I know you won't move to Sydney. It was just a fantasy, I guess.*

GP: *If you get divorced and we ever find ourselves in the same country again, I'll see you in a heartbeat. I promise.*

SG: *Unless* you're *married.*

GP: *I doubt I'll ever get married. I don't understand how you sustain a marriage for a lifetime.*

SG: *I think* we *could find a way.*

GP: *You don't think our chemistry is because we're doing something we're not supposed to do? Because of the risk?*

SG: *No, darling. Maybe in the beginning, but our connection has only gotten stronger with time. I can only imagine how wonderful our relationship could be if we could have uninterrupted time together.*

GP: *It's sad to think that last week was probably the last time.*

SG: *It doesn't have to be, but yes, I know what you mean. I realise I'm a world away.*

GP: *At least we have IM.*

SG: *Hey, will you send me some pictures?*

GP: *What kind of pictures?*

SG: *You know what kind.*

GP: *Seriously? You just saw me and took photos. Don't you have a fresh image in your mind?*

SG: *What can I say? If I can't have you in the flesh, I'll take the next best thing.*

GP: *We'll see.*

SG: *I'm getting hard just thinking about it.*

■ ■ ■

Later that evening, after returning from a dinner party where I watched two famous actresses push three pieces of asparagus from one side of their plate to the other as though it were a choreographed ballet routine, I decide to indulge Simon's request. Although we get along like we've known each other for years and have well-matched sex drives, one reason I am so drawn to him is his desire for me. It seems endless. Even on a regular day, where I'm dressed down and have my hair in a ponytail, he makes me feel like a temptress. I've come alive since meeting him and stepped quite far out of my comfort zone on numerous occasions only to realize that I love it. So taking a few sexy pictures doesn't seem like such a big deal after what we've already done.

I decide to do a few different looks, thinking about the right angles and flattering light ahead of time, creating an atmosphere that's more *Playboy* than *Penthouse*. After taking a few shots on my bed, holding my Sony digital camera with my outstretched left hand, I start feeling aroused knowing how happy they are going to make him. After my photo shoot is finished, I scroll through the results, deleting the bad ones and keeping the best few. I don't always love photos of myself, but these are pretty good. In the morning I'll email them to Simon and wait for his reaction.

■ ■ ■

I can't believe it, but it's actually happening. Rebecca is getting married. Not to the snowboard instructor but to Scott, a West Point graduate who is sweet, funny and absolutely crazy about her. I'm the maid of honor, so it's been a busy few months planning the bridal shower, doing the requisite bachelorette party (we're all slightly traumatized by what we saw during the "male revue" in San Francisco) and accompanying her to dress fittings.

I'm the only single girl out of the six bridesmaids, so there have been a lot of sweet looks and comments like "Don't worry, Georgina, you're next." I'm not sure I want to be next. I can't imagine wearing a tiara or sleeping with one person for the rest of my life. I can barely handle wearing the bridesmaid dress, a floor-length, sage green number made from a polyester blend that is meant to look like satin. The color flatters no skin tone known to mankind. Rebecca has many amazing qualities, but style isn't really one of them.

I keep my mouth shut, as there have already been plenty of comments from Scott's side of the family and Rebecca's Bay Area posse about me living in L.A. and having such a "glamorous" and "exciting" job. At the shower and bachelorette weekend I was interrogated on all things celebrity, even though the events were supposed to be all about the bride.

"Who's the biggest bitch you've met?"

"Is Tom Cruise really short?"

"Have you ever hooked up with one of them? I would!"

"How do you talk to them? I would be so nervous!"

We're just a few weeks away from the June wedding, and since this is Rebecca's last L.A. visit for a while we're hitting Burke Williams for a spa day, which is a rare treat for me. Rebecca's moving to Washington, D.C., right after the wedding, and much as I hope we'll stay close, I know it will never be the same. Different time zones, different lives. Scott got an offer from the Department of Homeland Security that he couldn't refuse, and Rebecca, a burgeoning architectural photographer, says she is ready to be back east again. She wants to have kids immediately. D.C. is not Manhattan, but I'm happy if she's happy.

In the spa sauna, I fill her in on the few dates I've been on in the last couple of months. There was the stand-up comedian who had a terrifying case of road rage, the newly sober Associated Press reporter who always insisted on meeting me at a bar to test his boundaries, and the creative director who asked me to please wear knee-high boots whenever I was in his presence.

"What is wrong with these people?" Rebecca says, clearly appreciating Scott even more every minute.

Near us, a trio of fortysomething women are complaining about their children's nannies. "It's like everyone who ever had an unresolved issue comes to L.A.," I say.

"The only common denominator is that they are all obsessed with Wilco. I don't get it."

"You need a real man, Georgina. No offense, but do guys who listen to Wilco and Death Cab for Cutie really know how to fuck?"

I laugh and think she may be on to something. Her fiancé did two tours in Iraq and completed last year's Ironman.

"I met one really nice guy the other night, but he lives in Northridge. I can't do that commute," I tell her.

"How far is Northridge?"

"I don't know. Maybe twenty miles north, but it would take an hour each way with traffic. Who has time for that?"

"You'd better stick to a five-mile radius."

"Plus it's probably twenty degrees warmer. Sometimes I feel like I just don't have the energy required for dating in Los Angeles."

"That reminds me," Rebecca says, perking up and removing her towel. "Do you ever hear from Simon? Whatever happened to him?"

It's odd to hear someone say his name out loud. I have kept that secret for so long, buried deep under countless nights and weekends of work, dead-end relationships, random hookups in bars, and dates that were about as fun as doing my taxes. Bec was always a fan of Simon's even though they never met. I tell her we email once a year or so and that he's still in Sydney.

I know he must follow my career, at least on occasion, because he usually writes to comment on something of mine in print, as I'm still freelancing for the *Times*, or to warn me that a new editor I'm working for is a complete prick. In these emails he always asks about my love life, which I think is just a way for him to turn the conversation to anything sexual, but I don't indulge him with any stories. So many of our IM conversations turned pornographic once he moved back. It was fun for a while, but I eventually lost interest since he was still married. I didn't want to be part of his infidelity any longer, even if it was just over a computer network. Last year I finally cut off communication and told him to call me when he was divorced, thinking it would never actually happen.

"Not really," I say. "Once in a blue moon. That all feels like a hundred years ago."

Rebecca and I part ways so we can each get a massage, and make a plan to meet back in the oversize whirlpool that's currently inhabited by ladies in their fifties and sixties who appear incredibly comfortable with their nakedness. A pretty and petite masseuse named Theresa introduces herself and leads me with her hand on my shoulder to a candlelit treatment room downstairs. I spend the entire fifty minutes thinking about Simon—who must be able to sense this from 7,500 miles away, because within a week there is a message from him.

■ ■ ■

Because of the seventeen-hour time difference and fact that we haven't heard each other's voices in almost two years, I am a bit gun-shy to call him back. His voicemail sounded upbeat so I don't think anything is wrong, which means I can justifiably give myself a full twenty-four hours before placing the call.

Since Rebecca is swamped with wedding stuff, I call my friend Lourdes, an up-and-coming family attorney who lives in my building. "Hey, are you busy?"

"No," she says. "I just got back from hiking Runyon Canyon."

"That's impressive."

"It's such a fucking *scene*. Parking's a nightmare and you have to overhear the worst conversations, but the view is worth it. I have to remember to bring headphones next time to block out the *beyotches*." She always makes me laugh.

"I was wondering if I could come upstairs real quick. I just want to run something by you."

"Sure, as long as you don't mind that my hair looks like a rat's nest."

I grab my keys and phone and take the rear staircase up to her unit, which is slightly bigger and nicer than mine. Normally I wouldn't befriend someone in the building in case things took an awkward turn, but Lourdes is too interesting to ignore: Harvard grad, speaks French and Spanish, handles celebrity divorces and custody agreements, hosts a Scrabble Club and appeared on a few episodes of *Beverly Hills, 90210* as a teenager.

"Hi," I say, giving Lourdes a quick hug before plopping down on her fancy Italian sofa, the kind you can only have before becoming a parent.

"So what's up?"

"I never told you about this guy, Simon, I used to date when I first moved to L.A., who moved back to Australia a few years ago."

"Why are Australian guys so sexy?" she immediately asks.

"Well, for every Hugh Jackman there is a Crocodile Hunter. But yes, I know what you mean. That's partly how I ended up in this…situation."

"Okay, lay it on me," she says, leaning on her breakfast bar.

"I'm not going to sugarcoat it, and you're the only person I've ever told this to, but he was married at the time," I tell her. "I was twenty-two, and it was an intense affair that lasted a few months. I saw him another time when he was back for work."

"Wait, let me get comfortable for this," she says, smiling and joining me on the sofa. "This sounds juicy."

I can tell by her body language and tone that she is unfazed by a story involving a young woman and a married man. Her billable hours practically depend on this phenomenon. Since I haven't told Rebecca the whole truth about Simon and me, it feels like a relief to say it out loud to someone.

"We stayed in touch over the years, but I didn't think it was right that we crossed the line again if he was still married," I explain. "A lot of our IM conversations were hot. I mean, isn't cybersex or sending dirty photos back and forth still cheating?"

"Yes," Lourdes says, "but you are on different continents, so I don't think it's as dangerous as what you were doing in person."

"I think I grew up a little in the process and just knew it wasn't right. It didn't feel good anymore, so I put an end to it."

"So now what?"

"He just left me a voicemail, and I have a feeling it's to tell me that he finally got divorced," I say. "I can't imagine any other reason for him to be calling."

"And you're worried that he's going to want to start things up again?"

"Yes."

"How would that even happen? Would he move back here?"

"I don't think so, because he has children." I wait for the judgment to arrive any second now, but it doesn't.

"Oh, well then it sounds like there's not much of a future. I don't think you can actually date someone who lives in a different country, seeing as you rejected that cute guy for living in Northridge."

"I guess I just don't know how to handle what he's going to tell me," I say. "If I met him in a parallel universe where he was single, maybe a little closer in age, I would do anything to be with him, because he's an incredible guy."

"How old is he?"

"He must be forty-six now."

"You know, divorced guys always want to remarry immediately," Lourdes warns me. "They can't be alone."

"I knew you'd have insight on this topic."

"These men, especially the powerful and successful ones, can barely function without a woman," she continues, laughing. "I get it. I mean, I would love a wife who could cook, clean, raise the kids, do all the Christmas shopping and find time to blow me. Well, you know what I mean."

I laugh again, which releases some of the tension I was feeling. "I'll call him back and let you know what he says. I guess I was just nervous thinking he might expect something from me that I'm not prepared to give."

9

"Is this the world's most beautiful journo calling?"

Just hearing his voice makes me quiver. It's clearly a sense-memory thing, as my actress friend Kimberly would say.

"Still a smooth talker, I see."

"It's so lovely to hear your voice again. It's been too long."

"You too," I say, pacing the living room like a mental patient.

"Do you want me to ring you back?" he asks, knowing how expensive the call is.

"No, don't be silly." I'm earning double what I did back when Simon was living here. "So, how are things?"

"All is well," he says. "Work is busier than ever. I'm now with the Sydney Broadcasting Company, in charge of a motley crew. It's a lot of trimming budgets and managing egos. What about you, darling?"

"Things are good. I moved to a new place last year and have a funny upstairs neighbor who reminds me a bit of Rebecca. She gets me out of the house. Work is going well. I'm doing more celebrity profiles, so I don't have to stand on so many red carpets. I just filed my first cover story on Kate Hudson. I'm still freelancing for the *Times*."

"I'm so pleased for you," he says. "You deserve it."

"Thanks."

"Well, I suppose I'll just get right to it then. The reason I rang is because you once told me to call you when I was divorced."

I don't take another breath until I hear him say the words.

"And I wanted you to be the first to know that I am officially separated," he says.

"I'm not sure what to say to that."

"The divorce could still be a year off. We have to work out custody and the financial settlement. But I thought you would be happy to know that it's a reality."

"I'm happy for you," I say, and mean it.

"Well, thank you, but aren't you a bit chuffed for yourself?"

Silence.

"Georgina?"

"Yes?"

"I think this impacts you as well," he says, sounding concerned by my lack of a response. "Don't tell me you've gone and fallen for some young bloke."

"No, I'm not with anyone."

"I just thought that now we could try to give it a real shot. You know, go public instead of hiding."

"In which country are you envisioning this happening?" I ask.

"It would have to be here, I'm afraid," he says. "I can't leave the kids or my job. My barrister said I'm likely to have to give Clare around half a million."

"I didn't know you had that kind of money," I say, stunned by my frankness and the actual amount.

"Well, yes," he says, "there is something to be said for giving way to youthful ambitions."

"Aside from the logistics of me emigrating, how on earth would you introduce me to friends and family? How would you explain me turning up out of the blue?"

"I don't think it would require that much of an explanation," he says.

I wonder how someone so smart could be so naïve, thinking that friends' wives and nosy neighbors would welcome me without question. "Simon, you don't think people might find it suspicious that a twenty-years-younger American girl from Los Angeles—where you recently lived—has conveniently shown up in Sydney to keep you company during your separation?"

"Well, we would have to figure all of that out, I suppose."

"I don't mean to be such a downer, but I don't think I can just up and move to Australia. What about my career?"

"You could continue writing here," he says. "Maybe break into travel writing."

"I've just started making a name for myself," I continue. "And my parents would be devastated to have their only child living so far away."

"It's not like I'm asking you to move to Iraq, Georgina," he responds defensively. "Some would consider Sydney paradise."

"I know, I'm sorry. Okay, forget all the commonsense stuff." I sigh and lie on my bed so I can ask the real question I need the answer to. "You don't worry that the reason for our connection was the fact that we never settled into monogamy?"

"I have never once had that worry," he retorts.

"Things were just so intense when we were together. It seems impossible to keep that up, so to speak, for years to come."

"What if it was even better? If we were together, it could be so much better in countless other ways."

It would be nice to do regular things that couples do.

"You didn't tell Clare about me, right?" I ask.

"Of course not," he says. "And I never will. Trust me, she wants the separation as much as I do. I think she's already got her eye on an old colleague of ours."

"But how will you explain *me*, especially if I am living with you? I assume you are asking me to move in?"

"Georgina."

"What about your kids? I don't know how to help raise kids. I don't even have siblings. I'm sure they would despise me."

"Look, why don't you just take some time to think about it. Just digest the separation news for a bit before killing the idea altogether."

"I feel like I'd be taking all of the risk and you would reap all of the rewards. How will I find a job, or friends, or a life? I can't just be arm candy."

"Darling, you are getting a bit carried away here," he says. "I'm not asking you to move here to be my companion for work dinners. I want us to try having a real, adult relationship where we could come out from the hotel rooms. I could help you with the expenses, of course."

"I don't feel comfortable with that."

"Fine," he says, clearly getting frustrated by my stubborn independence and play-by-play analysis. "I'm just saying that I would be there to help you in whatever way you needed *because I love you.*"

"I love you too, Simon," I say quietly. It's the first time I've said it to him.

I imagine how insanely romantic it would be to just pack up and leave my life here. I enjoy writing profiles and freelancing, I've made a small but quality group of friends, and my parents live two hours south. But aside from those things, there is nothing tying me down to Los Angeles. I could write from anywhere, and Australia wouldn't be as much of a culture shock as, say, India. But still. Saying yes to Simon would mean uprooting my life for a man. My college self would not approve of this.

"I wish I could see you right now," he says. "I'm getting aroused just hearing your lovely voice."

"Is this how television executives in Sydney talk at work?"

"I can't help it." He laughs. "This is what you do to me."

"I see age is doing nothing to curb your libido."

"You must come to Sydney," he says. "At least to visit first. And we could take it from there."

"That sounds like a better plan," I say, relieved. "I do have some Virgin frequent-flyer miles."

■ ■ ■

"So, what happened with the Australian?" reads a text from Lourdes the next day.

I invite her to my place for dinner as I was hypnotized by an episode of *Barefoot Contessa* earlier and decided on a whim to replicate the Tuscan-style menu. I go off to Trader Joe's in search of ingredients and spend an hour preparing everything. By the time Lourdes gets home from work, the entire apartment smells of garlic and butter.

"Look at you," she says, eyeing my apron and seeing my domestic side for the first time since we met last year.

"I figured it would keep me busy," I say, opening a bottle of Pinot Grigio. "So I wouldn't just sit and obsess on Simon."

"Did he ask you to be with him?" she asks me.

"Yes. He's separated, not divorced. Big difference."

"That's a bit tricky. I don't know Australian law, but divorces can take years."

"That is one of my many concerns," I say. "I spent twenty minutes giving him a lot of reasons why it wouldn't work, but we agreed that perhaps I should at least visit and see how it goes."

"I would just be certain that it's for the right reasons," Lourdes says, "and not just because he doesn't know how to live alone."

"Good point."

"So what are you, exactly, to each other?"

"I don't know. He's not my boyfriend. We've never said we can't see other people. It's an unusual situation with no road map."

"Don't take this the wrong way," she says, "but it seems like a lot of trouble to go to for a confusing, are-we-or-aren't-we relationship. You could have plenty of those right here in L.A. He's not promising you anything."

"If I went, he'd be offering me the chance at a happy relationship, but we've never spent more than twenty-hour hours together, so it's a huge leap," I say. "I have my best friend Rebecca's wedding next month in New York, so I'm not going anywhere before then, that's for sure. I'll just have to figure it out after that. "

■ ■ ■

Rebecca and I are in the bridal suite at the Four Seasons in New York City. "You look absolutely beautiful," I tell her as she surveys herself in the mirror.

"These fake eyelashes are going to be the death of me," she says, fussing with her veil. "I can't believe this is actually happening, G. Who would have thought that *I* would settle down at twenty-six?"

"No one." That Rebecca is about to become a wife feels like an abstract concept to me.

"I think Kevin is into you," she says of Scott's best man, a fellow triathlete who lives in Maryland and talks a lot about his regimented diet and various supplements. "He's a great guy."

I know what she's trying to do. She thinks if I can spark something with Kevin, then I can get married, move to the East Coast, and we can all live happily ever after. "I'm the only single bridesmaid," I tell her. "Who else is he going to be into?"

"Don't be ridiculous. A million guys would line up to be with you."

"Yeah, the lines are practically wrapped around the hotel," I deadpan as I help her into the petticoat of her dress.

The wedding photographer, who is so upbeat it's like nails on a chalkboard, encourages us to "be natural," "laugh like she just told you the funniest thing" and "put your head on her shoulder."

"Sandra," Rebecca sighs. "Just let us be ourselves and snap away. Georgina will not put her head on my shoulder, no matter how many times you ask."

"Whatever you want!" Sandra enthuses. "After all, you're the bride and therefore you get whatever you want. It's your day!" I look at Rebecca and know she can read my mind.

"I could not do this if you weren't here," she says quietly.

"Are you nervous?"

"No, actually, I'm not. Mum is driving me insane, but aside from that it's been pretty smooth, don't you think?"

"Absolutely," I agree, though I have nothing to compare it to since this is the first wedding I've been in since I was a flower girl at age five.

"I didn't need to have such a fancy wedding. I mean, we could have just gone to the courthouse and had a fun party, but I figured it would be easier if I let my parents do their thing. Their thing being showing off to their friends."

"I can't believe your parents put me up here. I think my room costs seven hundred and fifty a night. I feel bad."

"Don't worry about it," she says. "They can afford it."

"I know, but I could have stayed somewhere else."

"I needed you close-by, G. I insisted and they had no problem with it."

The daughter of a venture capitalist and a homemaker-turned-philanthropist, Rebecca was closer to her nannies growing up than to her own parents. Mrs. Fraser is an elegant woman, always dressed to the nines and hosting fabulous charity events, but she is on the icy side. I can't recall ever seeing Rebecca and her embrace or share a meaningful moment throughout the entire wedding-planning process. Rebecca's father is a bit warmer, especially after six scotches, but at one Christmas dinner I spent with them in New York I caught him staring at my cleavage, and I've stayed far away from him ever since.

They weren't exactly thrilled about Scott being the one for their daughter—I'm sure they would have preferred a member of a Manhattan family dynasty. But being typical WASPs and knowing that Rebecca is rebellious enough to run off and elope, they got on board soon after the engagement and decided to play up Scott's good looks and military service instead of the tiny Indiana town he comes from.

"Well, the venue is amazing," I say to Rebecca, even though I agree that it is pretty over-the-top for a photographer and a government worker. "Everyone is going to have the best time."

"I just hope Scott's not too overwhelmed by it all," she says. "I mean, I'm used to this outdoing-the-Joneses bullshit, but he grew up on a farm. A literal farm, G. His family must be like, 'What the fuck?'"

"I know." I laugh. "His mom told me that the rehearsal dinner was fancier than any wedding she had ever seen in the movies."

"That is so embarrassing."

"In all fairness, the rehearsal dinner was fancier than any wedding any of us have seen in the movies," I joke.

"That's why you're marrying him. Because he's nothing like the guys from Spence or even from Orange County. He's who you want, not who your parents want."

She steps into her dress, a simple, strapless lace Vera Wang gown I helped pick out, and instantly I tear up. She has never looked more beautiful, and I am happy for her. Truly.

■ ■ ■

"Scott and Rebecca have chosen to write their own vows to express their love," says the judge, an old friend of Mr. Fraser, who is officiating the ceremony. "Scott, please turn to your bride."

Scott takes out a cream-colored index card with a gold foil monogram on the back that the high-priced wedding planner had clearly arranged for him. "Rebecca, I promise to listen to you and learn from you. I will celebrate your accomplishments, support your dreams and will love you unconditionally," he begins, his voice slightly shaky. "I vow to trust you, respect you and be faithful to you. I will be the best husband that I can be and promise to help you load your gear whenever you have a shoot. I will care for you and our future children, stand beside you and share with you all of life's joys and pains, from this day forward and all the days of my life."

I can't see Rebecca's face since I am standing directly behind her, holding our heavy bouquets, but do see her wipe away a tear, which in turn makes Scott a bit emotional, before beginning her own vows.

"Scott, you are my best friend. I promise to love you when we are together and when we are apart. I promise to laugh at your dumb jokes and not get mad when you are playing Xbox until two in the morning. I promise to support and respect you and to be by your side through all the days and nights to come, no matter how tough the road may get. I will always put you first and remember why I chose you and you chose me. I will always remember how it felt to marry you in front of our family and friends. My mum always told me that my prince would come, and here you are. I love you, today and forever."

After the ceremony concludes and they are pronounced husband and wife, Rebecca and Scott walk back down the aisle, disappearing into their new life together. Kevin, the best man, offers me his arm and escorts me to the cocktail reception, where I catch up with a few of our college friends and Rebecca's handsome older brother Robert, whom I've had a crush on since 1996. I down a glass of champagne fast, as I know my toast is coming up once we get to the reception. Since I don't know 95 percent of the 300 people here, I'm not as terrified as I'd expected to be.

After an hour, the bubbly wedding coordinator leads us into the contemporary reception space that's been outfitted with thousands of white lilies and votive candles. It's an ethereal dream and takes my breath away for a moment. The formality of it all makes the wedding and commitment feel incredibly real. The Frasers have spared no expense.

We sip Veuve while dining on Maryland crab cakes, lobster bisque and an herb-roast rack of lamb.

After sitting through Kevin's slightly inebriated and awkward best-man toast, during which he alluded to Rebecca's wild past on several occasions, I hear my name announced by the DJ and know it's showtime.

"Hi," I say, adjusting the microphone to my height while realizing I am standing in front of countless members of Manhattan's elite. I tell myself to ignore them and just focus on Bec. "I am so honored to be here this evening to celebrate my best friend Rebecca's marriage to Scott. At this age, and particularly at weddings, people like to ask me if I'm seeing anyone special. I imagine they are trying to find out if I've been lucky enough to find my soul mate, the love of my life. I guess I never thought about it that much, because I feel like I already met my soul mate when I walked into Middle Earth my freshman year of college and met Rebecca. Yes, the dorms at University of California, Irvine, are named for a place where Hobbits live."

I get a few laughs from the handful of people in the room who get the reference.

"From the beginning, Rebecca and I got along like a house on fire, even though I was from a sleepy beach town where I went to public school and she was from the fancy Upper East Side and an alumna of Spence," I continue. "I had never met anyone like her. She was so charismatic, opinionated and funny—traits that are usually absent from most freshmen girls' personalities. We lived together throughout our college careers, except for the year I spent abroad in London, the highlight of which was her visit. We shared a love of books, *Seinfeld* reruns and proper cups of tea. And while we've lived apart since, I in Los Angeles and she in San Francisco, we still managed to talk every day and have racked up a few free flights on Southwest visiting each other over the years. One Sunday morning last year, she called to say that she had met a kind, handsome guy with large biceps and really white teeth. I knew we were in trouble."

I look at Scott, his arm around his new bride, and he is beaming.

"When she said 'G, you have to meet him,' I knew she must have really liked this guy. During my next visit, Scott won me over instantly with his quiet confidence, charm and service to our country. And of course I loved seeing him stand whenever Rebecca would get up from the table, or how he'd walk on the street side of the sidewalk as we strolled through the Marina District. They don't make guys like Scott in California."

A couple of college pals boo in mock outrage, so I smile and mouth "Sorry," which gets a laugh.

"So Scott, not only did you win me over, but I think you've won everyone over because of who you are. It's easy for everyone to see why she picked you. And Rebecca, I just want to thank you for being my best friend all these years. You're my favorite person for many reasons: You're quick-witted, smart, talented, passionate and my number one fan. Why wouldn't I adore you? But the thing I admire most about you is your ability to say whatever is on your mind and make decisions without worrying about anyone's approval. I would like to be more like that one day."

I know I'm getting to the end of my speech and feel relaxed.

"In addition to inquiring about my love life, people also ask me if it's hard or lonely being an only child. I often respond that I don't have a sister, but I have you."

As I raise my champagne glass for the toast, I see Rebecca crying, which makes it impossible for me to hold it together. I give her a quick hug, wiping my tears away, before heading back to my table.

Even though I mean every word I've just said, I can't help but think that this sort of happy ending just isn't in my cards. Simon claims he would marry me tomorrow, in a ceremony just as beautiful as this one I'm sure, but that's easy for him to say one month into his legal separation and before he's spent even a entire week with me.

■ ■ ■

"How was the wedding?" Simon asks immediately when I reach him on his cell after I return home from New York.

"It was perfect. She looked so beautiful, and Scott was so proud to marry her. It was all pretty magical. I was more emotional than I expected."

"Aw, that's sweet. How did your speech go?"

"It was fine. I got a few laughs and a few tears, so I figure that's a win. Rebecca was really pleased with it, and that's all I really cared about."

"I'm sure you were fantastic," he says, always in my corner, much like Rebecca. "Did it make you think about getting married one day? I always thought that if anyone could make the institution of marriage more attractive, it would be you."

"It did almost the opposite. Watching Rebecca and Scott made me realize that I am not ready for all of that yet. And as happy as I am for her, it felt like it could be the end of the way things are between us."

"It's only natural that you'd be emotional. After all, she's like a sister to you, and now she's moving across the country."

"And she wants to get pregnant soon," I add.

"That is a mistake," Simon says. "She should enjoy the love and lust of being a newlywed."

"You don't know Rebecca. She does whatever she wants and doesn't look back. There is no telling her what to do."

"You both are still so young," he marvels. "You've got your whole lives ahead of you."

"Well, it's funny you say that," I begin.

"Why's that, darling?"

"It's not just because of the wedding, but I have been doing a lot of thinking about our situation. In fact, I spent the entire six-hour flight home just thinking about us and trying to work it all out in my mind."

"And?"

"I just don't see it working, Simon. I'm sorry."

"I was afraid you were going to say that."

"If you were still in L.A. or if your kids were younger, then it could be different I'm sure, but it's too much with the way we started. I just can't get comfortable with it, no matter how hard I try."

"I feel like I'm being punished because I was married," he says.

"I don't want to punish you. You are an incredible man. I feel like I'm a better person because of you. I'm definitely more fun and confident."

"We broke a lot of new ground together."

"I loved being with you, and I still care about you a lot. I'm sure I always will."

"But not enough to visit and see what it could be like?"

"It's not that," I say. "A visit will complicate things further. I know if I come we will have an amazing time and you'll take me to unforgettable dinners and kiss me in front of the Opera House and we'll go home and fuck for hours."

"That's the spirit, darling."

"I just mean that of course it will be wonderful, but it won't be reality. It will be like a vacation. That kind of visit isn't indicative of what it would be like for me to leave my family, friends and career, and come into your world."

"I suppose you're right about that."

"No one, aside from two girlfriends, even knows you exist," I continue. "My parents have never heard your name. I'm not sure how I could explain it now. I've always done the right thing in their eyes. This might be too much for them to handle."

"You sound firm in your decision," he says.

"As much as it pains me to say, yes, I am."

"Then I have to respect that."

"I appreciate that."

"Can we still stay in touch?"

"Of course. Why wouldn't we?"

"And if you ever change your mind, I will be here," he says quietly.

"What's that saying? If you love something let it go, and if it comes back it's yours forever? Or something like that?"

"And if it doesn't, then it was never meant to be," he finishes. "That's just something people say to make themselves feel better."

"I'm saying that what's meant to be will be."

"It's not like you to speak in all these clichés."

"It's because I don't know what else to say."

"It's okay, darling," he says. "I understand."

"Thank you."

"But I won't wait forever."

■ ■ ■

After freelancing for the *L.A. Times* for a few years while keeping my gig at *InStyle*, the newspaper has finally offered me a job as a columnist for its Sunday magazine. It's the biggest thing to happen to my career and was announced in a fancy press release and on media blogs. Bidding farewell to celebrity interviews was like a weight, albeit a very attractive one with lots of perks, being lifted off my shoulders. Perhaps it's because I now keep normal daytime hours or that I'm just happier and therefore more open, but I've finally met someone worth caring about, and it's looking like it could be serious. Justin is creative, funny, sexy, smart, age-appropriate, and most importantly, not married.

On our fourth date, on the patio at a Mexican cantina in West Hollywood, Justin told me he wanted to be exclusive. Lourdes and everyone around me had me believing it couldn't be this easy. There had to be head games, shocking revelations and dramatic starts and stops. But there, under the string lights and over good tequila, we decided to go for it. My first real boyfriend since John. My first real boyfriend in the city where I've lived for five years. My first real boyfriend where it just feels right.

Two months into my new job and relationship, I see an email from Simon first thing when I wake up, after not having been in touch for nearly a year. Our calls became emails, and our emails eventually became nothing. Now that he was officially divorced, I figured he had met someone.

I wait a moment before opening his email. I am nervous about corresponding with him for fear of messing things up with Justin. I still think about Simon, probably more than I should, and I'd be lying if I said he didn't make regular appearances in my dreams. But it's not that kind of note.

From: Simon Grant
To: Georgina Park
Date: March 9, 2006 at 9:35 PM
Subject: Some news

Hey Georgina,

I know we haven't really spoken since the divorce, but I felt like I should tell you that I am getting married again. Can you believe it? Maybe you can. Are you still against the institution or just opposed to marrying me? Just teasing you. Every so often, I see one of your stories, and I feel so proud of you—not that I had anything to do with it, but I know you had aspirations for something more permanent at the Times, so it's a big deal. I love watching your career flourish. You write so well, and the weekend column you do is outstanding. I quite enjoyed the recent piece on the performance artist bloke. I hope they are paying you on time.

Clare and I are on good terms and managing the kids equally. She fell in love with someone and life is good all around. Now that some time has passed, I truly understand your reasons for not coming to Sydney to be with me, but I often wonder what could have been. Do you? You probably wouldn't want me now. When I first met you I was a thin, idealistic foreign correspondent, and now I'm an out-of-shape, gray-haired, pragmatic television executive.

What I want to say, Georgina, is just that I feel better for having met you. Every moment with you was delightful, and I never regretted any of it, even that last visit in Century City where we didn't sleep for a minute and I was like a zombie at our big meeting the next afternoon in New York. I wish I were able to see you one last time. To see the woman that you have become. I'm guessing a lot has happened in your life since we last spoke. How is your love life? I do hope you are happy. If you were so inclined to share, I would love to hear.

Love, Simon

■ ■ ■

From: Georgina Park
To: Simon Grant
Date: March 10, 2006 at 08:16 AM
Subject: Re: Some news

Hi Simon,

I'm not surprised you're marrying again. Nearly 80 percent of divorced people do. I just hope you took some time to sow your wild oats. (I don't need the details, by the way.) Thanks for keeping up with my career here and there. As you know, being a journalist means you have to know a lot about everything, but I really enjoy writing my column because I meet so many types of people who I never would otherwise. Half of the stories are assigned, and half I get to pick. I'm not sure that anyone even reads the newspaper anymore, but knowing that you are checking up on my writing skills from another hemisphere makes me smile.

I don't know if you saw my profile on that hotelier last week, but I so wish I could have written the true, behind-the-scenes story instead of a puff piece (he's an advertiser, so I was asked to tread lightly—so much for journalism, right?). He had three different female assistants of various ages at his beck and call, and an Egyptian girlfriend with jet-black hair and kohl-rimmed eyes who had to have been 40 years younger than his seventysomething self. He treated them all like slaves but would smile at the end of each command, as though that made it okay.

We met at his L.A. hotel, but he insisted on showing me his home in Holmby Hills so I would understand how his design philosophy was a "24/7 way of life." As we were speeding down Sunset in his one-of-a-kind Aston Martin, I thought we were going to die going around one of the bends and

I would be forever linked to him by a cruel fate. At a traffic light, a Star Line tour bus pulled up next to us and a group of European tourists started taking photos as he egged them on. I was mortified.

Luckily I made it out alive, but I had to endure at least fifteen phone calls from the aforementioned assistants, who were clearly being forced to check in on every aspect of the article. It was all a bit of a nightmare, but he was so pleased with the story that he sent me a gift card for $1,000 to use at any of his properties around the world. Since we aren't allowed to accept gifts at the Times, *I had to return it. I was furious; I think I earned it on that one.*

People often ask me how I deal with writer's block, but I've honestly never had it. There is always something to write, especially in L.A. The piece I'm filing tomorrow is on an all-girl car gang in Boyle Heights. They gave me a major once-over as I pulled up in my Volkswagen and floral-print dress, but by the end of the interview they were asking me to stay for a barbecue. I felt like I got initiated into the Pink Ladies, except these chicks were all Latina and have jail tattoos. Anyway, work is going well, and I don't miss the celebrity stuff. At all.

As for love, yes, I'm with someone, and things are getting serious. We're talking about moving in together, which would be a big step for me. He's the first person I've dated who truly wants what's best for me (no offense) and it's all been incredibly smooth sailing. Almost feels too good to be true. You know it's hard for me to find that spark with people, and I really don't want to mess it up, so I hope you understand that's why I can't be in touch more. He's a musician and junior high school teacher, and I'm happy. So it seems things have worked out just fine for us both. Good luck with the wedding and everything else. She is a lucky woman.

Cheers,
Georgina

JUNE 2013

10

Obama's in town again, so I know I shouldn't leave the house unless I absolutely have to. Plus it's a Friday, which means driving anywhere will be ten times worse. Traffic in Los Angeles is one thing in life you can always count on. I'm lucky to still be working from home, now a lovely 1930s Spanish-style cottage with dark hardwood floors and rounded plaster archways that I own, but I still pop out during the day to see my editor, have lunch with a friend, check out a new exhibit or do an interview.

I typically file two to three stories a week, including my Sunday "Movers & Shakers" column for the *Los Angeles Times*, which, if it goes smoothly, leaves me with a good amount of time to mess about in the city I've called home for the last thirteen years. On Fridays I always go to see an eleven o'clock matinee of a documentary or an independent film by myself. It's usually just a handful of retirees and me, and it's the best.

Trying to see a movie at any other time is an exercise in torture. You have to purchase tickets well in advance, even if the film came out weeks ago; you're lucky if you can find a parking space three levels down, where the air feels like death; and it's impossible to find a nearby restaurant that isn't already packed with diners. There's no such thing as spontaneity here. Not in a city of nearly four million people.

While I like to stick to my routines, I've already accepted that presidential gridlock means a movie today is not going to happen. When Obama was in town a couple of years ago, I got trapped in my car for over two hours on Sunset Boulevard. People were standing on top of their vehicles, desperate to see what was going on up ahead. I was convinced it was more than just the president being in town because it was a spectacle unlike anything I had seen in my time here. It was Britney Spears being released from UCLA Medical Center– or Michael Jackson dying at UCLA Medical Center–level madness. Going into hour three, when I finally saw the stream of police cars, flashing lights and the Secret Service, I was ready to ditch my Volkswagen on the street, walk home and call it a day.

It was the first time in years I'd lost my cool, and it was over something as completely out of my control as a presidential motorcade. Once the traffic lifted, I made the short drive home exhausted. You would have thought I had actually done something aside from sitting in my car, where I survived on a bottle of warm water and a protein bar a neighboring passenger handed me (probably the nicest gesture I have experienced in a city not known for its kindness). That night, I looked at the orange Obama sticker on my fridge with hate.

Because the city has a massive multiyear project to widen the already massive 405 freeway, the president now takes Marine One to get to his fancy fundraisers in Brentwood, but the streets are still congested because Friday is the worst traffic day, whether Obama is here or not. Since he's speaking on the Westside, surface streets will be closed, so I'm happy to stay in today and get some work done. It's finally warming up, so I crack open my office window and stare at the eucalyptus trees across the street as their branches sway a bit in the permanent ocean breeze. Bougainvillea leaves dot the front yard, but the wind will eventually carry them elsewhere.

I live near Santa Monica Airport, about twenty blocks inland from the beach, so it's normal to hear biplanes, private jets and helicopters throughout the day. It took a while to get used to the sounds, especially after living for nearly 20 years in apartment buildings where I never heard anything resembling nature or air traffic—just a nearly deaf Ukrainian neighbor yelling at his wife, and the stressed-out public defender stomping around upstairs at 6 a.m. I'll take the planes.

I spend the morning combing through my favorite blogs while rotating Françoise Hardy, Nancy Sinatra, the Velvet Underground and Neutral Milk Hotel on Spotify. I read a few online stories in the *Los Angeles Times*, where I have been a freelance journalist for eleven years, and check out the top headlines in the *New York Times* and the *Wall Street Journal*. I sort through my inbox, which is filled with messages from our always freaked-out photo editor, who is trying to set up a shoot with a difficult architect I recently interviewed. There's a Gagosian Gallery show that Lourdes has emailed me about, and I note the date on my calendar. Then I catch up on an "All Things Considered" podcast.

Buried in my spam folder is an email forward from Emily. She thought I'd like to know that David, my first junior high school boyfriend, just had his third baby boy. I'm not on Facebook, so I know nothing until someone tells me. There's the obligatory hospital shot where the tiny infant is swaddled in a pale blue-and-white-striped blanket, looking adorable next to his exhausted mother. I wonder if David and his wife are as in love with each other as they are with the new baby.

I see that David has aged quite a bit since I last bumped into him, at a Phoenix show at the Hollywood Bowl a few years back. The outdoor amphitheater is one of the best things about living in L.A., but apparently the 17,376-seat venue still isn't big enough to prevent me from running into someone I've dated. I haven't gone once this summer for that very reason. It's too much to handle at this point.

But back to work. I am in the midst of researching a story about the popularity of Native American–inspired fashion and how this may or may not be okay (it's not, really), or "culturally sensitive," as my editor put it. Companies such as Urban Outfitters are selling Navajo rompers, belts, backpacks and even panties. Who takes a fashion trend all the way down to the underwear? Apparently the same girls who wear feathers at Coachella and braided friendship bracelets like I made twenty-five years ago at summer camp.

I email a few local boutique owners and designers whom I consider work friends to get their two cents on the matter. I also leave a message for the Navajo Nations PR firm and hope someone there will talk to me. Usually they do. I'm not sure if it's because everyone wants their fifteen minutes or they respect the *Los Angeles Times,* or if it's because I am not a threatening, hard-hitting journalist. Maybe all the above.

No one is saving their newspapers anymore. Everyone just reads online, if at all, and though I may have a two-page spread in the country's fourth-highest circulated newspaper's weekend magazine, no one acknowledges it. Oftentimes not even the people I write about—politicians, designers, authors, city officials—say anything in the form of thanks or criticism. So it's almost as if the stories don't exist. Everyone is on to the next thing; their attention span is getting shorter with each passing day, with every click of the mouse.

But if you google my name, you'd see more than fifty pages of my stories, so there is a digital record of sorts (until the link is broken, and then that's that). Bloggers, celebrities and people with large followings on social media are taking the role of journalists. Things have changed so much since I started in 2000, because of the recession, technology and our culture. But it's okay. Nothing can stay the same forever. And I've written more than I ever imagined possible. I'm satisfied; it's enough for me. I'm getting a bit sick of it all, to be perfectly honest.

■ ■ ■

I have lunch after working for a couple of hours. Today it's leftover quinoa. It's funny how half of the conversations in this city seem to revolve around this Spanish grain, the taste equivalent of the word *neutral*, but since I became a vegetarian last year, it's sort of a staple. I hear the helicopters before I can take my first bite, and see them from my living room window. Obama? It's annoying, as I'm trying to eat and watch an old *30 Rock* I have on DVR. It continues for at least twenty minutes and now there is more hovering in my neighborhood.

I turn on the news to see if I can figure out when he'll be out of the area, but instead I learn there has been a shooting. The KNBC reporter is standing outside Santa Monica College, just blocks from here. I recently started swimming there a few times a week since the weather has been so warm. I like it because I don't have to talk to anyone. No one can hit on you when you're underwater. You don't overhear annoying women complaining about their weekend housekeepers. I go up and back, staring at the long black line on the pool floor. The only downside is that when you're swimming you can't ever get away from your thoughts, as there is no complicated play to focus on or teammate to high-five. It's just you, the chlorine and your racing mind.

Since I now see four helicopters, I know it's something big. It could be a mass shooting. Or is it to do with Obama? Please, don't let it be Obama. It's times like this when I hate being home alone. The shooter is down, they say, but someone else is in custody. Could there be two or more people responsible for this?

A local reporter on the scene says one or two shooters have claimed multiple victims in Santa Monica and that there's a burning house near the local college that authorities think could be connected. I'm on my iPad looking at Twitter since the news will be on the social networks faster than on TV. I hate trying to guess, but I have a strong feeling it's going to be a disturbed white or Middle Eastern male. I secretly pray it's not an Asian guy. After Virginia Tech, Long Duk Dong and small-penis jokes, I feel like Asian guys have enough to deal with.

The authorities are not releasing the names of any victims. I don't know anyone who would be at the campus today, but the newscasters are saying shots were fired into a bus, at cars and at passersby, and they keep mentioning the nearby fire because apparently someone heard gunshots before the flames. There are millions of people in L.A. on any given day, so I won't know anyone involved. The helicopters persist all afternoon. I can't work like this but I don't want to go outside, so I call Rebecca.

"Oh my God, I was just going to call you. I just got an email from CNN," she says before I even say hello.

"I can see the helicopters from here. Everything's going down like ten blocks away," I say as I shut the window and check to be sure all of my doors are locked.

"Don't leave the house. There could still be a crazy shooter running around."

"I won't. I can't believe this is happening again," I say quietly.

It's only been six months since the Sandy Hook shootings and all the talk of gun reform. The country has never been more divided. My friend Kimberly, who plays a minor character on a hit TV show, just lost half of her followers on Twitter because she said we needed to do something about gun violence. People also threatened to stalk, rape and kill her. So that's how things are.

Rebecca and I catch up on her kids, talk a bit about our upcoming 20-year high school reunions (you couldn't pay me to attend) and say our goodbyes. She feels extra far away. In college we would have been watching this unfold together. After sitting on the couch for hours, I turn the television off, feeling desensitized to the excessive coverage, and start reading *Vanity Fair* to take my mind off things. I always flip straight to the Proust Questionnaire on the back page. This month it's Christine Baranski. I always dreamed of writing a story for them, the kind that spans eight pages and pays four dollars per word, but I don't have the fire in me to even think about pitching.

In three weeks I start teaching a Writing for the Web course at UCLA, so I'm busy these days: researching, putting together a syllabus and bookmarking relevant links that we can go over in class. It's part of the Extension program, so pretty much anyone from the community who can afford to take the class can do so, as long as there's room. I have twenty-three students as of today and will be teaching on the north side of campus, just off Sunset Boulevard. I'm excited for the change of pace. After being a journalist for twelve years, it'll be nice to share what I know.

As much as I love writing for the *Times*, working for the newspaper hasn't been the same since the bankruptcy, about five years ago. I've gone through more editors in the last year than in my entire career, and they cut my rate by 25 percent. The class means an extra seven grand for ten weeks of work, and I could use the money; I can easily juggle both jobs. Lourdes always teases me because I probably work thirty hours a week compared to her sixty as a high-powered divorce attorney. I can bum around in yoga pants all day while she wears $1,200 designer suits.

Because of the recent shooting at Santa Monica College, everyone is a bit nervous about being on campus, but it seems as though it was an isolated incident courtesy of a disturbed young man (isn't it always?) who couldn't process his parents' divorce and possibly (positively?) had mental issues.

I've been briefed on how I can and cannot interact with my students: no hugs or physical contact unless someone is grieving or the situation is comparably severe;

no adding or accepting students on social media until the class is over and grades are handed in; no sleeping with them. Obviously.

The office administrator sends me a list of the enrolled students a few days before school starts. There are names like Bentley, Sophia and Emma on the list. And there's one boy named Grant. Of course this reminds me of Simon, whom I haven't talked to in so many years I've now lost count.

With my first class just around the corner, I should be focused on finishing the syllabus, but instead I find myself messing around on YouTube. I decide to enter Simon's name to see what, if anything, will come up. So many options pop up on the screen that I'm not sure what to click first. I watch him at a panel discussion about an upcoming election in New South Wales. He's much grayer now, like he'd said, and a bit puffier, but otherwise the same. I smile as I watch him charm the uptight female host and spar with an obnoxious right-wing politician.

He's wearing a wedding ring, so I deduce that he did go through with the marriage and is still with her. Unless he's on to number three by now.

Jesus, I think to myself, he's in his fifties. I'm thirty-four. I remind myself that he ages just as I do, but the fortysomething-to-fiftysomething transition is not very kind to a man, especially when it happens with the click of a mouse. I watch a couple of old reports he has filed—a total treat, as YouTube wasn't around when we started seeing each other. I google him, but there are hundreds of pages of results and they aren't all my Simon, so I go back to the videos.

I seem to be the only person named Georgina Park who's doing something search-worthy, so whenever someone googles me, they find everything I've ever done, including my bad poetry from a summer workshop between freshman and sophomore year of college. It can be quite humiliating.

I'd love to finally see what Clare looks like. Like Simon's, her name is also common on the Internet, and so I resist entering it into the search bar. I was always curious to know if she was beautiful. Not that it would mean anything. Would I excuse myself a bit more if she was frumpy? She probably was and is lovely. I find it oddly comforting knowing that she moved on and found someone. I can imagine Simon wasn't the perfect husband and father. He once mentioned that he was the fun one and that Clare was the disciplinarian when it came to the children. God knows what fallout there was from him being so "fun."

All I gathered from those months spent in bed together and chatting behind computer screens was that she had short blonde hair, a fair complexion, small breasts and a Catholic background. It figures he would have chosen me, with my wavy, long, dark brown hair, golden skin, curvy figure and no religious background to speak of (my parents opted to let me decide for myself; my decision was *no thanks*). You don't have an affair with someone who reminds you of your wife, Simon said once.

Before I put Clare and Simon out of my mind once more, I call Rebecca. It's harder to reach her these days, as she is quite busy reconciling her role as a full-time mother of three, including twin girls, with her work as a successful D.C. photographer, which sends her to New York and London often. Luckily I catch her alone; her kids are at the neighborhood pool.

"Remember Simon?" I ask.

"Of course."

"I just googled him."

"Why didn't I think of that? I always used to ask you what he looked like and you never had a picture, which drove me crazy."

"I still don't, but thanks to the Internet you can see more than a photo. You have to add his network name to find him."

"Oh my God G, he's old," she says.

"He's fiftysomething now. Crazy, right?"

"He's so not your type."

"I don't really have a type, do I? Click on the image search."

"Well, John was your age, very conventionally handsome, a surfer, and played guitar. Justin was really cute and a surfer and a drummer—and your age. And the guy you're dating now is one of those things, too, I imagine." Due to Rebecca's insane schedule and the time difference, I haven't been able to tell her much about my personal life.

"Forget photography and just become a psychic," I say.

I've also failed to mention that I'm actually dating *two* guys, Ethan and Mike, both of whom are in up-and-coming bands, a pattern I've subconsciously mastered ever since the breakup with Justin in 2010. After three years together he wanted to get married, but my gut said no anytime we would start to discuss it. Yes, I told him, I was happy with him, but I wasn't ready yet. No, I wasn't sure if I would ever be ready, but I loved him very much. I just needed some time to think about it.

"You're not ready to get married, or you're not ready to get married to me?" he asked.

"I am honestly just not ready to get married. It's not you, babe. You know I adore you."

Seeing the pain in his face, I remembered back to the first time we met—in a cemetery, of all places. A film organization began hosting free screenings on a sprawling lawn at the famed Hollywood Forever Cemetery, and I decided to pitch a story on the unusual event. Hundreds of Angelenos would bring blankets, picnic baskets and wine, as if they were enjoying a classical concert in the park, to view classic films like *Lolita* and *The Postman Always Rings Twice* within a stone's throw of mausoleums and tombstones. I brought Lourdes and a few of her girlfriends with me to check it out, and on a neighboring plaid blanket was Justin, doing the same with his friends. I was immediately interested. He was handsome but not too handsome, with a sly smile, kind eyes, and dark brown hair cut in a 1950s style. After learning he was a junior high school teacher, I was sold. We chatted through the entire screening of *His*

Girl Friday even though I love that movie, and by the end of the night I had given him my number.

"I thought every girl wants to get married. Isn't this what you do after three years of dating?" he'd asked, raising his voice and grabbing at the back of his neck like it was in knots.

I thought Justin was pretty close to perfect. I considered a lifetime with him and couldn't think of any red flags. We always had fun together; he supported my career and was kind to my parents. We didn't have Simon-level fireworks in the bedroom, but who does after three years?

"Anyone would be lucky to marry you," I said. "I love living together and sharing our life. I want to be with you. I'm just a little nervous about forever, you know?"

"No, I don't."

I'd hurt him badly but thought we could get through it, like we had gotten through his father's slow death from cancer in our first year together. I suggested we go to counseling, but instead he packed his things and moved out while I was in Seattle for a journalism conference. He just bailed, like I was a one-night stand he desperately wanted to get rid of. He refused to see or talk to me even though I called and wrote for days, so it felt like a death that I had to mourn. My friends and parents didn't understand, since we "seemed so good" together. We were. Justin and I had the same taste in music, books, films and people. We hated the same things, too. It was almost too easy. But for some reason, I just couldn't take that next step. I could already envision being the one to ruin the marriage, which terrified me, and I didn't want to do that to him.

I tell Rebecca about Ethan, the keyboardist whose band is playing one of the small stages at this year's Warped Tour. He thinks it will be their big break. I think it will be around the time we stop seeing each other. I'm not competing with twenty-three-year-old groupies who wear floral rompers.

I met him in April at Coachella, also known as the sweatiest forty-eight hours of my life. Most of the time I was stashed away in a media tent that had some air conditioning, thankfully, but the desert music festival reaches triple digits even before you add in the thousands of hipsters living their own personal Woodstock. Ethan was one of the only guys in all of Indio, California, who was not sporting black-rimmed glasses, a 145-pound frame or a beard.

"I knew it," Rebecca says smugly. "I swear, Georgina, you could put together a supergroup of the band guys you've dated."

"Well, there are a lot of musicians here. Can I help it if stockbrokers and lawyers don't approach me? Trust me, I would love nothing more than to date a normal accountant who works regular hours and has a good credit score."

We watch a few more YouTube clips together. "I'm not saying Simon's not attractive—he just looks ultraconservative, like all the politicos here," Rebecca says, and I can't deny it. "I can't really picture you two hanging out together."

"He's not how he appears. He's very liberal and open. But yes, physically, he made *me* look edgy, and I am so not."

"You have your bohemian ways," she reminds me. "I mean, your parents went to Berkeley. Some of that San Francisco hippie culture had to have rubbed off on you." Maybe Rebecca *does* know about the two guys somehow. "Wow, here's a photo of him with the prime minister," she continues, clicking away on every link she can find. "He's a total power player, I will give you that. What made you think of him today?"

"I don't know. I was working on my syllabus for the new class, and there's a boy in the class named Grant. It hit me that I haven't heard from Simon at all in like seven years. He used to check in from time to time."

She laughs. "Is that what we're calling it now? He wanted to marry you. I wouldn't call that 'checking in.'"

"I guess not."

"Didn't you tell him to stop contacting you?"

"Yes. Because of Justin. He didn't feel comfortable with me staying in touch with an ex, and I had a hard time having a platonic relationship with Simon, even online."

"Well, no offense, but why *would* he just want to have a friendly, innocent relationship with someone on the other side of the world? I don't talk to any of the guys I used to sleep with."

"Good point."

"That's what I'm here for."

"We just had a very unusual relationship. Part of me thought I would still know him down the road, even if we were living totally different lives in separate hemispheres."

"I'm not sure you'd even be attracted to him now. You look the same, but he sure doesn't."

"Maybe. Maybe not."

"You were what, twenty-two years old?" she asks. "That's so young, Georgina."

"I always secretly hoped I'd see him again, even if it was a decade or two later."

"Then he'd be even older."

"Anyway, how are Scott and the kids?"

■ ■ ■

I don't usually get nervous speaking in front of an audience. After you've had to ask Robert De Niro inane red carpet questions and watch his face curl into an expression that says he's incredibly disappointed with whatever life choices led you to be interviewing him, a little public speaking is nothing. But I feel some anxiety on the first day because I haven't been in an actual classroom in many years, and never as The Instructor. There are bound to be good students—after all, they are paying to take this class during a perfect L.A. summer, where it's seventy-two degrees and sunny pretty much every day. But there will also be know-it-all types who wouldn't be in the class if they actually knew it all. Since it's a continuing-education class geared toward working adults, there could be eighteen-year-olds fresh out of high school and seventysomething grand-mothers who are finally pursuing their dreams of writing.

I stress a bit over what to wear. I don't know if the classroom is air-conditioned or whether I'll be standing or sitting. What do professors wear these days? It's a writing class, not physics, so maybe I can be more casual. I settle on a knee-length, striped Madewell dress with cap sleeves and black ankle booties. I want to come across as friendly and cool, but not too friendly or cool. I'm hoping for the best.

■ ■ ■

After class, I put the syllabi back in my bag and collect my stuff so I can head out. Two twentysomething women—bloggers, they tell me—are waiting to chat with me. "Are you going to cover monetization?" asks the perky bru-nette, clutching her folder against her chest.

"We'll get into that later," I tell her. "There's not a lot of money out there unless you have a big following and can sell ads."

"What about creating content for bigger blogs?" she asks, hopeful.

"Blogs like The Huffington Post don't actually pay their writers," I say. "Most sites don't pay. You might get ten cents a word, somewhere, if you're lucky."

"That is so depressing," the blonde friend chimes in.

"I know."

After saying goodbye, I walk toward the parking garage when a slightly disheveled guy from the class approaches me.

"Hi, Miss Park?"

"You can call me Georgina."

"I've actually been a fan of yours for a long time," he says, looking at his feet. "I've read all of your columns since I was in high school. When I saw you were teaching this class I had to take it, even though I'm not really a writer."

I am not technically famous, but this does happen sometimes. People read something they like, or connect with me for some reason, and feel like they know me. Anytime my column is published, I receive impulsive emails from total strangers (because we can all be found in an instant these days) that fall into three categories: complimentary ("I never miss your column and think you are smart and witty"), critical ("you claim that Chef Kaye is one of the city's best, but I cannot agree with that statement because I had a terrible experience at his latest restaurant"), and creepy ("I want to worship your feet").

"Remind me of your name again?"

"Jacob," he says.

"Well, I look forward to having you in class, Jacob."

"Um, I was also wondering if you have time to grab a coffee or something," he asks, one eyebrow raised.

"I don't, I'm sorry." My tone makes it clear I won't have time tomorrow, either.

"Okay," he says, dejected. "Well, I guess I'll see you soon. In class."

"Have a good day."

I get back to my car, turn on the AC and double-check to make sure no other students are going to be popping out to say hello. I'm pleased with how the first day went. I decide to celebrate at home with a glass of sauvignon blanc before going to my office to plan the next class.

11

"Bec, I need you to call me the second you get this," I say to her voicemail. "I'm okay. I mean, I'm not okay, but I'm not dying or anything. No one has died. But please just call me as soon as possible."

I click the off button on my phone and notice that my hand is shaking, which never happens. Adrenaline is racing through my body so fast it feels like it was shot through my blood vessels with a bow and arrow. I feel like I might be sick. It's a beautiful afternoon in my little house, but acid rain might as well be coming down because I want to curl into a ball in my closet and never come out again. I'm not dramatic; Rebecca always says I'm the most even-keeled person she knows. If I do raise my voice or get emotional for a moment, it's for a good reason, like almost getting killed merging onto Wilshire because some lady was putting mascara on while driving.

I wish Rebecca would just call me back. Fuck. I'm going to go insane if I don't talk to her. Since I've always been a bit of a loner, I don't have a posse to conference-call in these types of situations. It needs to be her. Instead of pacing or crying, I simply stare at the wall, noticing small indentations and faint cracks I've hadn't noticed before. As if that will do anything to fix the situation.

"What's wrong?" Rebecca asks the second I answer.

"Thank God you got my message. I am freaking out and possibly having a panic attack. I have never had one so I don't know, but my throat feels like it's constricting, and my hands are shaking."

"Just breathe, Georgina. Tell me what is going on. Please."

"I just got home from teaching my class and needed to prep for the next one, so I opened my UCLA email account," I explain. "They give you one so you can communicate with students and send assignments. Stuff like that."

"Okay. And?"

"So it's not like my Gmail. There's no spam or joke forwards from my mum; it's just used for school business."

"That makes sense," she says.

"Today when I opened the account there were normal emails from a couple of students who had questions, and then there was one from a strange Yahoo address with no name associated—just an initial, numbers and an underscore. I figured it had to be someone in my class, since no one else would be emailing me here. I opened it and it was a photo."

"Of what?" Rebecca asks.

"Of me." I'm on the verge of tears. "It was a picture of *me*. A picture that I sent Simon years ago. One where I'm in lingerie."

"Oh my God. Wait, I don't understand. How would somebody have this photo?"

"I have no idea. There was no message. It was just the photo. It is so embarrassing, Bec," I continue, trying to catch my breath. "I'm on my bed, topless, holding my breasts together in one hand and wearing a lace thong."

"Well, do you think it was Simon? Maybe he thought he was being funny or flirty?"

"No, he would have definitely written something. And why would he use this new email address? I've had the same email for almost ten years and he always wrote me there."

"It has to be Simon. Maybe he forgot your old email address. I mean, it's been years, Georgina. He could have misplaced it, googled you and up come with this publicly listed email for your class. That makes sense."

"It was from a spammy-type email. Like one you'd get from a Nigerian scam artist, or someone telling you that forty million dollars are waiting for you. Simon is way too smart for that. He knows what UCLA is. He wouldn't dream of doing something like this."

"Maybe he had a few drinks and thought it was funny. Simon is the only person that makes sense."

"I know it's not him. Why would he randomly contact me today, of all days?"

"Is your face in the picture?"

"Yes. And very clearly, I might add."

"Then we have to do something about it."

"You don't find it incredibly creepy?"

"Of course I do. The timing is so odd. Didn't you just starting teaching a few weeks ago?"

"Yes, it's been three weeks, and we still have seven weeks to go."

"And we were just talking about him recently, remember? That is strange. Do you want me to talk to Scott?" she asks.

Scott still works in the Office of Intelligence and Analysis for Homeland Security. The thought of him knowing I sent anyone this photo is mortifying, but I say yes. "Just find out what I can do or what I should do. Please."

"It's going to be okay, you know?"

"No. I don't know that. That's not the only photo out there, by the way. It's the only one that they sent. But Simon had more explicit photos of me. Naked ones. Oh my God, I am never going to live this down."

"It's so unlike you, Georgina."

"That's the thing. It's the only time I ever did something so stupid, and it comes back to haunt me ten years later. The last time I even emailed with Simon was at least seven years ago."

"This might sound silly, but are you positive it is definitely *you*? It's not Photoshopped or something?"

"I've never been more certain of anything."

■ ■ ■

Today in class we're talking about sites like Slate and Gawker. I'm trying my best to stay focused, appear normal and actually do some teaching, but inside I'm still obsessing about the photo. I knew it was me the second I saw it. The Agent Provocateur heels I used to wear were a dead giveaway. It makes no sense. Even if someone broke into Simon's secret dirty-picture file or stole his laptop, how would they know who was in the photo, and why would they email it to me? My reporter's brain will not shut off, even as I talk with my students about traffic rankings and the difference between unique visitors and hits. They're surprisingly engaged. I must be acting my ass off.

As I listen to an older student talk about an essay she wrote for The Daily Beast, my mind starts wandering. I have to get to the bottom of this for my own sanity, or else I'll be of no use to anyone.

It's been twenty-four hours since the arrival of the email, which I printed out before deleting. The last thing I need is to have UCLA investigating me for receiving soft-core porn via their network. I try to take my mind off things and prepare for next week's classes, but it's futile. There's another email waiting for me after class, and this one includes a note.

> *From: _H1036*
> *To: Georgina Park*
> *Date: July 11, 2013 at 4:31 PM*
> *Subject: Hi*

Georgina,
        You know I can ruin your life.
Sincerely,
Me

My heart sinks into my stomach and my mouth goes completely dry. There's no chance on earth that this is coming from Simon. He is many things, but conniving and vengeful he isn't. He would never speak to me that way, even as a joke. Whoever is doing this is after me for some reason.

I haven't heard back from Rebecca since she spoke to Scott, but I can't just sit here while these emails continue to come in each day and paralyze me with fright. Maybe it's a stupid move, but I have to write back.

From: Georgina Park
To: _H1036
Date: July 11, 2013 at 4:47 PM
Subject: Re: Hi

If you're going to ruin my life, can you at least communicate with me at this Gmail address? UCLA has strict policies about content and will likely just delete my email account altogether, so if you want to say what it is that you need to say, write me here instead. I don't know how you obtained the photo that you sent me, but I own the copyright to it, so please keep that in mind.

From: _H1036
To: Georgina Park
Date: July 11, 2013 at 5:11 PM
Subject: Re: Hi

No problem. This nude one of you in heels from behind is my favorite. Your ass looks great.

■ ■ ■

"What did Scott say?" I ask Rebecca when I finally reach her.

"You might not like it," she says.

"Why?"

"He thought that the first thing you should do is contact Simon, because apparently guys sometimes upload these types of pictures to different websites to share with other people. There's something called revenge porn. I know you think he wouldn't do that, but maybe he did, and maybe someone got fixated on you for some reason."

"There are pictures on the Internet that are about five thousand times more graphic than this photo, so that makes no sense to me. Simon and I didn't end on bad terms. Why would he want to hurt me?"

"I don't know, Georgina," she says, sounding exhausted. I hear her kids playing in the background. "I'm just telling you what Scott said. Maybe Simon told someone your name for whatever reason. It could have been fairly innocent. Also, Scott mentioned that you technically own the copyright if you took the picture."

"I know, I told them that already."

"What do you mean?" I can tell she disapproves of me responding to the mystery writer. "Don't you think it could incite him further?"

I explain that I couldn't wait any longer and that even though it seems ridiculous, I've at least gotten the person to stop contacting me through the university email system. "There's a second photo. And it's worse."

"How many are there?"

"I don't know, exactly. I remember Simon taking a few of me in a hotel once, but these are different. They're from when I lived in that duplex by Wahoo's. I can tell by the bedding. It was way after he left Los Angeles. We stayed in touch for a while, and apparently the size of the Pacific Ocean wasn't enough to stop us from doing what we needed to do."

"I get it, Georgina."

"He wanted them and I wanted to give them to him, but I never thought in a million years that anyone else would ever see them," I explain as my eyes well with tears. "I mean, he's an award-winning journalist who has interviewed heads of state and suspected terrorists. He knows how to be discreet. I didn't think I needed to lecture him on the topic. It was understood. He knows I'm very private."

"Then maybe someone got the picture on your end and not his?"

"Is that even possible? The photos were from two computers ago."

"Don't you wonder if those guys at the Genius Bars look at all your stuff when you take your computer in?"

"I don't know what I was thinking," I say, my stomach tightening up. "I feel like crawling in a hole."

"You weren't thinking. Look, people do this all the time. Don't think for a second that Scott has never sent me a dick pic."

"Seriously? I don't want to think about that."

"I delete them so the kids won't find them and need a lifetime of therapy."

"If this doesn't get resolved immediately, *I'm* going to need a lifetime of therapy."

"Well, you'd better talk to someone," she says. "What about Lourdes? She's a lawyer."

"No, I don't want to call her." Rebecca is simply trying to help, but I'm too wound up to think about telling other friends. "This is all feeling very sinister. I'm scared."

"I can't even imagine who would want to do this to you. I know you keep a close circle of friends, but you certainly don't have enemies. You're a good person."

"I'll try Simon right after we get off the phone."

"Scott said not much can be done at this point. He asked if you knew how to track an IP address."

"No, I don't."

"Okay, he'll email you how to do that. At least then you'll be able to tell where they're emailing you from."

"That would be amazing. Thank you, Bec. I'm sorry, I haven't even asked how you're doing."

"I'm fine. I actually have nothing to report, which I'm sure sounds like the best thing ever to you right now."

"I have to get this under control, like, tonight."

> *From: Georgina Park*
> *To: Simon Grant*
> *Date: July 11, 2013 at 10:35 PM*
> *Subject: Urgent*
>
> *Simon,*
>
> *It has been so long. I know this is totally out of the blue, but I'm in the midst of a real crisis. I'm sure you remember that I used to send you pictures many years ago. Someone has at least two of them, and they're taunting me with them. I don't know what they want or why they have them in the first place, especially as they're from a decade ago. I am not accusing you of anything, but I have to ask if you know anything about this or can imagine any reason why this would be happening to me now.*
>
> *Did you leave them on a laptop with my name somehow attached? Did someone hack into your email at some point? Or did you ever show them to someone, for whatever reason? I won't be mad, I just need to know the source of this so I can get it contained. I know it's been years*

*since we've spoken and that this must sound a
bit crazy, but it's happening and I am incredibly
upset. I'm teaching at UCLA this summer and
don't want this to come out in any way. Aside
from my parents and a few real friends, my career
is all I have.*

*I don't have any enemies that I know of, and
Rebecca is the only person who knows about you and
me. And she knew nothing of these photos until yesterday. I would appreciate anything that you can do
to help.*

*Sorry I'm not writing with happier news. I
hope you are well, and I'd love to properly catch up
once this nightmare is over.*

Georgina

I go to get a glass of ice water, and when I return to my
desk I see there is already a reply.

From: Mail Delivery Subsystem
To: Simon Grant
Date: July 11, 2013 at 10:39 PM
Subject: Delivery Status Notification (Failure)

*Delivery to the following recipient failed
permanently.*

------End of message------

I blink at the screen, puzzled and concerned. Simon surely would have included me in a mass change-of-address email. I stare for a few moments longer, feeling helpless, before closing my laptop.

12

In addition to working full-time and teaching, I now have two mysteries to solve. Who is sending me these emails, and where the hell is Simon? I'm consumed by the situation day and night. I'm having trouble sleeping, which I never do, and sometimes wake up at three in the morning wondering when this person is going to send the photos to my department chair at UCLA, or to my father.

What could they want? They haven't made any demands, but I suspect something is coming down the line. I haven't told anyone aside from Rebecca, but I'm preparing myself and living in a constant state of dread. The fact that they used my UCLA address makes me think it's someone who doesn't know me personally. So that eliminates about 300 people and whittles it down to around 7.12 billion.

I don't know why my email to Simon bounced back. I didn't use his old work address. He's had the same personal

Hotmail address since we first met. I suppose he could have changed with the times and switched to Gmail. I look for him on Facebook, LinkedIn and Twitter, but no luck.

I have a feeling he isn't into social media, especially now that he's a fifty-six-year-old high-level executive, not an on-camera personality who needs to interact with viewers. He probably values his privacy since he is well known. I do, too. I'm not on the aforementioned sites at all; I just have a work-mandated Twitter account with a measly 563 followers. The comments section of my online stories is bad enough; now we have to let the readers send us tweets every time they don't like something, or need to share an opinion because they can rarely do so in their real lives?

I email Rebecca to let her know Simon's email account is defunct. I can usually find anyone or anything I want online, but discovering his new email address is proving to be impossible, and I'm so distracted by fear of the situation that I can hardly think straight. The next morning, Rebecca tells me to call Simon's network and just ask for him. That's Reporting 101, and I mentally kick myself for not thinking of it sooner. I look up his network's website.

It's already tomorrow afternoon in Sydney. I've made hundreds of cold calls as a journalist, but this one feels particularly awkward. I haven't called Simon at work since he told me he was legally separated, and I'm not prepared for getting his voicemail or speaking to an assistant. I never imagined that I would call Simon unexpectedly after seven years, let alone have to conduct a minor investigation regarding some softcore photos he hounded me for.

But I can't blame him in the slightest. I did it. I was proud of how I looked in the snaps, and I knew he would love them, so I clicked send.

I don't have an international plan anymore, so this phone call is going to cost me a small fortune. Fuck it, just dial. I would give my life savings of $7,342 to get rid of these pictures for good. I find the number for the head office in Sydney and start pressing numbers with quivering fingers. My heart rate speeds up and my stomach starts doing flips like it used to when I would speak to him, but this time it's for all the wrong reasons.

It's always odd hearing a different type of ring than you're used to. Breathe, I tell myself repeatedly. I immediately hear a prerecorded voice saying this call may be recorded for quality control. Just what I need.

"Good morning, SBC," says an upbeat woman with that charming Australian accent.

"Hi, I'm trying to reach Simon Grant."

"I'm sorry, there is no one by that name here. Is there someone else I may connect you to?"

"Are you sure? I'm certain that SBC was where he was working. This is the Sydney Broadcasting Company, right?"

"Hang on a minute," she says.

After a brief hold, a man gets on the line. "Who may I ask is calling?"

"My name is Georgina Park," I say. "I'm calling from Los Angeles. I'm looking for Simon Grant."

"May I ask what it is regarding?"

"It's personal," I say awkwardly. "I'm an old friend."

There is a long pause.

"I'm so sorry to have to tell you this," he says, "but Simon passed away back in 2010."

I drop the cordless phone, and it hits the hardwood floor with a loud thud. I cover my mouth with my hand in disbelief. Am I going to pass out? In this moment I've forgotten about the pictures, the strange emails and the fact that someone is messing with my sanity and possibly my livelihood. All I can think is: Simon. He died, and I didn't even know, because no one would know to tell me.

I need to make sure it's real. What if another Simon Grant worked at SBC? I quickly type his name into the Google search bar with the word *obituary*, and there it is.

I see his picture, and I see Clare's name, and the kids', and his job, and that he loved watching cricket and collecting wine. After staring at the screen for several minutes, mouth agape, I sit in my office chair, staring past the computer to the hedging outside my window.

I've lost people before. You grieve, you go to a funeral and share sweet and funny stories about the person, and it gets a little bit better. You write a letter to the loved ones, expressing what the person meant to you. You might even set up a scholarship in their honor or start a golf tournament to raise money for cancer research. I know the drill. I've been through it. But that's not going to happen here. How do you grieve for a married former lover whom no one really knows about?

It is too late to call Rebecca, or anyone for that matter, so I get in my car and find myself heading toward Simon's former home in the Palisades. I turn off the Jenny Lewis CD that's blasting out of the car speakers, as it's just going to make things worse. I only went to his house that time when Clare and the kids were out of town, and it was a lovely place. But I had a hard time relaxing, knowing I was in *her* home, with her stuff. I felt ashamed as I left early the next morning. Simon wanted to share something personal with me—his home—but I saw it as violating Clare and their kids' privacy and space.

I remember there were no photos up of the family. Maybe Simon had removed them because he knew it would bother me. If so, how does it feel to physically erase your family so that your twenty-two-year-old lover can come stay over? Is it exciting, or do you feel like a horrible person? I'm sick at the thought. What were we thinking? It was so risky. What if a neighbor had seen my car parked there overnight and casually mentioned it when she returned? Why didn't Simon just stay at my place that night? I can't remember, and it doesn't really matter now, does it?

I haven't been in this particular neighborhood in twelve years and am shocked that I remember the street name. I go to nearly every corner of Los Angeles for the stories that I write but couldn't tell you the name of the avenue I was on last week for a profile of a top local author. After winding up a hillside lined with massive magnolia trees, I arrive. The Craftsman-style house is a little smaller than I remember but still more amazing than any home I will ever live in on a freelance journalist's salary. There's a black Range Rover in the driveway, and I see a neighbor walking a pair of goldendoodles across the street. I just sit in the car for a few moments. For the first time in many years, I miss Simon.

My eyes fill with tears, and I know I should get out of here before someone notices me, but then I start truly crying, and there's no turning back from the floodgate now. I'm hysterical, releasing more tears in my car outside Simon's old house than I probably have in a lifetime. I couldn't drive like this even if I tried. So many memories come flooding back. I can't stop thinking about the way his face looked whenever he saw me. That impish smile. The sadness is heavier than anything I could have predicted. I guess I always thought in the back of my mind that I would hear from him again, that I would have a chance to say something, anything, to him again, even just an email or IM just to say hi.

After ten minutes of this, I'm able to compose myself enough to drive. I find a few napkins in my glove compartment and check my red and swollen eyes in the rearview mirror. I look like I've been through a battle. It's nearly midnight and I am absolutely exhausted. The stress of what is going on is manifesting itself in a pounding headache and sharp pain above my shoulder blades. I take Palisades Drive back down to Sunset Boulevard and start heading back to Santa Monica.

Once I reach Pico Boulevard, I see a billboard for AshleyMadison.com that reads, "Life is short. Have an affair." I feel like I'm going to be sick as I turn up 16th Street. How could this have happened? Simon was still young. Why didn't I learn of his death when I was googling him? His poor children. Was he alone when he died?

I catch myself zoning out at a red light on Ocean Park when the black BMW X5 behind me honks aggressively. I feel like getting out of my car and telling the driver that I just found out that the second man I ever slept with is dead. I am heartbroken.

The minute I'm home I go back to the obituary, as if it's going to reveal something different upon a second reading. As I look at Simon's photo, a serious, professional shot that looks presidential, I think about all the times we were so happy and carefree. I remember his Polo aftershave and how lightheaded I would feel when he kissed my neck.

The obituary tells me things about Simon I never knew. The small town in New South Wales where he was born before his family moved to Brisbane. How he became a journalist at the age of twenty-one. That he was the youngest of four children.

I begin to feel guilty that I didn't ask him more about himself when we were together. How can you be so intimate with someone that your body aches for every inch of him, yet you don't know if he has brothers or sisters? My whole life revolves around asking people questions, but I forgot to ask Simon some of the most basic ones, which I now regret. I read on, learning that he wrote a second book with a colleague in 2006, and that he was twice divorced. I wonder why he never told me about the second divorce. Embarrassed, maybe. Or too busy fucking everything in sight, perhaps. I'll never know.

It doesn't say much about his time in Los Angeles, only that it was one of the many places he lived during his busy and successful career. There is, of course, no mention of the unique and memorable relationship he had with a young aspiring journalist, no sentence about how they must have exchanged thousands of messages over the years and told each other things they'd never uttered to anyone else. And there's nothing about the off-the-charts sexual chemistry they explored together, trying anything and everything they could think of.

As close as we were for a time, I realize that in the story of Simon's entire life, I was probably just a short footnote, a drop in the ocean. Someone he pursued to escape a loveless marriage and perhaps indulge a midlife crisis. It could have been a million others, but it happened to be me because I was the girl on her own at that screening and I said *Okay*. No one in his world ever knew about me, so it's almost as if our time together never existed. I try my hardest to remember each instance we were together, but I can't. It was so long ago that I can only think of a few specific images and conversations, which play like a highlight reel in my mind, but I see his warm eyes and remember the shape of his jawline easily.

Tears begin to flow again, making it hard to read the screen, as I consider all the relational nuances we'll never have. I feel sad that I never saw his handwriting. And that we never wished each other a happy new year. I don't know his favorite meal or the name of his best friend. I feel bad that I cut off communication because of Justin. It seemed like the right thing to do at the time, but maybe it hurt Simon's feelings, something I had done before. He even suggested that we eventually get married, which I dismissed as if it was a silly joke, but he was serious. Timing is everything, they say, and Simon and I were never in sync when it came to pursuing a real relationship.

I remember back to the only time I was ever truly mad at him. He stood me up for a prearranged meeting at my place during lunchtime and didn't call or email to cancel. I sent him a curt note, essentially threatening to never see him again, and he wrote back the next morning, explaining that his daughter, Hannah, had been rushed to the hospital with appendicitis the previous morning. His phone died, and he wasn't alone for the rest of the day or evening. His daughter was okay, but it was terrifying for their family. I felt like the world's worst person and realized that no matter how cool I played it, I was in over my head with this affair. I wish I had told him so. Aside from that incident I was always acting a bit, never wanting to be vulnerable with him. Now that I'm raw, for anyone to see, he's no longer here.

Feeling jet-lagged even though I've only been to the Palisades and back, I get into bed, still wearing my damp, tear-soaked shirt. I finally fall asleep at two in the morning, desperately hoping to dream about him.

13

Before I attempt to track the IP address of this strange email account, I do some regular old-fashioned Internet sleuthing by first googling the address. Nada. I type it into Facebook to see if it's associated with a profile, but nothing comes up. Whoever it is was smart enough to use a virgin email account. It's been two days since the last photo was sent to me, and just over twenty-four hours since I found out about Simon.

Last night I woke up every hour with my heart racing. It would take me another half hour to fall back asleep. My body can't turn off its fight-or-flight response. I'm ready to go at any second. If I can't get some real sleep soon, I'm going to have to ask my neighbor Eli for a Xanax to knock me out. I really hate being alone during nights like these, but it isn't a good time to ask one of the two guys I have been casually dating to come over. I don't share anything real with them; we just have superficial fun. I call one of them when I've been alone for so many nights I can't count them anymore, and then I go as long as I can without having to call again.

I'm teaching this afternoon and have to act like a normal person. I will park in Lot C, make the short walk through North Campus and speak animatedly before the class, as though my biggest problem in life is that I have to pay ten dollars to park but don't get reimbursed by the university. I feel sympathy for all the teachers I've had over the years. Their students never knew if they were having a horrible day, if they were worried about their child who was home sick with a fever, or if their husband had just left them. We never cared.

I also feel bad that I haven't called my parents in a couple of weeks. We usually talk every Sunday morning and Wednesday evening, a ritual that began when I moved out at seventeen, but I let their last two calls go to voicemail and texted them that I was swamped. I was in no condition for a peppy talk. As an only child, I'm often stuck in a cycle of guilt, as I can't rely on a sibling to pick up some of the slack of their loving attention. My parents wanted to have another child, but it wasn't in the cards. I tell myself I will call them soon. I just want to get this situation resolved. I look at my phone and see a text from Rebecca.

I just got your message. I am so sorry. Call me when you get out of class.

"Hi," I say quietly.

"I can't believe it, Georgina."

"I know. I don't really know what to do. I don't know anyone from his life to reach out to or say I'm sorry. And the fact that it was three years ago makes me feel like I don't have a right to say anything to anyone."

"Of course you do. People lose touch."

"Even though the photo debacle might have happened because of Simon in some way, I was counting on him to help me figure it out. He would have helped me," I say.

"Of course. He always seemed to care a lot about you, even after things didn't work out."

"I think it's hitting me so hard because I always secretly thought we could have ended up together, even after years of not talking. The possibility of trying out a real relationship is gone forever. It was something in my back pocket, especially after Justin, but now I am truly on my own. All the soul mates have left the building."

"That's heavy, G," she says, sighing.

"I just wish I'd known something was wrong. If I knew he was sick I would have gone to see him."

"Maybe he didn't want to be seen. Do you think he mentioned you to any of his friends? Is there anyone you could reach out to for information?"

"I doubt it. I never met anyone from his life, and he never met anyone from mine."

"Sorry if this is the wrong time to bring this up, but I was thinking that it sounds like he could have been married," Rebecca says. "It's weird that he never introduced you to anyone, and you guys never really went out in public much. Did you ever think that?"

Long. Awkward. Pause. I have never lied to Rebecca, and I don't want to hide this anymore.

"Yes," I say. "I mean, yes, he was married."

"Did you just find that out reading the obituary?" she asks in horror.

"Rebecca, no—I mean I always knew that. I was just too embarrassed and ashamed to tell you that at the time."

I can hear her judgment through her silence.

"Or anytime after that, I suppose," she snaps.

"I know you're probably disappointed in me, but honestly I can't deal with you being mad at me on top of this."

"I have to go."

■ ■ ■

From: _H1036
To: Georgina Park
Date: July 14, 2013 at 12:11 PM
Subject: Re: Hi

I would consider not making your photos public if you do something for me. I know these pictures are old. I'd like to see some new ones. Take them from your webcam.

■ ■ ■

From: Georgina Park
To: Rebecca Fraser
Date: July 14, 2013 at 1:37 PM
Subject: So sorry

Rebecca,

I'm so sorry if you are hurt by my revelation. I know it was wrong, but I can't change something that happened ten years ago. I was inexperienced and totally charmed by him. I don't know what else I can say about it. I'm not trying to make excuses; I was old enough to know better.

You were the only person who even knew that Simon existed. He was not happy at the time, obviously, and ended up divorced years later. His wife fell in love with someone else and is a successful TV producer in Sydney. She never knew about me and never will.

I don't know why I couldn't tell you, because I can tell you anything. I know you wouldn't have judged me, but I think I just wanted to keep it between Simon and me. I struggled with the right and wrong of it all, vacillating between feeling bold and ashamed. The connection I had with him was unparalleled; it was something chemical that I can't really explain.

Maybe it was the perfect convergence of love and lust and timing. I've been looking for that feeling ever since and haven't found it—not even with Justin. It wasn't the danger of being caught (although of course *that can feel exciting at times); it was how he made me feel.*

When we were together, I was free. Free from being the good girl. Free from being my parents' daughter. Free from always doing the right thing. I was my real self with him.

The whole naughty-picture thing and Simon's death are punishment enough. Maybe it's retribution from the universe. You know how much I care about you and our friendship. If you want to talk about it further, I will tell you anything you want to know, or if you want to never discuss it again, that's fine, too. Take whatever time you need.

Love,
Georgina

From: Rebecca Fraser
To: Georgina Park
Date: July 15, 2013 at 3:58 AM
Subject: Re: So sorry

Georgina,

I am not mad at you for sleeping with a married man for a few months. Who hasn't? It's like a rite of passage for smart, independent women who mature faster than their male counterparts. You intimidate most men as it is, so I understand that a 23-year-old douchebag wouldn't have cut it for you.

It just caught me off guard, because you never hide anything from me. I couldn't believe that you could keep a secret like that for so many years. It scared me, actually, because I thought I knew everything about you. I'll call you soon—promise.

Love you,
Bec
P.S. I just wanted to say that I don't think this Simon's death is retribution from the universe, Georgina. I'm surprised you would say such a thing, given that you're not religious. You know better.

■ ■ ■

"G?"

I'm relieved to hear Rebecca's voice. "I'm so sorry, Bec."

"You don't need to say anything else. I think the reason I reacted the way I did is because I'm almost certain that Scott is in the midst of some sort of an affair of his own."

"What are you talking about? That can't be true."

"I mean, he's in intelligence, so of course he knows how to hide his tracks, and I have no real proof—just a feeling. So the idea that two of the most important people in my world could be lying to me felt pretty shitty. Then throw three screaming kids into the mix. It's not a great week over here."

I'm mortified. "Oh my God. I've been so wrapped up in my own little soap opera that I had no idea you were dealing with this, Bec. How long have you suspected something?"

"Only very recently. We haven't been super connected lately, but he's been acting strange, dressing nicer and wearing cologne," she says. "It's like some bad *Cosmo* article about the warning signs of cheating."

"I am so sorry. I've lost faith in humanity. I never thought Scott of all people would do something like that. He's supposed to be one of the good guys," I say. "Apparently we are all capable of doing bad things. Let's hope it's a misunderstanding, but I've always thought that you have minor psychic abilities, so if you are right, we will deal with it—together."

■ ■ ■

From: _H1036
To: Georgina Park
Date: July 16, 2013 at 08:31 AM
Subject: Re: Hi

Do you not think I'm serious? In case you were wondering, I know you live on Ocean Park, teach at UCLA and write for the L.A. Times. You like behaving like a little slut, don't you?

From: Georgina Park
To: _H1036
Date: July 16, 2013 at 08:42 AM
Subject: Re: Hi

No pictures will be taken. The ones you have are essentially illegal. I have a lawyer. If I hear from you again, I will take action, so please fuck off.

■ ■ ■

This morning is the first chance I've had to attempt to track the IP address. It's also the day I find my first gray hair—no surprise there, considering my stress levels this week. The latest emails from my mystery tormentor sound angry, and I wonder if they're coming from Simon's ex-wife Clare. It seems ridiculous, since they divorced in 2005 and she is a successful producer who has better things to do.

I call Rebecca to run the theory by her. "Maybe she had some of his old things, like a laptop from that time, and only now got around to going through it."

"But three years later?" She sounds skeptical.

"Good point. There could have been some file with all our old emails or IMs. I know I saved some of them."

"Imagine the rage you would feel finding out that your husband cheated on you, only now you're already divorced and he's dead," Rebecca says. I cringe at the thought. "There are no answers and no good explanations."

"Honestly, I would expect more from her. I always respected Clare, which sounds contradictory since I was fucking her husband, but I would imagine that she is above all this."

"I actually think it's the second ex-wife, because she most recently had access to his things and may have been jealous, thinking that the affair went on while she was with him," she says. "Who knows what Simon told her about you."

"What I don't get is this: Say you have these few photos you want to keep because they remind you of good times or serve as some sort of digital scrapbook. Do you really transfer them over, from computer to computer, cell phone to hard drive, for years?"

"Apparently he did," Rebecca says. "I used to keep a diary of everyone I ever slept with and would even write little notes about them, like if they had a hairy back or giant balls."

I burst out laughing, and it feels so good to release some of the tension that's taken up residence in my chest the last week. "That is the first laugh I've had in days," I tell her. "I guess it's possible. It's just weird because I wouldn't have thought Simon would hang on to the pictures so long after they were sent—men aren't usually so sentimental. The timing makes no sense, since he's already been gone for several years."

"Are you going to talk to a lawyer? Or maybe you should call the FBI."

"They won't do anything. Ask Scott—do you know how many thousands of people are victims of stuff like this?" I say, realizing how jaded I sound. "First I'm going to do the IP address search, and depending on what that says, I'm going to call the LAPD and see what they suggest doing. Just to at least have a record of it, in case I end up dead."

"Georgina, don't even joke like that," Rebecca says sternly.

"I'm sure the guy won't kill me," I assure her, "but he knew I lived on Ocean Park. That made my head spin."

"The fucking Internet. You know if you buy a home, anyone can see the price and address, and even Google Earth it to see the color of your door and the type of trees you have out back."

"Whatever is going on, whatever the motivation, it feels like they're saying 'You think you got away with something ten years ago, but you didn't.'"

"This is getting insane."

"I could always pretend I was doing a story on revenge porn or something, you know, to find out what the next steps would be without actually outing myself. I have a few contacts at the LAPD and could easily get a detective on the phone."

"That is not a bad idea," Rebecca says. "But while you're at it, please make sure you set your alarm and leave everything locked. This is just crazy."

I bought a small house two years ago, when the market was at an all-time low and I had come into a bit of money—$125,000, to be exact, thanks to a gift from a deceased, childless aunt I wasn't really close to. I felt strange about accepting money I hadn't earned. As much as my parents love and support me, they insisted that I start working as soon as I was of legal age, and I had to work throughout college as well. They always instilled in me that I had to take care of myself and should never rely on a man.

I didn't want to be frivolous, so I agreed to accept the money knowing I would do something completely sensible and risk-free with it. Every advisor I talked to said the same thing: real estate. It turns out they were right. I recently had a couple from San Francisco ask if I would consider selling my house for $200,000 over what I paid for it.

"You know what is also really upsetting me?" I say as I straighten items on my desk into perfect right angles.

"What could bother you more than X-rated photos of yourself floating around the Internet?"

"I'm upset with myself that I never pursued the relationship. Simon wanted to, but I always said no. I had every excuse possible to not move to Sydney: I couldn't be a stepmother, I didn't want people to think that I broke up a marriage, I couldn't fully trust him given where we started."

"Well, those are all legitimate arguments," Rebecca says, always on my side. "It would have been a huge risk to up and move to a foreign country where you knew no one."

"Since I was so young, I blamed a lot of what I felt for him on inexperience or naïveté," I explain. "I didn't realize it was real until it was too late."

"Please. You have never been naïve a day in your life," she retorts.

"Well, now that he's on my mind so much I feel an ache inside, like an emptiness. It's heartbreak, you know? I loved him, but it was a hopeless situation."

"That might be true," she says, "but you are in a crazy state of mind right now. Obviously you're having a lot of feelings. You're grieving, G."

"I just can't believe he is gone."

"I promise someone else will come along one day and you'll love him in a way that makes you realize he's who you have really been waiting for," she says. "You'll look back on Simon, and even Justin, and know that those were just warm-up acts for the real thing."

"That would be nice," I say, not actually believing her. I've been dating for over a decade and I know what's out there. I've never found the feeling I had with Simon on that very first night in the hotel, where the desire radiating between us must have been palpable to anyone sitting within ten feet of us at that French restaurant.

"And think about it. Even if you and Simon ran off into the sunset, the age difference would have eventually caught up with you. I mean, can you imagine hitting your prime in your forties and he's on the decline? How would you have even explained how you two met? And do men like that really change? If things fizzled out, would he just find someone else?"

"I don't know."

"Okay, wait. If you're thirty-four he'd be, what, like fifty-four?"

"It's easy to remember because it's a twenty-year age difference. It was."

"I read this thing on Cup of Jo—it's like a rule of thumb for dating. The post said that you take the older person's age, so in this case fifty-four, then divide it in half and then add seven. And that's the biggest age difference you are allowed to have."

"Okay, so twenty-seven plus seven is thirty-four."

"And you're thirty-four. Wow, so I guess it's okay after all."

"Okay with whom?" I ask, starting to laugh.

"The Internet and me, apparently."

"I'll keep that in mind going forward."

"And something I've been wondering lately: Why couldn't Simon be alone?" she asks. "Like, why didn't he just divorce his first wife instead of waiting to find you? And when you made it clear you weren't going to marry him, he just marries someone else right away?"

"I don't know," I say wistfully, knowing I am in no state to fully analyze Simon's emotional issues at the moment. "He was against divorce and wanted to make it work for the sake of his children. I guess he hadn't really been alone since he was at university. Let's change the subject. What is going on with you and Scott?"

"It's not a great time at the Fraser-Mitchell household," she says. "I confronted him about the emails, and instead of explaining and apologizing, he attacked me for snooping. He was very defensive—and angry too."

"So what do you do now?"

"We are supposed to have a *talk* later tonight, after the kids go to sleep." I hear the dread in her voice. "I can hardly look at his face right now, and it's so hard with the kids because we have to act normal for them."

"Well, call me after if you need to," I tell her. "I'll be up."

"You have a lot going on," she says. "Not sure you need *this* on your plate too."

"I could say the same to you."

14

Right after hanging up with Rebecca, I follow the IP-tracking instructions Scott sent me earlier. I open the last message from _H1036 and follow the steps carefully. Once I have what I need, I enter it into the bar of the website he forwarded me. I scroll down and see a bunch of what looks like gibberish. But about nine lines down there's a nine-digit number that's separated by periods. Bingo.

I cut and paste the IP address back into the website, and up pops the information. I was convinced it would be untraceable. After all, if you're going to blackmail some-one, you'd better do it right. But no. Here is the hostname, server, country, state, city and even the fucking latitude and longitude of where this computer is physically located. I don't want to get too excited, since this psycho could be using any smartphone, laptop, iPad or computer on earth. Just because you find the IP address doesn't mean you find the person who typed those emails. Today the *Times* ran a story on a child-pornography bust that was traced to a public library. The police had to set up a video camera to see who was actually sending and receiving lewd material. Libraries are apparently so empty these days that no one noticed the perv among them.

In addition to the geolocation information, there's even a map. I am floored by what I see. The address is on campus at UCLA. I dial Rebecca's number as fast as my fingers will possibly move.

"It's someone on campus," I blurt out, so proud of my detective work that I could scream.

"You're shitting me!" she exclaims. "So it can't be the first wife or the other wife."

"Not unless one of them has taken up graduate work in a foreign country."

"This is absolutely insane, Georgina," she says excitedly. "Lucy, do not hit your brother or you will be in time out. Sorry, Georgina, hold on, Scott wants to talk to you."

"I'm not sure that's necessary right now…"

Rebecca and Scott are in a weird place, but I appreciate the fact that he's still willing to help me. He knows it means a lot to Rebecca. Scott and I have never been particularly close. Although I have always liked him, he's never warmed to me. I think I symbolize Rebecca's past, which includes bouts of promiscuity, and I know he thinks we talk on the phone too much.

"Georgina."

"Hi."

"I couldn't help but overhear. I just wanted to tell you that we've been seeing cases where pictures are stolen from victims via a hacked computer or cell phone. Those photos may not have come from the person you sent them to. They could very well be from your own computer."

"I'm starting to realize that, but I don't have those photos on my computer. They're from ages ago."

"I can call in a favor," he says. "I think you should talk to a federal agent, just to weigh your options."

"I appreciate it. Let me just see if I can track down the physical computer. If I can't, then the next move will be the FBI. I hate the idea of a case being opened, or this being on the official record, if I can contain it myself."

"It's better to be safe," says Scott, as little Lucy screams in the background. "Trust me. You want to do the right thing here."

It's funny hearing this from a man who *hasn't* been doing the right thing for quite some time now. Rebecca finally found proof of an affair in the form of more than 200 emails to a secret Gmail account Scott accidentally left up on their shared computer. So much for the slick intelligence officer. He swears that nothing physical happened between him and this woman, and we almost believe him. Rebecca quickly read as many messages as she could and there was no mention of sex, but what's extra hard is that she has met the woman—it's a coworker of Scott's who is shorter, heavier and less attractive than she is.

"One last thing. You should probably put a piece of tape over your computer's camera. People have figured out how to hack in that way and can even watch you without that little green light being on."

"You have to be kidding me," I say, recalling all the times I've changed clothes in my office or simply sat around working in nothing but a flimsy nightie. "Thanks for the tip. Can you put Rebecca back on for a sec?" I hear her take the phone.

"As soon as we can find an hour to ourselves, we're going to couples counseling," she explains in a low voice before saying goodbye. "With the kids and my business, I don't really have time to deal with this. I'm pretty sure the last time we had sex was six months ago, so what did I expect was going to happen?"

It stuns me to hear Rebecca talk this way; she was always such a sexual being. In college she was the first one to tell me the best position to be in to have an orgasm, and she owned a mini collection of sex toys I stumbled upon in our senior year. I had never seen anything other than a vibrator, so I must have looked confused by the shapes, sizes and textures of her assemblage. She just laughed. Rebecca was the first person to show me a porno and sleep with a bartender from our favorite spot in Newport. She was always comfortable and devil-may-care when it came to sex. And she never shied away from talking about it. She often wanted details about my sex life that I wasn't comfortable sharing. I always saw her as the wild one.

This revelation isn't helping me believe in the institution of marriage, either. I already have my doubts, perhaps because of rising divorce rates and the fact that several of my friends who were once carefree and happy grew into nagging and constantly annoyed wives. Granted, Rebecca has three kids under six, enough to put a strain on even the healthiest of marriages, but still. Lourdes told me that some of her male clients put minimum sexual requirements into their prenups. Only in L.A.

I hang up the phone after thanking them profusely and feel a new swell of guilt. I could easily be placed in the same category as the woman who is having this emotional affair with Scott. Just because Rebecca's going through a bit of a sexual slump doesn't entitle him to seek excitement elsewhere, although Clare's apathy toward Simon was enough for me to account for our behavior.

But because of Simon, part of me understands what Scott must be feeling. He married a fun-loving, self-described nympho and ended up with a frazzled mom who will take sleep over sex every single time. What do you do if you've taken the vows, for better or worse, and your spouse stops sleeping with you? What if that period is temporary because of young children and you know it will get better so you don't want to leave, but you simply have to be touched by another human who isn't drooling, crying or screaming? You'd probably think it would be easier to just have a little fun on the side. Maybe it wouldn't even be physical. It could just be a flirtation to give you an ego boost, to know you can still get it if you want to. No one will ever find out, except that they will.

I'm going to campus tomorrow and find myself actually excited, in a rather sick way, to try and solve this myself since the IP address is definitely at UCLA. It's still hard to quiet my mind from wondering if this person is in my class or if it's some sort of obsessed fellow instructor, though neither makes any real sense. I wanted to be a crime reporter growing up, so let's see if I have the stomach for it. For the first time in weeks, I feel a bit settled. I may even sleep through the night.

As my head hits the soft, cold pillow in my queen-size bed, I start thinking I could go back to yoga. My teacher recently left a voicemail to check on me since I usually never miss her 7 a.m. class every Monday, Wednesday and Friday in Mar Vista. I love the studio because it's cozy and no one is wearing Cartier Love bracelets like at their Santa Monica outpost. It's nice to know that someone would notice if I really did disappear. I'm starting to feel like everything might be okay.

■ ■ ■

It's 11:53 in the evening and I've already been asleep for an hour when I hear a rap at the door. I've pretty much dropped off the face of the earth socially, so it isn't Mike or Ethan, the two guys I've been seeing. After making up excuse after excuse and finally texting that I was dealing with a death in the family, I stopped hearing from them. They both know better than to show up unannounced.

The adrenaline is instantaneous. My senses are immediately heightened, my hands feel a bit numb and I'm acutely aware that whatever is on the other side of that door cannot be good. And it keeps knocking.

I tiptoe my way to the kitchen in the dark and grab one of my huge Wüsthof kitchen knives. I can hear my heart beating as if in stereo. Why didn't I opt for the $400 doorway camera that ADT rep was selling? I have the phone in my other hand, ready to call 911, but what am I going to say—that there's someone knocking at my door? I text my neighbor Eli, whom I'm friendly but not too friendly with, although I'm not sure he'll be awake since he works strange hours, telling him there's someone outside my door who was not invited. Immediately his light comes on, and I've never been so happy to live near someone who is a mixed-martial-arts enthusiast. I'm relieved that whatever is going to happen next will at least be known by someone.

I see Eli step onto his front porch when the motion-sensor light goes on and hear his deep voice in conversation with another man. "Dude, she's out of town," Eli says casually.

"She invited me here," a strange voice says as I tiptoe to the door to look through the peephole.

"*Who* invited you?"

"Georgina. Georgina Park."

"Well, I don't know what to tell you, brother," Eli says, playing his role so well that I wonder why he isn't an actor instead of a research assistant at a chemical lab in El Segundo.

"Sorry man, I didn't mean to wake you. This doesn't make sense. I was in touch with her in the last hour. She was up for it. You know what I mean."

"I can tell her you stopped by when she gets back. What was your name?"

"Owen. We met on Plenty of Fish."

My heart nearly stops. I've never had a profile on Plenty of Fish. I run to my computer and go to the site. I have to create a free account to get access, so I make up a fake profile using my real email address and start ticking boxes. There are what seem like millions of profiles to sift through, so I'm not sure I'll be able to find myself, but I narrow it down by age, race, location, occupation, and then...*boom.*

My work headshot that runs with my column appears next to my name, along with the headline "Ready for Anything!!!" The creepiness factor of seeing someone posing as me on some second-rate dating site is off the charts.

After texting Eli, thanking him and telling him I will explain later, I fill out the "Report Image" form, typing well over 125 words per minute. Apparently I'm not the first person whose photos are being used without consent on this site. It occurs to me that I haven't even Google Image–searched my headshot or the other photos I took for Simon. Part of me is scared to see what damage this asshole could have done in the last few days. An X-rated photo on the Internet is like finding an ant in your kitchen. It means many more are on the way.

I first upload my work photo and am relieved to see it only next to articles I've written, a conference I attended a few years back, on a blog about Asian-American writers and on my Twitter page.

Not even the Plenty of Fish profile is coming up. For now.

■ ■ ■

From: _H1036
To: Georgina Park
Date: July 18, 2013 at 07:16 AM
Subject: Re: Hi

You know what I can do. I want new photos, or else I am submitting the old ones to thedirty. com and letting them know that you are a UCLA professor. By the way, I haven't told you how hot you look in the photos. I like the one of you on your knees, looking up, mouth slightly open. It gets me excited.

■ ■ ■

I take Scott up on his offer. I'm already terrified that a strange man who was clearly promised something turned up at my door at night, and now the threat of TheDirty. com, the controversial gossip website that can ruin you for life, means it's time to get real help. I pull up the screen-shot of the IP address, which I still can't believe is coming from somewhere within the mini city that is UCLA, and text Scott the info, asking him to call me as soon as he can. There has to be some law against impersonation (*Yeah right*, laughs everyone who's ever been catfished), at least when it comes to arranging a booty call without consent. Part of me wants to go to UCLA IT Security, but then the information will certainly get out to my department chair, something I'm still desperately hoping to avoid.

I think of Hunter Moore, the jackass behind the now-shuttered Is Anyone Up? His site was like TheDirty on crack. It featured user-submitted nude photos—usu-ally of ex-girlfriends or former conquests—along with screenshots of the subjects' real names, links to their Facebook profiles and any other available contact info. I remember watching victims share their devastating sto-ries on Anderson Cooper's show. There was no reason-ing with Hunter Moore, who posted thousands of images over the years and described himself as a "professional life-ruiner." Conveniently, he also ran a business that helped get the pictures taken down for a fee. His defense was something along the lines of "No one forced you to take the picture." Moore eventually sold the site to an anti-bullying group, claiming he had turned over a new leaf. An FBI investigation determined that he had paid a hacker to steal victims' photos, and he's since had a flurry of legal charges thrown his way.

Articles on revenge- and stalker porn are becoming more commonplace by the day. Reading story after story, I cringe for myself and these other girls and women who thought they were doing something sexy or cute for their boyfriend and are now being terrorized on a daily basis by men who have serious issues with women. I read their stories, which are far worse than mine, and think about pitching a story on the topic. Some of the girls are underage, and one killed herself because of the humiliation, shame and bullying she endured for months. While I wait to talk to Scott, I scan a Huffington Post story about California State Senator Anthony Cannella's new bill that would make it a misdemeanor to post or distribute sexual pictures or videos without the subject's consent.

But for now, these sites are getting tons of traffic and ad revenue, and they're largely immune to criminal prosecution. I read about victims who have lost their jobs, friends, families and souls because of this sort of thing. Luckily my twelve-year-old pictures are not graphic, but they are still very embarrassing. The thought of my editors, family or friends seeing them is enough to make me physically ill. If this person really submits my photos to TheDirty.com, they will certainly be posted (who can resist the UCLA and homewrecker angles?), and I will probably have to change my name. Don't think the worst, I tell myself.

It's hard to believe I've been living this terrifying life for only a week. It feels like a full-time job, worrying and creating scenarios in my mind of having to talk to some old-school male detective who doesn't know what an emoji is and would probably judge me for taking the photos in the first place. The lack of sleep, constant worry, anxiety and distracted hack teaching are starting to catch up with me. I know I need to nip this in the bud before the photos are disseminated and unable to be erased from the interwebs. I constantly have to remind myself to breathe.

I take a stab at answering some of my emails, which have been piling up for days, and tell an editor I need an extension on the current story I'm working on (an is-this-really-newsworthy profile of a new space downtown where a bunch of artists, designers and creative types are working together). I write myself a reminder to go by Eli's later to explain my situation. I've suspended all my regular activities and pretty much leave the house only to go to campus, which I don't feel safe doing anymore knowing my email stalker may be there.

I've never felt unsafe on the fairly main street in Santa Monica where I live. It's a few blocks from a hipster coffee shop and an always packed vegan café. All kinds of people park their cars along Ocean Park, from Santa Monica College students to residents to customers visiting the nearby restaurants. But with all that is going on, I've been looking at each car closely and jumping at every little sound, whether it's a bird chirping or a baby crying in the nearby park.

Since I haven't gotten a reply from Scott yet and have nothing going on today work-wise, I decide I should get out for an hour just to take a walk around the neighborhood. I grab my headphones and blast an old Sleater-Kinney playlist. Anything that can stifle the thoughts racing through my head at a hundred miles an hour is a good thing. When I arrive back at my front door, which faces Eli's front door off the main street, I notice a freshly washed black Mercedes that looks a bit too nice to be parked on our block, but I dismiss my paranoia.

The second I turn my key into the lock (a supposedly impossible-to-crack, $400 version used by top Israeli security experts, at least according to my non-Israeli locksmith) and crack the door open a few inches, I hear footsteps and can physically sense someone coming toward me. I quickly turn around and see an attractive guy, about five foot nine, with thick brown hair, looking right at me.

"Hey, Georgina," he says like we know each other.

My eyes widen and I freeze with fear. This isn't a delivery person or my usual postal worker. I'm positive this is another Plenty of Fish situation and that this guy recognizes me from my photo. I'm ready to explain how my unknown stalker duped him and apologize for the inconvenience, thankful that it's broad daylight and not one in the morning.

But the next thing I know, he is making contact with me. Stunned, I tense up, attempting to block him from the doorway while he uses his body weight to push me inside the house. It's not much of a struggle. He closes the door behind us.

"What are you doing? You need to leave," I say, firmly but in a neutral tone, wondering to myself why I'm not screaming in horror. Why can't I scream? What is wrong with me? Scream, dammit.

"You beg me to come over and then tell me to leave? I don't think so."

"I never asked you to come here," I say, breathless. "Whoever told you that was impersonating me. I don't know who you are."

"You're such a dirty little whore, aren't you?" he asks, reaching for something in his back pocket.

I'm convinced it is a knife. Or a gun. But it's a plastic zip tie, the kind you see cops sometimes use. I don't see a weapon. I have a giant knife in my kitchen, but no matter how strong I've become from years of yoga, I'm not going to be a match for this man.

"Please," I beg. "I swear I don't know who sent you here, but it wasn't me."

"Shut up, you whore," he says, looking me right in the eyes. "You know you want this. You are such a little slut."

He turns me around and binds my hands behind my back with the zip tie. I start thinking of how I can talk my way out of this. Everything I've ever read about preventing rape—don't wear a ponytail as it's easier for an attacker to grab you, don't sit in your car in a parking lot, don't leave your drink unattended, walk with purpose—is of no use in this moment. I remember hearing a security expert on a

Dateline-type show say to never let your attacker take you to a second location. But what did he say about being in your own home? Why can't I remember that part?

"You wanted an aggressive guy, right?" he says. "Well, here I am."

"Please, I beg you. I don't know what you're talking about. I have never communicated with you. I don't know your name."

"Shut up, bitch. You know my fucking name."

I try taking in as many details about him as I can. He doesn't have any scars or tattoos. He has nice olive skin and straight teeth. He's wearing a typical button-down found at a million stores in America, and well-fitting jeans. He looks like a Westsider. His hair is slightly oily. I notice he is wearing a gold wedding band. He looks like someone I could know under very different circumstances.

"I don't," I say, my voice starting to tremble.

"Say it."

"I'm serious. This is a horrible mistake. Please just let me explain for two minutes."

I am not crying. I am still not screaming. I am trying to rationalize with him. I am desperate for life to remain as I know it.

"Get on your fucking knees."

"Someone is stalking me. They set this up. Did you actually ever speak to me?"

"I talked to you," he says, grabbing the hair above the nape of my neck and lowering my body onto the floor. "And now we're going to stop talking."

He jams three of his fingers into my mouth, and I see the outline of his erection through his jeans. Realizing this is my only opportunity to convince him I'm serious and not role-playing, I bite down on his fingers as hard as I can.

"What the fuck?" he screams. "You fucking bitch!"

"I'm sorry, but whoever you spoke to was *not me*. You have to believe me. Look, my husband is going to be home any minute."

"Just shut up, or I'm going to make you shut up."

"My husband is on his way home and he will kill you. He worked all night and will be here any minute."

"Oh, you want to play that game?" he asks. "Does your husband know you're a little whore who begs strange men to come fuck you in the middle of the day?"

"I'm not kidding. I'm not playing a game. I know this isn't your fault. You have to understand that whoever set this up with you *was not me*. Whatever they told you, it's not true."

"But you *are* Georgina."

"Yes."

"I talked to you this morning and you know it, so drop the act, okay? It's getting fucking annoying."

"Look at my phone. You will not find your texts. My phone is right here in my pocket. You were texting someone else. I promise you. I'm trying to help you out here before you do something that will land you in jail, or dead."

I'm on my knees in my own living room with my hands tied behind my back. Tears start streaming down my cheeks. I'm terrified of what's going to happen next. He reaches into the small pocket in the waistband of my black leggings, and I get the chills from feeling his breath near me. The hardwood floors make kneeling painful, but I feel a glimmer of hope as he checks the number against his own phone and realizes it's not the one he was texting with. I sniffle audibly so he knows I'm crying.

"I don't know what you're trying to pull here, but it's not cool."

"Please just leave before it's too late. This was all a huge mistake. I know it's not your fault. I don't want you to get in trouble."

His domineering persona visibly exits his body, and his pulse races through his neck, which has the tiniest bit of brown stubble. I sense that he's not going to hurt me. Then it hits me what has happened. He simply answered an online ad thinking it was his lucky day to indulge in a little role play. Free daytime sex. Maybe he's done it before; maybe it's his first time. Either way, it was his chance to do the things he can't do with his wife.

"Fuck," he says. "I have to go."

He looks more scared than I am, and he's so caught up in getting out the door as fast as possible that he doesn't cut the zip tie or give me the number of the person who just put a rape hit out on me. But he does leave the door wide open. I sit there for a few more seconds until I hear his Mercedes peel out.

15

No more waiting to hear back from Scott. No more trying to be my own Nancy Drew. At this point I don't care what humiliation I have to endure to stay safe. I'm past the point of trying to contain it. My parents are definitely going to know. I could end up on the front page of my own newspaper if I don't do something this second. I push myself up, my knees cracking, and bolt onto the street. I almost run straight into a Guatemalan nanny who's pushing a double stroller holding adorable twin boys whom I've clearly startled. One begins crying immediately, while the other just stares and frowns at me.

"I need you to call 911!" I say loudly, begging her with my eyes. *"Por favor, emergencia."*

She hesitates for a moment, probably because I've scared the shit out of her, but seeing my hands tied, she starts dialing. She holds the phone up to me as I give my address to the female operator. I describe what's just happened as though I was telling a simple story. It's like I am watching the entire episode from outside my body.

Within minutes, two Santa Monica police officers pull onto Ocean Park, and I see joggers and young moms looking our way. I'm not mortified or embarrassed. I no longer care what anyone thinks. The nanny stays with me until the police arrive, then says "*Lo siento*" and continues on her way with the twins. I ask the policemen if we can go inside and they say yes. Officer Tanaka, the younger of the two, immediately offers to cut the zip tie, which feels like the best release of my life.

"Thank you," I say, shaking out my aching wrists.

He gives me a closed-mouth smile that seems to say *Sorry for all of this.* "Is there somewhere we can sit?" he asks.

"Yes, yes, of course," I say, motioning to the living room.

"What's your name?" Tanaka asks after taking a seat. His partner stays near the front door.

"Georgina Park. G-E-O-R-G-I-N-A."

"Korean?" he asks, and I wonder why every Asian person I meet has to play this guessing game.

"Yes."

"Do you need to go to a hospital?" he asks, raising an eyebrow.

"No, no, I'm fine. I mean, it didn't go that far. It's just my wrists. Nothing else happened."

"Well, we can still take you to the hospital to get checked, just in case."

"There was no sexual assault. I think I know what happened. It's a long story," I say.

"Do you know the person who was just here?"

"No."

"Can you describe him for me? You know, his height, hair color, eye color, stuff like that."

"He was about five nine, with brown hair and brown eyes," I tell him. "He has nice teeth, looks professional and is probably in his early thirties."

"Okay, great," Tanaka says, writing furiously on a notepad.

"He had a gold wedding band that was scratched a bit. He was wearing a light blue button-down shirt and dark-wash jeans. Ethnically, I would guess Italian or Greek. A Mediterranean type."

"Did he have any tattoos or scars you can recall?"

"No. He was clean and polished. I don't think he's a real rapist," I explain, immediately realizing I've just made a sweeping generalization. "I think he was tricked by someone who was impersonating me."

"Well, even if that's the case, we still need to bring him in for questioning. It's best that we document everything when it's fresh in your mind and gather evidence. It's better to have it and not need it than to need it and not have it."

"Wait, there's something else," I remember. "I'm pretty sure he was in a black Mercedes with a license plate that started with a 6M, but I could be wrong."

"That's great, Georgina," Tanaka says, motioning to his partner.

The older officer immediately puts out a brief description of my assailant and his car over the radio. I reiterate that I don't believe that he is a true rapist, just someone who was tricked into the situation. But the officers explain that we don't know for sure that it wasn't criminal solicitation or conspiracy to commit a rape. They are treating this as a big deal and not a petty misunderstanding, and for that I'm relieved.

"If you could tell me in your own words what went on here, that would be great," Tanaka says, police report in hand, ready to take my statement.

I recount the entire story quickly, still hyped on adrenaline and thinking how bizarre it is to see uniformed officers in my own home. Lourdes wouldn't think it strange since her brother is a NYPD cop, but I'm not used to being around law enforcement of any kind.

Two more police cars arrive. Officer Tanaka tells me they're holding the scene for evidence. I'm getting slightly panicked at the thought of more and more people showing up at my home. I'm told that a detective will be assigned to this case and will contact me.

"What if that isn't for hours? This can't wait."

"Do you have a safe place you could stay tonight?"

"Yes," I barely muster.

Of course I'm tempted to drive straight to my parents' house, but I might give my dad a heart attack if I tell him the truth. As much as they tend to keep their emotions in check, something like this is bound to set one of them off, and I don't want to end up consoling them instead of being consoled.

I have another idea. I don't want to wait until tomorrow.

"Evidence is here," I hear one officer say to another.

After some awkward introductions and even more strange men in my bungalow, the work begins. They collect the orange zip tie, take photos of the marks on my wrists, the doorway and other areas of my home that don't seem relevant to me. I watch as they swab my cell phone for his DNA and dust for prints since the guy wasn't wearing gloves. *Surreal* is the only word I can use to describe the situation. Even though they are all polite and straightforward about what needs to be accomplished, it feels like a violation. By the time it's over, I realize it's been three hours.

Before the officers leave, I remember that I still have the IP address and go to my office to retrieve it. "It's somewhere at UCLA, but I don't know where," I tell them. "When you trace it there's no specific location given, but it's on the UCLA network, so I'm sure their IT security department can figure it out if they know a crime has been committed."

"That is very helpful," Tanaka says. "I'll pass it on to the detective."

"If you have a couple minutes, I'll print out the emails, too."

"Go for it."

I head back to my office and go to the password-protected folder on my computer where I've been stashing the correspondence. "I told you this all started as soon as I started teaching, so I'm starting to believe it could be a student in my class, even though that makes no sense," I explain, handing over the pages. "There's a guy named Jacob who stares at me a lot when I'm talking. He once tried to get coffee with me after class, but I said no, and I feel like when the quarter is over he is going to actively pursue me. He just has that vibe where he can't read the room—seems clueless to the fact that I would not be interested and that it wouldn't be appropriate to date a student. Let me grab my class list for you, just in case."

"Well, the detective will look at everything and everyone who could be responsible," he assures me.

As soon as the door shuts behind the last policeman, I burst out crying. It's as though the adrenaline has finally left my body to take a much needed break elsewhere. I'm weeping alone on my couch. I have no desire to call Rebecca, my parents or anyone else. I just want to cry.

After ten minutes of sobbing I realize I need to pack a bag. I assemble a few changes of clothes, some toiletries, makeup and a notepad. I grab my MacBook, set the house alarm and lock up. I jaywalk across the street and up toward the coffee shop, where I quickly go online. In the back of the shop are two cameras filming what looks like a date.

"It's some reality-show pilot for Bravo," says the pretty waitress, rolling her eyes. An enormous eagle tattoo rises out of her black, low-cut top. "Can I get you something?"

"No thanks," I say, then remember that I'd better order something if I'm going to use their Wi-Fi. "I mean, yes, I'll take an iced tea."

I check around to make sure no one can see my computer screen. I only see girls in expensive workout ensembles chatting about their Pressed Juicery cleanse ("Thank God coffee is allowed!" one shouts) and an older man sipping an espresso while staring out the window. I immediately log on to Plenty of Fish, where I sign in with the fake profile I made the night before. I use the access to search for Owen, the guy who came to my apartment and spoke to Eli. I had gotten a quick look at him through the peephole, although it was dark and I was terrified. I remember he was somewhat attractive, average in height and slight in build. I go to the search bar and start selecting options for gender, age range, ethnicity, body type and city. I throw in the name Owen, which gets so specific that only six results come up. I quickly scroll through them all. I'm shocked to find my midnight visitor staring back at me.

His profile says that he is an occasional smoker with an athletic body type. He's twenty-eight, five foot nine and Christian. His personality: "Adventurer." He has a dog, doesn't do drugs, and his longest relationship lasted five years. His intent? "Wants to date but nothing serious." He drinks socially, eventually wants children and has more than a few grammatical issues in his "About Owen" section. I click on the green "Contact This User Now!" button and pray that it works.

Then I go online to look for a hotel. In what may be one of the biggest coincidences in my life, the Century Plaza comes up immediately, at $258 for the night. With the click of button, I have a reservation. Since there's no way I can drive at the moment, I order an uberX car from my phone. I take a deep breath.

I text my mum from the car and say I'll be sure to call tomorrow. I need some time to process everything before I talk to her.

■ ■ ■

I arrive at the Century Plaza and am given a key to a room on the sixth floor. I haven't been here since visiting Simon so many years ago, under drastically different circumstances, and figure it's the safest place I could be for now, as no one would expect to find me here.

I take a hot shower, and when I get out I realize I haven't eaten anything since breakfast. I might as well make a meal out of the minibar so I'll have energy for later. After chowing down on a protein bar and a bag of gourmet popcorn, I flop on the bed wearing a plush robe and a towel around my head. I open my laptop and am surprised to see that Owen has already responded to my message.

Feeling a little rebellious, I type a message back to him, explaining what happened to me today. The detective won't like it, but the journalist in me can't sit idly, just waiting. I click send and anxiously wait for the next reply.

16

I feel like I'm on my way to meet a subject for a story, something I've done hundreds of times over the last decade. I have my standard black leather tote bag, my notepad, my favorite black ink Paper Mate Flair pen and a list of questions. After feverishly explaining the situation to Owen in a second email, I'm grateful he's willing to meet with me, even though he knows he won't be getting laid.

I picked a busy chain restaurant at the nearby mall that I would normally never frequent because of the crowds, noise and ridiculously large portions of things like Irish nachos, but right now it feels like the best place on earth to meet. I arrive first and request a table toward the back so we can speak freely. Owen is about ten minutes late, but he's there, which is all that matters. I offer to buy him a drink and he orders a beer. I'm on my third glass of water.

"Do you mind if I record this?" I ask him, pulling out my iPhone and clicking on the Voice Memos button.

"Um, well okay, I guess so," he stammers. "I've never been recorded before."

"You didn't do anything wrong. I'm not going to do anything with the recording, I assure you. It's just been a crazy day and I don't want to forget anything."

"I know, but..."

"You're not in any trouble, I promise."

"This is really fucked up."

"I'm not going to argue with you there."

"I feel really bad about this," he says. "You must think I'm a horrible person."

"I don't think anything like that, Owen," I say, attempting to gain his trust by saying his name and empathizing with him. "You did what any normal guy would do, and I don't blame you for it."

"I mean, I don't go around doing this every day."

"Of course not. All I need from you is the phone number of whoever you were in communication with yesterday. Just tell me what happened."

"First we were just emailing through the site," he explains. "And then I said I wanted to talk to you."

"That makes sense," I say, smiling, trying to make him feel comfortable.

"But you, or they, didn't want to talk at first, which was a red flag, I guess, but she kept writing back and was very forward."

"Yeah."

"It seemed a little too good to be true," he continues. "You know—that someone like you, like that, would just ask me to come right over after a few flirtatious messages. Even girls who are down usually want to meet at a bar first, to be safe."

"Right."

"My buddy had a similar thing going online, and when he showed up, the girl invited him in and then her boyfriend robbed him."

"That's awful."

"So there was part of me that thought this might be a trick or something."

"Well, I'm sure there are girls who do that sort of thing, but you felt safe enough to go to the house. Was there a reason for that?"

"I just said for her to text me the address, you know, to make her prove that she was real, and I gave her my cell phone number," he says. "I googled the address and a website came up that said the owner of the house was Georgina Park, so I figured that was all the confirmation I needed."

"Wow," I say, stunned by the amount of information that can be ascertained in a matter of seconds.

"So I just thought, what the hell, why not? I was really nervous knocking on the door, and when there was no answer after a few minutes, I figured something was up. It was too easy."

"And then you talked to my neighbor," I offer.

"Yes," he says. "Cool dude."

"He is. Can I see the number?" I ask politely, not wanting to drag this out any longer than necessary.

"Sure. Here you go."

I write it down, double-checking that I have each digit correct, and take a photo of his phone with my own. "Thank God you saved it."

"I texted the number a bunch last night, asking why they didn't answer the door, but there was no reply for hours, so I figured it was all a joke or whatever. I was pretty embarrassed."

"Did you ever get a response?"

"Yeah. Super late there was a text that just said sorry and that we should try getting together another time, but I didn't write back."

"Well, I'm so sorry you were dragged into all this," I tell him. "You certainly didn't deserve to be."

"I'm deleting my profile tonight," Owen says.

"I don't blame you one bit for wanting to, but could you wait a couple days, just in case they try to contact you again? If she does, please let me know immediately and I'll pass the info on to the police."

"Okay."

"Thank you so much. This has been so helpful."

Owen reaches for his wallet, but I insist on picking up the six-dollar tab. "Thanks," he says, looking down at the table sheepishly. "Good luck with everything. It sucks that you have to deal with this."

He gets up and I shake his hand, hoping I never have to see him again. Having the cell phone number in my hand feels like holding a winning lottery ticket. I'm so tempted to call it myself, just to hear the voice and then hang up, but I know I can't.

■ ■ ■

It's almost 8 p.m. by the time I walk back to the hotel. I'm worn out and exhilarated at the same time. I don't want to leave these four walls for the rest of the night, so I decide to treat myself to room service and a bunch of TED talks on my laptop when my cell phone rings. A Detective Mendoza introduces himself as the officer the state has assigned to my case. He explains that the man who was at my house about ten hours ago has been picked up and taken down to the station house, where they want me to make an ID right away. The thought of seeing him again makes my skin crawl, but Mendoza assures me that he won't see any part of me and it will just take a few minutes.

"I'm so glad you called, because I now have the phone number of the person who set up both visits," I explain breathlessly, reading out each number carefully.

"How did you get it?" he asks, suspicious.

"I tracked down the guy from last night who thought he'd talked to me on Plenty of Fish," I tell him. "His name is Owen, and I just met him at the mall in Century City."

"Are you kidding me?" the detective says disapprovingly. "That was very dangerous, Georgina. Please don't do anything like that again."

"I couldn't wait until tomorrow."

"I understand. Now let me do my job."

"So what can you do about the number?"

"Even if we put a rush on this, it'll be a few hours or even tomorrow until we're able to subpoena the cell phone record. I'll get on it now, though."

"I appreciate it, thank you," I say. "I'm staying at a hotel tonight and you're the only one who knows that, so I'll be okay."

"Okay, good. I can come pick you up and bring you here, or we can send a patrol car for you."

"I can get there on my own, no problem. Just give me the address."

■ ■ ■

The elevator can't come fast enough. The sooner I make the ID, the sooner I can come back to the hotel and try to get some sleep. By this time tomorrow, the police will at least know whose cell phone made the calls. I want to be certain that the number this guy was given is the same as the one Owen had. I hop in one of the taxis waiting outside the hotel and head west on Olympic Boulevard, relieved that the cabbie doesn't ask me why I want to go to the Santa Monica Police Station.

During the ride, where we pass production companies and auto body shops, it occurs to me that in all of my years of reporting, I've never set foot in an actual police station. I'd be more excited if I were visiting as a journalist, not as a victim. I text Detective Mendoza when we are a couple of minutes away and let him know I'll be arriving in a white cab.

I can smell the salt water in the air once I step out of the car. Even though it's a summer night, it's breezy and cool, and I'm glad I thought to bring my cashmere cardigan when I fled my house. Wrapping myself in a little cocoon makes me feel better.

The station, a modern, gray building, is perched on a small hill among palm trees. It's steps from the touristy Third Street Promenade, City Hall and the Santa Monica Pier. During the day, this area is swarmed with tourists and homeless people. I'd never noticed the compound before now.

Detective Mendoza, a fortysomething man with droopy but kind eyes, a well-groomed black moustache and an extra fifty pounds on him, greets me out front. I never expected to have my own detective at any point in my lifetime. Not when I was a girl writing in my baby blue Louisa May Alcott diary. Not when I was at the beach with Emily in high school, getting more freckly with each passing day. And certainly not when I was doing my first big profile story on Kevin Costner.

Detective Mendoza shakes my hand and gives me a smile that says *Nice to meet you but sorry we are meeting under these circumstances.* My mind connects the dots—he has seen the emails and the photos of me and read my statement—but I'm not embarrassed. Motioning for me to follow, Mendoza walks past a bank of nondescript cubicles and empty offices. I'm surprised by how little the station resembles the ones I've seen on television or in movies. It looks more like a '90s-era corporate office, with its copy machines and gray and white color scheme. I smell new industrial carpeting.

Mendoza leads me into an unmarked conference room, where he pulls out a worn office chair with uneven arms and gestures for me to sit. "Can I get you some water?" he asks. "Or coffee?"

"No, I'm okay right now, thanks," I say, unzipping my tote bag.

"We've seized his phone, so we have the number of the person he was texting with. And you have a number as well?"

"He googled my address and saw that Georgina Park owned the house, so that was all the verification he needed." I pass him a torn page from my black Moleskine reporter's notebook. "He never actually spoke to anyone, just texted back and forth. Here's the number Owen gave me."

I fill Mendoza in on everything I know, and he catches up quickly. We chat for about half an hour, and I give him any detail I can think of that could help, and he takes pages of notes. While he writes, I look at the fine lines around his big brown eyes, and his calm demeanor slows my mind down a bit.

"This is very thorough," he says with a smile. "I know you're a journalist, so I guess I shouldn't be surprised, right?"

"Anything I can do to speed up the process."

"How long have you been a writer?" he asks, attempting to connect with me.

"For more than ten years."

"What do you write about?"

"You know these whistleblowers and journalists who are taken as political prisoners?"

"Yeah," he says, eyes widening.

"I do the opposite of all that."

"Well, that's nothing to be ashamed of," Mendoza says.

"Oh, I know. When I was younger, I thought you could only be a real journalist if you were covering really serious subjects like crime and war. I'm not giving up my life for a dollar fifty a word."

"So what do you write about, then?"

"I have a column called 'Movers and Shakers' that focuses on unique, interesting and powerful L.A. residents," I tell him. "Sometimes I profile city leaders. I actually did a Q&A with your police commissioner once, but I didn't come to the station. We just did a phoner."

"I've seen it before," he says. "The Sunday magazine, right?"

"Yes." I smile for the first time today.

"I've never met a columnist before," Mendoza says. "Cool."

"I've never met a detective before."

After our chat, he gets down to business. "So like I told you, we picked up the suspect this morning and he's here, but we need you to do an ID first."

"Is he already under arrest?"

"We cuffed him when we brought him in about an hour ago, and he was read his rights, but not he's not under arrest yet," he explains. "Right now he's just a suspect here for questioning."

I perk up. "Can I watch the interview?"

"That's definitely not standard procedure," he says. "We don't let victims watch questioning."

"But it's my case and I'm here," I appeal. "You know I work for the *Times*. I can handle it."

"We videotape interrogations, so it may be better if you just watch that at a later time."

"Please." I can see he's racking his brain on the pros and cons of letting me come with him. He excuses himself for a few moments, and then a different male detective joins me in the room to supervise the ID. I guess they don't want any bias involved in the process. The atmosphere immediately shifts to formal and stiff.

"Miss Park, I'm Detective Samuels," he says, barely making eye contact. "I'm going to show you some pictures."

"Okay."

He presents me with a sheet of paper with six images on it. "Do you recognize anyone?"

It takes all of two seconds for me to positively identify the man whose slightly sour fingers I can still taste in my mouth. "Yes."

"From where?"

"From my house on Ocean Park today, around eleven in the morning."

"Could you point him out to me?"

"Right there."

I want to know who the other five men in the pictures are, but I don't ask. He thanks me and is on his way. Detective Mendoza returns and confirms that I've identified the man: Will Tisdale of Marina del Rey, who is now sitting in an interrogation room down the hall. The thought that we're under the same roof again is almost too strange to process, but I'm relieved to this time be in the company of a burly detective with a weapon who can easily shield me from any sort of danger.

"How are you doing?" Detective Mendoza asks. "Do you need a moment? Can I get you anything?"

"I'm fine, but I really want to watch the interrogation," I insist. "There's two-way glass, right?"

He scratches his head, and I notice a few beads of sweat at his hairline. "Okay, but if you feel uncomfortable at any time, I want you to come back here."

"I promise."

"I hope I don't regret this," he says. "Follow me."

We head down a long hallway and my heart starts racing, not out of fear but from sheer excitement and curiosity, as I know we're getting closer to the answer. The polished floors smell of Pine-Sol. After a few moments, we're inside a small room with two wood chairs that looks onto a larger interrogation room. After opening the door and grabbing a chair for me, Detective Mendoza leaves. I'm staring at my would-be attacker, who looks much less threatening than he did earlier today. There's a string hanging from the top buttonhole of his shirt, and he nervously purses his lips, which look a bit chapped.

I watch Detective Mendoza head inside the room and introduce himself to Will, who's seated directly across from him at a large folding table. I never thought that the man who called me a whore earlier would have such an innocent-sounding, one-syllable first name.

"Look, I just want to get out of here as fast as possible," Will says, glancing at his silver Patek Philippe watch, clearly agitated that this interview has messed with his original plan of wild sex with a complete stranger. "I didn't do anything wrong, so can we just get on with this?"

"Of course," Mendoza says, opening a file and placing a legal pad on the table.

Will puts his forehead in his hands, which are shaking ever so slightly. "Fuck my life," he says. "Why did this happen to me?"

"You were read your rights earlier, so you know that you have the right to remain silent."

"Yes, but I didn't do anything wrong, so I have nothing to hide." Will's voice has the faintest trace of a southern accent. "I mean, you're not going to arrest me, right? I can explain the whole thing very easily."

"I can't make you any promises," Detective Mendoza explains. "But if you want to tell me what happened today, that would be helpful."

"I wish I never went online today," Will says, picking at his designer jeans.

"You say you thought that Miss Park was the woman who arranged for the meeting," Detective Mendoza says empathetically. He's holding a pen in his right hand, which resembles a small catcher's mitt.

"I even spoke to her briefly. I thought it was totally legit."

"So this misunderstanding isn't actually your fault," Mendoza offers. "You were only doing what she asked of you, right?"

"Exactly." I notice Will's left foot tapping rapidly underneath the table. "I saw an ad on Craigslist early in the morning, in the Casual Encounters section."

"I see."

"And the picture was hot, so I thought I would shoot her a note."

"And then what happened?"

"I sent her a few photos of myself. We messaged back and forth a few times, and things got extremely sexual fast."

"How so?"

"She was saying all the stuff she wanted me to do to her."

"What kind of stuff?"

"That she had a rape fantasy and wanted to be roughed up a bit," Will says. "She specifically wanted to be tied up. She said she needed a very aggressive man who had no regard for women."

"I see," says Mendoza, writing more notes on his legal pad. The leather strap on his Timex watch looks worn. He deserves a nicer watch, I think to myself.

"It's not like I have no regard for women," Will continues, "but I was willing to play the part for the sake of her fantasy."

"Did she ask you to bring anything specific?"

"I didn't have any handcuffs or rope or anything, so I just stopped by the hardware store on my way over and bought the zip ties, since she repeatedly asked to be tied up. She sounded straight out of *Fifty Shades of Grey*."

I'm watching the conversation unfold like my own personal *Law & Order: SVU,* only Ice-T is nowhere to be found. My detective looks more like a high school football coach, with his expanded waistline and military haircut.

"I have to get home," Will declares, running his hands through his thick hair and staring at the eggshell-colored ceiling. "My wife is going to be furious if I'm not back soon. We have a six-month-old daughter."

"Sure. I just have a couple more questions and then that will do it."

"I mean, I got screwed over here, too," Will says. "If things had progressed further, I could be doing twenty years."

"I understand."

"I just wanted to get laid. I've never done anything like this before. I'm out of work at the moment. I was bored."

"Let's just get through these quick questions, okay?"

Will doesn't ask about my well-being or seem overly concerned with tracking down the person who set up the date and is the reason he's currently sitting in an airless room at the Santa Monica police station. I'm relieved that he seems genuine and is not an actual rapist, but I can't imagine how the rest of the day would have gone had I not been able to convince him. He seemed like a natural, considering he claims it was his first time showing up for something like that.

Just then I see a text from Eli, who is home from work.

G, there's a guy hanging around outside your front door. What do you want me to do? He looks like he's waiting for you to come home.

■ ■ ■

After Mendoza finishes with Will, I tell him about the new development, feeling far more terrified and less confident than when he last saw me. "I think there have been more men going by my place," I say, trying my best to appear strong, but I'm absolutely sick to my stomach, wondering how I'm ever supposed to go back home knowing that half of the male population of L.A. may have my address. "My neighbor says there's some guy outside now."

"Georgina, I think this would be a good time for you to meet with one of our victim advocates," he says. "She can refer you to counseling services that we offer, or—"

"I appreciate it," I say, immediately cutting him off. "But since we have the phone number, can't you just call this person's phone right now? If there's an ad somewhere, it has to be taken down, or this is going to get out of control."

"I promise you that I will do everything possible to help you. Let me give you a ride back to your hotel."

"Okay, thanks," I say, too scared to be alone with even a taxi driver right now.

We hop into Mendoza's gray Buick LaCrosse, which has a radio mounted in the dashboard, and get on the 10 East. "What if you have to chase someone?" I ask him.

"See those switches? They make the headlights and taillights flash," he explains. "And there's a siren switch, too. Otherwise it's just a normal car."

As we ride on the freeway, Detective Mendoza makes small talk with me, trying to be kind in an extraordinary situation, but I can't stop wondering if there are ads or profiles on more sites aside from Craigslist and Plenty of Fish. Since I haven't seen the ad Will referenced, I have no idea if this person is using the Simon photos, my headshot, shots of someone else or a mix of them all. The fact that this person is giving out my real name and address to strange men is the worst of it all. I can already see one of these guys googling my name, realizing I'm a somewhat known person and harassing me in the Comments section of my next column. Even if this case is resolved tomorrow, how can I sleep in my own home again?

17

The phone in the hotel room wakes me from a deep sleep. I answer groggily.

"Georgina?"

It's ten in the morning, but I was up until five, thinking, worrying and analyzing every word I could remember from Will's interrogation. I saw his angry face over and over in my dreams and every time I awoke.

"Hi," I say, recognizing Detective Mendoza's voice immediately. "What's going on?"

"Well, we were able to find the owner of that cell phone, and I think you are going to be very surprised—shocked, actually—by who it is."

I sit up so I can brace myself. My stomach is queasy at the thought of a venerable, experienced detective telling me something is surprising. "Who is it?"

"Hannah."

"I don't know a Hannah," I say hurriedly, flipping through my mental catalogue of students, fellow instructors, neighbors, yoga friends, old classmates and colleagues. Then.

"Oh my God."

"You know who I mean?" he asks.

"Yes."

I feel as though I've been punched in the stomach and struggle to take my next breath. Six-year-old Hannah. A little girl with blonde curls and missing teeth. I saw her picture only once, for maybe five seconds, but when Simon mentioned her on occasion, his face always lit up.

Detective Mendoza breaks the silence. "Are you okay, Georgina?"

"Yes," I lie.

"I'd like to meet with you today, if that's okay. You know I mean Hannah Grant, right?"

"Yes. I can't believe it," I say, experiencing the biggest shock of my entire life while simultaneously feeling relieved at having an answer. "Yes, I know who she is. I mean, I don't know her. I've never met her, but she's the daughter of a former—she's the daughter of someone I used to know. The man I told you about, who had the pictures."

"Yes, she told us all about it."

"I had no idea she lived here." I try doing the math on her age. "I don't know how she even knows who I am. She certainly shouldn't."

"She's an incoming freshman at UCLA. She moved here a few months ago from Australia," Mendoza explains.

"She was first staying with family friends nearby, but now she's in the dorms on campus for summer school, which explains why the IP address is on their network."

"So you've picked her up already?"

"Yes, earlier this morning. She's very scared and confused," Mendoza says. "I got the sense that she can't believe she went as far as she did. She seemed relieved that you were okay."

"Interesting," I say coldly.

"I had a female detective from our department talk to her," he continues. "She was able to bond with Hannah and get her to take her through everything that happened—the emails, the photos, the ads. Hannah placed multiple ads, I'm afraid."

Breathe. Keep breathing.

"Did you videotape her interrogation?" I ask.

"Yes, but I don't think it would be beneficial for you right now," he says. "She was terrified to be in a police station, I can tell you that much."

"I just want to know that I can watch it if I need to."

"Well, we'll cross that bridge when the time comes."

"I'm getting out of town for a bit, but I need to go by my place first. Can you meet me there?"

"Of course."

"I'd feel better if you were there."

"Me too."

The moment I hang up the phone, I run to the bathroom and throw up. Sitting on the cold marble floor, I replay everything in my head: the night I met Simon, learning that he was married with children, how he made me come with the touch of his hand, how he said he was falling in love with me, how he asked me to move across the world to be with him, how he said he wanted to marry me. Eventually I drag myself off the floor, brush my teeth, pack up my toiletries and shove my clothing into my bag. I leave a few bucks on the nightstand for housekeeping and head to the lobby to check out.

■ ■ ■

An hour later I meet Detective Mendoza at my place, better known as "the scene" these days, so he can fill me in on everything. I need to get more clothes and whatever else I'll need for a few days, but I can't think right now. The only reason I can walk through the front door is because I have an armed, 230-pound man with me. "Do you want some water or something?"

"No, I'm fine, thank you," he says. "You have a very nice home."

"It's hard for me to see it that way today, but thanks."

Once we're seated at the dining room table, Mendoza begins. "Hannah told us that over a hundred people responded to the Craigslist ad." My eyes widen and my mouth falls open. "Will was the first one to actually show up. She felt overwhelmed by the response and decided to take the ad down after an hour or so, figuring she had enough guys on the hook. So I think you can feel a little better knowing there's no other ad currently up."

"So there were other men who were supposed to come by?"

"Perhaps she set it up like an insurance policy, in case one of them chickened out. From what I can tell, several men did agree to come and never showed up, but Will was pretty determined, I guess."

"What about Plenty of Fish?"

"Apparently she had already taken that down because so many men asked her to video-chat or meet up first, which she refused to do. I guess she liked Craigslist better, for whatever reason. Although she remarked that she received a lot of pornographic images."

"From the guys?"

"Yes. She was embarrassed discussing that, but obviously we were going to see it all anyway."

"I can't believe that over a hundred men were ready to participate in this sort of thing on a moment's notice on a workday morning."

"She assured us that there are no other ads in existence and seemed quite remorseful for it all. I think it's clear to everyone that she is not well."

"That might be the understatement of the year," I say.

"A team searched her dorm room and seized her computer, her phone and other personal items," Mendoza continues, and I wonder if he means voodoo dolls with my face on them. "So we will look at all the communication from the last week or two to be certain."

"I gave the officers all the emails yesterday. But do you need my computer, too?"

"That would be great," he says. "We'll try to get it back to you relatively soon."

"Everything is on this laptop," I say, showing him my silver MacBook Pro. "I just got it last month."

"How are you feeling about this?"

"I'm so glad it's over, but I can't believe it's *Hannah.* I mean, her mom is going to have to know. I'm going to have to answer some questions, I'm sure."

"Yes, I believe Hannah called her already."

"Oh my God," I say, dropping my head in my hands.

Mendoza folds his thick hands together. "So what do you want to do from here? You know we have enough evidence to place her under arrest and pursue a case."

"Do you have kids?" I ask him.

"I do. My son is a junior in high school. He screws up from time to time, but nothing like this."

"I just can't imagine how this all happened."

"We will figure it all out soon enough," Mendoza says. "I promise."

"I need to think about it." My head is spinning. "Let me think about it for a few days."

"Well, if you don't press charges, we have to let her go back to her dorm today. Is that okay with you?"

"I just don't know if I'm ready to decide this split second, you know?"

"I understand," he says. "Well, she's had a good scare. I don't think she'll be doing anything online if we let her go. You can always press charges at a later date, whether that's tomorrow or some other time."

"Okay," I say. "Let her go, then. I guess *something* has to happen to her. There have to be repercussions, but I'm not sure having her go to jail is going to be that something."

"She mentioned wanting to go back to Australia and withdrawing from school."

"That would be a good start," I say. "She needs help."

"I do think it would be good for *you* to talk to someone professional, too," he says. "You need support during something like this. If you were my daughter, I would insist on it."

"I need to tell my parents, too," I tell him, not exactly excited about hitting them with all of this at once. "I think I'm going to go stay with them for a while and then I'll find a therapist here. I promise."

"I'm glad." He smiles, the lines around his eyes deepening.

"This must be hard work, dealing with heavy stuff every day."

"There's never a dull moment, that's for sure. But I can't complain. It's what I always wanted to do."

"At least you work near the beach," I say, immediately embarrassed at having made such a flippant comment. Like he has the time to catch a few rays on his lunch break.

"It definitely beats the Rampart Division."

"Thank you for everything. Really."

"You're very welcome, Georgina."

"Can I ask you something I've been wondering about?"

"Of course."

"What really happened with the Santa Monica College shooter?"

"Everything you heard is what happened. He was a messed-up kid."

"Did you work that case?"

"I wasn't first on the scene or anything, but I worked the investigation, yes."

"I heard it was because he was upset about his parents separating."

"If you're thinking Hannah is like the Santa Monica shooter, that's a bit of a stretch."

"I just think men and women react differently to devastation."

"True, but the shooter was really sick. I mean, mentally. It's sad how many of our cases happen because people aren't getting the help they need."

"Maybe I can do a story on you sometime," I say.

"Who would want to see this face?" Mendoza laughs, breaking his serious composure for the first time since we met. He gathers his stuff up as I push the chairs into the table. "Is it okay if I give you a hug?" I ask, unsure of what the protocol is.

"Of course."

I have to stand on my tiptoes to fully make contact. Mendoza is soft, warm and comforting. He reminds me of Santa Claus. The Easter Bunny. A Disney character. I feel a bit better already.

"Well, I'll let you know what I decide," I say.

"Stay in touch and don't hesitate to contact me any-time, day or night. You have my cell."

"Okay."

"I'm going to wait outside until you've left."

"Thank you. For everything."

■ ■ ■

After grabbing a big canvas bag and filling it with enough clothes for a week, I wave to Mendoza, who is talking on his cell phone in his car, and get into my own car, driving for a mile before pulling over so I can do a search on Hannah on my iPhone. Her full Facebook page comes up immediately, and I'm shocked that it isn't set to private. She's pretty, with long ombre hair and clear skin. She isn't smiling in her profile photo, clearly trying to look a bit moody, but a quick scroll of her timeline shows nothing out of the ordinary. She appears to have friends here and at home.

She has Simon's nose. I can't look anymore.

I call my parents' landline and am relieved that my father is home. I try to sound like my normal self, saying I'd like to come visit.

"Of course it's okay, Georgina," he says warmly. "We would love to spend some time with you, especially as you've been so busy."

"Yes, well, I'd like to explain why," I say. "I'm actually coming now."

"Oh, okay—I'll be here, and your mum will be home by five. I was going to make a panzanella for dinner."

"That's perfect," I say, hopping on the 405. "See you in a couple of hours."

"Drive safe, Georgina."

"I will."

I've never been happier to step into our 1950s ranch house, which is just a few blocks away from the Pacific Ocean. I smell garlic in the kitchen and smile upon seeing my dad, who's wearing an apron that says "Man Bib."

"Hi sweetheart," he says, turning away from the stove to give me a kiss and hug.

"I'm going to go put some stuff upstairs, and then I can help you if you want."

"You just relax. How was traffic?"

"Not too bad. Took two hours."

"Your mum is on her way home. I let her know you were coming, and she couldn't wait."

"That's sweet," I say, instantly feeling guilty that I am about to ruin their evening one way or another.

■ ■ ■

"I wish I were here for just a normal visit," I say, alluding to the half dozen trips I make each year to see them.

Mum senses my sadness immediately. "Is everything okay?"

"Before I tell you what's been going on, I just have to preface it by saying that I *am* okay." I know how extra sensitive they are to my safety and health. "I am not in danger, and everything will be fine, eventually."

"You're making me nervous, Georgina," she says. My dad waits quietly.

"A year after I moved to L.A., I met a man I connected to immediately. I hadn't been dating much since John, and Simon was a real grown-up. I met him at a work event. He was a foreign correspondent for an Australian network, and we quickly realized that we were crazy about each other."

"Why is this the first we are hearing of him, then?" Mum asks.

"Because he was married," I say, my mouth going dry. "I hid that from everyone because I knew it was not okay and that you would expect more from me."

"That is very unlike you," she says. Dad's face moves from concern to disappointment.

"I know," I say, "and I can explain more later about why I think I was so drawn to him even though he was unavailable, but what's worse than that is the fact that I had sent him some private photos."

"What do you mean, 'private?'" Mum asks. "Nude photos?"

"Sort of," I say, thoroughly embarrassed. "Anyway, he moved back to Australia, and though we stayed in touch over the years we eventually went our separate ways, and I met Justin, and you know the rest."

"How old was this man?" my dad asks, alternately stretching his hand out and balling it into a fist as if he could punch Simon for whatever I am about to say.

"He was twenty years older than me."

"How dare he."

"Dad, I was old enough to know what I was doing."

"Georgina, there is absolutely no way that at twenty-two you knew anything," he says. "I have girls that age in class all the time, and they are just kids. I'm sorry, but he took advantage of you."

"That is a separate conversation to have. The reason I'm telling you all of this—and trust me, I never wanted to have to say any of it—is because last week someone began taunting me with some of those old photos. I thought it might be Simon, but in researching and tracking the IP address, I found out that he passed away in 2010."

"How awful," my mom gasps. "What happened to him?"

"Leukemia. It was so upsetting, especially considering what was going on, and I haven't had time to fully process his death, because this person who had my photos was posing as me on different websites, like Craigslist, and trying to entice men to meet up. By the time I realized this, it was too late."

Silence.

"Like I said, I am okay," I continue. "But there was a guy who showed up at my house and was forceful. He was under the impression that I had personally invited him there to have sex when of course I knew nothing about it. Luckily I was able to reason with him, but it was an awful few minutes."

It's too soon to give them the details. The shock and horror on their faces is enough.

"I called the police, and they were able to find out that it was Simon's daughter who was behind it all. She had moved back to attend UCLA and knew of me because she found those photos, and a letter from Simon, after he died."

"This is like a movie," my mum says, tearing up. "A horrible one."

"I know," I say, getting emotional at seeing her upset. "I'm so sorry for my role in it, but I didn't deserve what happened."

She gets up to give me a hug and sit by my side. It looks like a storm is brewing in my dad.

"Why didn't you tell us what was going on?" Mum asks.

"It all happened so fast. I was a mess. I haven't slept properly in days, and I didn't want you to worry. I was doing enough worrying for all of us."

"Well, all that matters is that you are okay," she says, wiping the tears from my cheek with her thumb.

I look over at my dad. His eyes are watery, something I've never seen before. "Dad," I say. "I'm sorry. I didn't want to upset you."

"I'm so sorry that you felt like you couldn't come to us," he says. "The thought of you dealing with this on your own is as upsetting as what you just told us."

"Maybe I should have come to you," I say. "Ever since the accident I've tried to be the model daughter, which is why I never told you about Simon. I didn't want you to be ashamed or think differently of me."

"We could never be ashamed of you. We're your parents and we love you unconditionally. One day, when you have your own child, you'll understand why we worry so much. You'll see how the love for your child is instant, and deeper than anything you could imagine. That's how we feel about you, Georgina." He's never spoken like this to me before, and it brings on a new level of emotion for me.

"I guess I always wanted to be strong. Even though I had you to support and love me, I wanted to do everything on my own and not come crying to you about it. I didn't want you to have to worry about me any more than you already did."

"We raised you to be strong, yes, but not to be a wall of steel. I often wished that you'd opened up to us more. Many times we felt a bit shut out of your life, particularly since the accident."

I'm surprised to hear him say this, but I understand. After all, I rarely tell them about whom I'm dating or what I do outside work. We usually stick to general subjects like our jobs, the weather and family gossip.

"I'm sorry for that," I say. "That's why I am here. I can't do *this* on my own."

My dad gets up to hug me. Feeling his tears on the side of my face breaks my heart into a million pieces. "All fathers want is to keep their daughters safe, and I'm sorry I couldn't do that," he says.

Emotionally exhausted, we agree that we will continue the conversation tomorrow. I get into bed, reading my old high school diary for entertainment until I'm too tired to keep my eyes open. For the first time since the photos surfaced in my inbox, I sleep like a baby.

■ ■ ■

"I have an idea," Mum says over breakfast the next morning. "Why don't we go to the fair today?"

"The three of us?" I ask, surprised, as we haven't done this since I was a child.

Held each summer at the Del Mar Fairgrounds, a short ride from our house, the San Diego County Fair is a popular summer attraction for tourists and locals. Along with rides and games, there's a car show, animals on display and exhibits. It isn't somewhere I would ever think to go unless I needed to entertain a group of children.

"That's a great idea," my dad chimes in. "Let's do it."

I agree. "I can be ready in half an hour."

Going to the fair is extremely out of character for my parents as well. As worldly as they are, they tend to enjoy staying in most nights, and when they do socialize, it's usually with intellectual types at dinner parties and book clubs. I can tell they are desperate to cheer me up and be there for me, and it's touching.

■ ■ ■

I'm still feeling sad, numb and exposed, but being surrounded by thousands of random people in broad daylight makes me feel safe somehow. There are too many distractions—a hypnotist, a giant Ferris wheel, Krispy Kreme cheeseburgers—for me to focus on my own thoughts, and for that I am relieved.

My dad and I throw darts at colorful balloons and try to drop Ping-Pong balls into goldfish bowls while my mum snaps photos of us on her iPhone. I watch as my parents get into an old-fashioned photo booth, kissing and making funny faces, and wonder if I'll ever find someone to share my life with. Right now, that feels completely impossible.

After a couple of hours we've had enough fun and head back to the car. "Have you thought about how long you'd like to stay?" my dad asks.

"At least a few days," I say, "if that's okay."

"Stay for as long as it takes," he replies, holding my hand as he did when I was a girl. "We're not going anywhere."

18

Yesterday I did something I haven't done since I was a senior in high school: I went to a therapist's office. Team Georgina—my parents, Detective Mendoza, and Rebecca—all agree that it is a good thing. I've been experiencing a solid amount of stress, fear and sleepless nights, and I'll do anything to start feeling better.

Barbara Stevenson came highly recommended to me from Lourdes, who probably has a Rolodex's worth of therapists to choose from due to her occupation and status as a native Angeleno. I figured I'd be more likely to show up if it was convenient, and her practice's office is just a few minutes from my house, so I took it as a sign. Normally I would do a solid amount of research before selecting a doctor, dentist, plumber or hairstylist, but right now I am unable to focus on reading Yelp reviews or asking for referrals from my inner circle. I trust

Lourdes enough to know that Barbara is a good place to start.

I made the short drive over and was feeling good about the fact that Barbara's building offered ninety minutes of free parking before it dawned on me that I was about to take an elevator five stories up to share my feelings with a total stranger. I briefly explained the Hannah/Will situation to Barbara over the phone last week when I booked the appointment, but I dreaded retelling the story from start to finish.

I was grateful that she didn't keep me waiting; anything longer than thirty seconds makes my mind race these days. The waiting room left a lot to be desired in terms of decor and style, and Barbara, who shook my hand and smiled warmly at me, wasn't how I imagined her to be. She has mousy brown hair, '80s oversize reading glasses and tanned skin. I would guess she's in her late fifties.

"I'll keep track of the time, so don't worry about that," she said once we'd sat down, she in an office chair and I on a plush love seat, with a coffee table between us. "Why don't you tell me a bit about yourself."

I felt myself go on autopilot. "I'm a journalist for the *L.A. Times*. I've lived here since 2000 and grew up near San Diego."

"Oh, San Diego is lovely."

"I just stayed there with my parents for a couple of weeks," I explained. "I needed that."

"Do you want to tell me a bit more about why you are here today?"

"Sure," I said, taking a deep breath and playing with the tassel of the blanket next to me.

As I told her the story of Simon and me, and Hannah, it felt like I was talking about someone else, or describing the plot of a recent Lifetime movie or an episode of *Dateline*. I was surprised I didn't cry—I've been doing plenty of that lately. Barbara took copious notes but also managed to hold eye contact most of the time. That impressed me. Before we had analyzed anything or come up with any solutions, the appointment was wrapping up. Even though it felt strange to be in her office, I liked her immediately and wanted to see her again. We had barely scratched the surface this hour.

"When do you want to come back?" she asked.

"As soon as possible, I guess."

■ ■ ■

"Good to see you again," Barbara says in her soothing, almost hypnotic voice. "How are you feeling today?"

"I'm sleeping for longer periods the last few days, which is good, but I'm not ready to go back to work just yet. I told my editor I needed a few weeks off, and he was fine with it. I haven't said no to a story in eight years."

"Well, I think that's smart, Georgina."

"It's hard to focus right now. I'm good for an hour or two and then something happens—a sound, or a UPS delivery—and I go right back to that day."

"That's extremely common, but I know it's still upsetting."

"I sometimes think I see Will when I'm just running errands, but of course it's never really him."

"Well, knowing he lives a few miles from you is certainly unsettling, but I think it's important to remember that he was only doing something he thought was okay with you," Barbara says. "He doesn't actually wish you any harm."

"I know. In a weird way, he's a victim of all this too, I suppose," I say. "Lately I've been meditating, too. It's funny because I always silently made fun of people for any sort of self-help thing, and now I realize how ridiculous that was. I feel like it's helping."

"That's wonderful to hear. How often are you doing it?"

"I meditate in the afternoon, when it's quiet around my house, for about twenty minutes. Sometimes it feels like a high, almost like an altered state."

"We call that transcendence."

"Sometimes I can't get my mind to quiet down or focus, but I continue anyway, because my yoga teacher said it's still doing me good."

"Do you think it is helping with your anxiety?"

"Yes, I do," I say. "I mean, it's not going to solve all of my problems, but I usually feel good afterward. At least for a little bit."

It's unusual to have someone ask me so many questions, since I'm the one who usually asks the questions. But am I giving the right answers? Barbara is not grading me on my responses, I remind myself, but I can't help wondering if I am reacting normally to all of this.

"And how are you feeling about what Hannah did to you right now?"

"I mean, she's obviously very disturbed. I'm sure she was traumatized finding those photos, so in some ways I feel bad for her. No teenage girl is equipped to handle something like that. But to think of what could have happened, and how many times she tried to make something like it happen, is just still so unbelievable to me. I mean, what if I actually had been raped? Would that have pleased her?"

"I know that must be so disturbing to even imagine."

"Do you think she's a sociopath?" I ask.

"I don't know enough about her to make such a diagnosis," Barbara demurs.

Part of me wants Barbara to just give me the answer. To say something like, "In my professional opinion, Hannah has a personality disorder, and you did nothing wrong." I am desperate to have some justification for Hannah's actions so that I can accept it and move on. I know Barbara will not give me what I want. I am going to have to work for it.

"Detective Mendoza said she was remorseful, and I guess sociopaths aren't remorseful unless they're just acting. So maybe she really is sorry."

"Does it matter if she is or isn't?" Barbara asks, jotting notes.

"Of all the things you could do to another woman, arranging for someone's rape is the absolute worst, aside from murder, right?" Barbara doesn't answer. "It's the kind of situation I never could have fathomed in a million years, and I'm pretty imaginative."

"I can understand how surprised you would be to find yourself in such a terrifying situation, especially as the photos were from so many years ago," she says. "But Georgina, I asked you how you felt about what Hannah did to *you*. Not your analysis of Hannah or *her* problems."

"Oh right, sorry," I say, fidgeting on the love seat. "It's hard to think about what she did to me without focusing on why she did it, and my role in that."

"That's okay," she says, smiling. "Just tell me how you feel."

"I'm not used to sharing feelings and emotions this openly," I explain. "I know we haven't gotten into my background very much since we just started."

"I'd love to know more about you if you'd like to share."

"My parents couldn't have any other children after me, so I'm like their one chance at success. I always subconsciously felt a pressure because of that. You know, to not mess up."

Barbara nods. "I see."

"They love me very much, but they didn't always show it in traditional ways. I was raised to be tough. Told that I could do anything boys could do, and if I had a problem, you just 'get on with it,' as my mum always says. I've only seen her cry maybe three or four times in my life."

"Really?" Barbara is scribbling on her lined pad again.

"Both of their cultures have that stiff-upper-lip mentality. You don't ask for help, you solve your own problems and take care of yourself, because no one else will."

"But they sound like they are helping you through this challenging time."

"Yes," I say, "they have handled this remarkably well. In some ways it's brought us closer together, and for the first time I can recall, I'm letting people help me."

"That's really wonderful. I'm pleased to hear it."

"I've been on my own for so long now that I sort of forgot what it felt like to have a community of people who care about me. I had a boyfriend for a few years and we lived together for most of that time, and it was really nice. But I managed to push him away, and I don't know why. Maybe that's something we can talk about later."

"Well, perhaps this tough shell you've had for so many years has something to do with it," she offers.

"Yeah," I say listlessly, surveying the ethnic art—wood carvings, embellished tapestries, African masks—on her walls.

"Sometimes we think it means we are weak if we depend on others," Barbara says. "Do you think that could be why you felt the need to do your own investigation rather than going to the authorities for help?"

"I guess I just don't like relying on people. If I can do it myself, why wouldn't I?"

"Well, I would suggest that when it comes to conducting a criminal investigation, a detective would certainly be far more experienced. It seemed like you didn't want to let him do his job."

"I was operating on pure adrenaline the day of the incident. I didn't want to just sit in a room when I could be doing something to speed things up," I say, feeling tears in my eyes. "I didn't want to feel like the victim. I know it was dangerous, but I had to try. I can't explain it. It's just who I am."

"So I'll ask you again, if you don't mind," Barbara says, passing me the tissue box across the coffee table. "How are you feeling about Hannah? About what happened?"

I dab my eyes and realize that I'm furious and sad and broken.

■ ■ ■

We have our fourth session two days later. I'm feeling more comfortable with Barbara and actually look forward to walking into the lobby, though I nervously hope I don't bump into any of the practice's other patients. I press the lighted button to signal that I'm there, and within a couple of minutes she appears with a warm smile. She asks me if have anything I'd like to discuss today. I do.

"I've been thinking a lot about Hannah and even feeling a bit of empathy for her, even though I'm still angry as well," I begin. "So it is confusing."

"That seems natural," Barbara says.

These past few days, I've been thinking that all bad behavior stems from some sort of hurt or pain. I've been thinking about the drug addicts on Skid Row, wondering what they ran away from. A child molester tells the *New York Times* that he was the victim of sexual abuse when he was a kid. The schoolyard bully at my godson Max's school is acting out because something is probably wrong at home.

I think about Hannah, who was so certain that I wanted to break up her family because of a few photos, and Simon, who felt entitled to an exciting sex life and got one, and Will, who figured that if some girl wanted to get roughed up by a stranger from the Internet, he might as well do it or someone else would.

"Hannah did what she did because she despised me for supposedly wrecking her family, and she was hurt and angry that she lost her father prematurely," I tell Barbara. "Maybe Will likes rape fantasy–type sex for some reason stemming from his childhood. Maybe he was made to feel small and now needs to feel powerful. Who knows? I guess it doesn't matter, now that what's done is done."

"That's very perceptive, Georgina."

"I was thinking about gang members as an example. They're tough and intimidating criminals who sometimes do horrible things, but at the end of the day it's because their families are not intact and the gang is a place to belong," I say, looking out the window at the traffic on the 405.

"I never thought of it that way."

"I did a story on a Westside gang last year. I didn't even know they existed in my neighborhood, but they do. In

Venice, Santa Monica, West L.A., you name it. I spent time with some of these guys."

"That sounds scary."

"They were actually really nice, but I'm sure I wouldn't feel that way if I were on the other end of one of their crimes. I guess what I'm trying to say is that if everyone felt loved, cared for and safe in this world, then things would be very different, right?"

"And I wouldn't have a job," she jokes.

But at what point do people have to take responsibility for their own actions? When do we say: Yes, these terrible things happened, but we are not going to ruin other people because of it. How much behavior can you blame on your family and circumstances? On being emotional or angry? What age is old enough to know better? Twenty? Forty? Sixty?

"You mentioned last time that the detective said Hannah wanted to apologize to you," Barbara says. "Have you given any more thought to that?"

"Yeah, that is not happening right now," I quickly say. "I think I've been gracious enough, all things considered."

"That is obviously your decision to make, but it might be beneficial to at least receive a letter or an email. Sometimes forgiveness is easier. You know, to officially close that chapter and move forward in life."

"I feel like I know all I need to know. I managed to get a transcript of her questioning, which she doesn't know. They don't normally let victims see that, but since I have a good relationship with the detective, I insisted and he allowed it as long as I didn't tell anyone."

"Anything you say here is confidential," Barbara assures me.

"I heard her whole side of it all and can appreciate that she's barely an adult and is troubled, which is why I didn't press charges."

"Is that the only reason? How do you think Simon would feel about all of this if he were alive?" Barbara asks, her face quizzical.

"I'm glad he didn't have to know anything about this," I say, feeling a lump in my throat and looking out of the window again. "He would have been completely heartbroken. I don't think he could have handled it."

"Of course."

"At the end of the day I'm not pressing charges, because I have no desire to go through the system with this case."

"Understandable."

"It would be so public, so on the record," I say. "I mean, imagine having to go in a courtroom and relive the whole thing again and put all of these sordid details out for a court reporter to transcribe and a jury of strangers to hear."

"It would be very difficult."

"Anyone could get their hands on the facts of the case, and I would never live it down. And having to face her? And probably her mother? I can't imagine doing that. I've done enough damage to their family, and they've done enough damage to me."

"It could feel like a re-victimization of sorts."

"I'm fiercely private as it is."

"Yes, you mentioned that last time."

"I write the story. I don't want to *be* the story."

"I see," Barbara says, adding to her notes. I want nothing more in this moment than to see her assessment of me, but I know that it's impossible.

"I'm interested in exploring why you are so private," Barbara says, and I realize it's time to tell her.

"When I was seventeen, three of my closest childhood friends were killed in a car accident."

"My goodness," she says, not writing anything. I can imagine she is thinking something along the lines of "Why didn't you mention this on day one?"

"It was a drunk driver, and they were sober. I mean, we used to drink a bit in those days, sneaking beers on the beach and going to parties, but it was early morning, before school."

"How did you find out about the accident?"

"I just happened to catch a ride that day with my other friend. But when we got to the beach, we didn't see them. So we got back in her car and went to go look for them. The wreckage was about a mile south, and police tape was already up."

"That is so tragic," she says.

"That whole time is like a blur," I continue. "I can only remember bits and pieces because I think I blocked out so much of the pain. I was absolutely shattered with grief."

"So how did you process such a devastating loss at a young age?"

"I saw a counselor, but it was too soon for me to open up. I didn't have the language to express myself and stopped going after a few times. I talked a lot with other friends from school, and of course my parents checked on me a hundred times a day, but it was very much a case of me being looked at as the lucky survivor, even though I wasn't even in the car that day."

"How so?"

"I was told incessantly that there must have been a reason I didn't get into the car with them, as though my friends made some cosmic mistake by just going about their day. Do you want to know the reason I didn't get in their car?"

"Of course I do."

"Because I had just bought a new CD, and Emily was the one with the CD player."

"Did you have any feelings of guilt because of that?"

"Constantly. I would wonder how such a small decision could be the difference between life and death. Sometimes I would question the larger meaning of it all, but I eventually realized there isn't one. The angels didn't need them. There was no bigger plan. Those are just things people tell themselves to feel better. It was a random, shocking event that would have happened to a different carload of people if it was even thirty seconds later."

"How did your family handle it?" Barbara asks.

"My parents became ridiculously overprotective, and how could I blame them? They were terrified of me driving and made it clear that I was to go to UC Irvine so I could be closer to home, even though I really wanted to go to NYU to pursue journalism. I think they were just as traumatized by the accident as I was.

"And how did that make you feel?"

"It felt like a lot of pressure," I admit, for the first time. "As if I had to live and pursue the dreams of my friends who died, but also had to be so careful in life because I was their only child and could be taken from them any minute. College was a welcome change for many reasons, and once I had some distance from the accident, I could understand that life was not like the movies or a fairy tale. It's complicated and filled with so much happiness and so much devastation."

"This is great progress, Georgina," Barbara says. "As we continue to work together, I think you may see how this tragic event helped shape who you are."

"Have you heard of Humans of New York?" I ask, referring to Brandon Stanton's popular blog that features portraits and short interviews of random strangers he meets.

"Yes," she says, perking up. "My son gave me the book for Christmas, and I loved it."

"Then you know he often asks people personal questions like 'What was the saddest day of your life?'"

"Yes."

"That accident was the saddest day of my life," I say, pinching the hem of my dress. "I will never get over it. I have learned to live with it, but I will never be okay with what happened."

"I am so sorry."

∎ ∎ ∎

Because I am still having some anxiety all these weeks later, Barbara teaches me a visualization technique. During my second session with her, she asked me what activity brought me pure joy and a sense of peace. Surfing, I told her.

"Why didn't you continue surfing when you moved to Los Angeles if it was such a big part of your life?" she asked.

"I think I was trying to reinvent myself by moving here, and maybe it didn't fit with my new life," I explained. "I never consciously thought about it, but I guess I wanted to be a sophisticated journalist and not seen as some sort of surfer babe."

"Well, I'm sure it's just like getting back on a bicycle, although I'd be terrified to find out," she said, laughing. "This technique I'm going to tell you about will be perfect for the beach. Close your eyes for a moment. Pretend you are sitting on the cool sand, looking out at the expansive ocean, and imagine that it holds your past, present and future."

"Okay," I replied, a bit skeptically.

"Over there is the day you were born," she said, her own eyes closed, "and there's your first day of kindergarten, and the night you went to prom. Then picture your present: your parents, friends, the work you do and the book you just finished reading."

"All right," I said, sneaking a peek with my left eye and closing it as soon as I saw she was still deep in the moment.

"Now imagine your future. You might take a vacation soon. Picture the future love of your life, the children you may have one day, or even something less serious that you're looking forward to, like the finale of your favorite television show."

"Okay."

"Then take your biggest worry and drop it into the ocean. See how tiny it looks?"

"Yes. I do."

"Your worry, whether it's Hannah, Will, explaining what happened to your friends or taking time off work, will seem much smaller compared to your huge and long life."

"Okay," I said, opening my eyes. "I get it. Thank you."

It's been working so far. I've been it doing every morning on the sand before I go surfing at Will Rogers State Beach. I got a new board, a six-foot-two, white epoxy funshape. And Barbara was right. After you've spent hundreds of hours in the water, reading the waves, paddling out, tasting the salt, popping up and riding, you don't forget how to do it.

I went back to my regular schedule at the yoga studio as well. Even though I started crying halfway through Friday's class, during pigeon pose, I figure that whatever can remind me to breathe and release negative energy is a good thing, and since I'm not working, going to my regular class is the least I can do. I'm not sure I believe in all the spiritual stuff, but I will try anything that will help me feel normal again.

"Take a deep breath from the tips of your toes all the way up through your chest," says Colette, a 105-pound

Midwest transplant who's my favorite teacher because she's the right mix of challenging and nurturing. "Now exhale from your chest all the way back down to your toes. Again. Deep inhale…hold it for a second…now exhale away all of your stress. Let the week just wash away."

Easy for her to say.

We do what feels like a thousand plank poses, and although my arms burn and my core starts to tremble, I like feeling strong. I've been struggling with my new status as a victim, wondering why I didn't do more to physically fight Will off when he entered my house. "You did the right thing," Detective Mendoza told me during our first conversation. "You're safe, and that's all that matters."

I surf on the days I don't go to yoga, and it's the only time in the day I feel truly happy.

"I know the water is freezing even in the summer—and aren't you afraid of sharks?" Rebecca asks during one of the three calls she now places to me each day.

"I have a wetsuit. Surfing is helping, and my therapist thinks it's a great idea. I can't believe I have a therapist, by the way, and I can now casually say things like 'my therapist says.' I am officially an Angeleno, after all these years."

"Well, I would make fun of you if I didn't absolutely agree that it was time to bring in a professional," she says. "Honestly G, you sound much better than the last couple weeks."

"The odds of being bit by a shark are one in eleven million."

"Did you just google that?"

"Yes." I laugh because she knows me too well. "And my chances of actually being killed by a shark are one in two hundred and sixty four million, so I'm not worried, and you shouldn't be either. It's scarier just driving back up San Vicente Boulevard with the entitled drivers of Brentwood."

"Okay, well, don't expect me to get in the water with you when I visit next week, but I'll watch and take pictures. Scott thinks it's so cool that you surf."

"You could at least go in knee-deep," I say, knowing I can guilt her into anything right now. "Nothing will happen to you. I'll protect you."

"Oh, fine."

■ ■ ■

Even though I have some dear friends here, like Lourdes, I haven't felt ready to discuss all the gory details with them yet, so it means everything that Rebecca is staying with me for a full week.

"I'm so glad you're here," I say as we hug curbside at LAX. "Thank you for coming."

"Don't thank me," she says, tossing her wheelie bag into my trunk. "This is my first time being away from the kids for more than a couple of days, and I'm not complaining. You know I love them more than life, but the thought of sleeping more than five hours makes me want to burst with joy."

I can't help but laugh. As someone with no kids and no snoring husband, I don't know how Rebecca does it.

"Of course I wish I was here under different circumstances," she says, turning serious for an instant, hugging me again.

"Yes, the whole thing was simply a ruse to get you out here," I say, trying to lighten the mood. "So what do you want to do? Do you need a nap?"

"Hell no, I don't need a nap," Rebecca says, applying ChapStick to her already dry lips. "I always forget how L.A. is a freaking desert."

I laugh and immediately feel the best I have since before the photo nightmare started. There is nothing quite like having your best friend by your side.

"Let's go to the beach," she suggests. "That's what I miss most about living in Southern California."

"Sounds good." We merge on the 405 Freeway North so we can grab some stuff at my place before heading to my secret spot, on the border of Santa Monica and Malibu.

After an unusually smooth ten-minute drive, we exit the freeway and Rebecca notices an IHOP. "I'm sorry, does that say 'valet parking'?" she says, incredulous that a pancake chain would need a professional car parker.

"L.A. loves its valet parking."

"And who are they?" she asks of the small group of Latino men standing near the underpass.

"Day laborers. I've never actually seen anyone pick one of these guys up to work on their homes, but it's a phenomenon on street corners and in Home Depot parking lots."

"Okay," she says suspiciously.

"You won't believe what Lourdes told me," I tell her. "You know how she's a divorce attorney? Well, she was representing an Orthodox Jewish woman, because her Hasidic husband was picking up day laborers and having sex with them."

"You have to be kidding."

"Lourdes said it's a real problem, because it's very down low and they're having unprotected sex."

She gasps. "Jesus."

"Are you hungry?"

"After that story, no." She laughs. "But I will be soon."

"We should pick up Kogi and take it to the beach. It will change your life, which sounds like hyperbole, but I'm completely serious."

"Yes, please. I think we could all go for a little life changing these days."

■ ■ ■

After sitting on the warm sand for a bit, I ask Rebecca what is going on with her marriage. Even though we talk a lot, the kids are always there, so it's hard to really go deep with anything.

"We've been going to counseling for a solid month now," she says, "which isn't as bad as I thought. The hardest part of it is just making the time, hiring a sitter and lining up our schedules."

"Who'd have ever thought we'd both be in therapy at the same time?"

"I know," she says, laughing. "We were probably the least likely candidates, but here we are."

"Has he fully come clean about everything?"

"Yes, definitely. I was right. There was no physical relationship, but there was an emotional one for sure, which in some ways hurts even more."

"Of course," I say. "It's still a betrayal."

"I was so angry for those first couple weeks that all I could think about was leaving him. The man I married would never do such a thing. I thought he was as honest as they come."

"Me too," I say, remembering their wedding day and how in love they were.

"Part of me wonders what would have happened if I hadn't seen those emails," she adds. "He swears he wouldn't, couldn't, cross that line, but it's hard for me to believe that."

"What does the therapist think?"

"He's been so great, helping us finally connect again, getting us talking openly and honestly. And I have to take some responsibility on my end as well. Scott brought up the fact that I often treat him like one of the kids, as opposed to my husband. After having Max we were still good, but the twins added a level of stress, and of course joy, that I never could have imagined. We went from man-to-man to zone defense."

"Well, you've done an amazing job with them," I say, thinking of my adorable godson and his crazy sisters. "And if you guys can survive this and stay connected, then you're only going to be a better, happier mom."

"Exactly," she says. "I just lost myself for a few years there. I mean, did you ever think that *I* would lose my sex drive?"

"Um, no." I laugh. "I have to admit I was shocked when you said you guys weren't sleeping together."

"Well, things have gotten back on track in that department, and I'm seeing him in a different light, like how I saw him when we first met. It's actually nice, dating your husband again."

"I'm so glad," I tell her. "I know it can't be easy, but it sounds like you guys are surviving it."

"We are," she says, placing her hand on mine for a moment. "But if he pulls anything like this again, I'll be out of there faster than you can say *trial separation.*"

"I'll help you pack," I joke. "But seriously, you know how I've never been the marrying kind?"

"How could I forget? I remember how in college, during your feminist awakening in that women's studies class, you would get real heated up about how marriage is an antiquated institution, how it was about ownership and protecting land, and how it's irrelevant to a modern society where people can live until they're ninety and have sex for fun and not just procreation. You were very passionate about the topic," she says.

"I was very impressionable back then," I admit. "I've been talking about this a lot with Barbara—about why I never seemed to believe in marriage when my own parents have a happy one."

"And?"

"Barbara thinks it could also be connected to the loss I suffered at a young age—a fear of fully letting people in because they might leave or die. It sounds so clichéd it's embarrassing, but it's probably true. And she, or I should say we, think that the affair with Simon did not help the situation. Having my second sexual partner in life, and someone I did care enormously about, be a man who was cheating on his wife was not healthy for my romantic psyche."

"I could have told you that for free."

I run a handful of sand through my fingers. "Lately I've been wondering a lot about what my life would be like if I never went to that film screening. Would it be better? Would I have still met Justin and said yes to his proposal instead of driving him away? Would I have children by now? Or would I have settled for something less because I didn't know any better?"

"I know this might sound weird considering what you've just been through, but I don't think the affair was right or wrong," Rebecca says. "It opened you up in a lot of ways and definitely helped break you out of your good-girl persona. You seemed more confident and happier after meeting him."

"He made me feel extraordinary. I started seeing myself the way he saw me. I can't regret it for that reason alone. He used to tell me that I saved him from drowning.

I would say that he made me feel alive. Maybe those are just the things we tell ourselves, and each other, to justify inconvenient desire."

"Well, we just need to find you a Simon type who is single and doesn't have a psycho daughter," Rebecca says. "Is it too soon to joke about her?"

"Probably."

"But seriously. You know from Justin that it is possible to fall in love with someone else. Simon may have been a soul mate, but he's not the only one in existence."

"Barbara said I'm too logical and could be more emotional. She thinks I shouldn't worry so much about divorce rates and stereotypes of marriage and should be open to whatever comes."

"Well, as someone who recently faced the worst moment in my marriage, I can say that it's worth trying," Rebecca says. "There are no guarantees in life, you know that. If you meet someone you fall in love with, who you think you could make a life with, then why not at least try? Maybe it will last ten years, or maybe it will last a lifetime. Marriage is not always easy, but there is something special about having someone by your side—being part of a team."

"Sometimes I miss Justin. But I wasn't ready then and tried to do the right thing. Now he's married to some Web designer."

"You say it like she's an arms dealer for Al-Qaeda."

"I'm sure she's great," I say, though I feel a tinge of jealousy. "He wouldn't settle for less. Plus, I had unresolved

Simon stuff to deal with before I could have married him, or anyone."

"I know you've been through hell, but maybe this will all be a good thing in the end," Rebecca suggests.

"It sounds crazy, but I think you're right. For the first time since college, I feel optimistic about the future. I'm not up for dating right this second, but I'm open to a new way of life, and that is progress."

"I'm proud of you."

"Thanks," I say, starting to blush. "You ready to grab a drink?"

"Absolutely."

19

I have never been happier to have someone staying in my home, because I almost fell off my chair after checking my email this morning.

"Bec!" I shout from my office so she can hear me through the noise of the hair dryer.

"What's wrong?" She runs in, her hair half wet.

"Look." I point to the bolded unread email in my inbox.

"Who is Clare Morrow?" she asks before quickly answering her own question. "Oh my God, G. Open it."

As much as I love Rebecca, I have to read it in private first.

From: Clare Morrow
To: Georgina Park
Date: September 3, 2013 at 06:11 AM
Subject: Thank you

Georgina,

First and foremost, I must apologise for everything that has gone on. You're probably still a bit shell-shocked from the entire experience, which would be completely understandable. I am so relieved that nothing more serious happened.

I know you don't have children, but I'm sure you can imagine how difficult it is for an already troubled teenager to deal with a divorce, much less the death of a beloved parent shortly after. This does not excuse what happened; it is just what set things in motion.

Hannah always blamed me for the marriage ending, and we've had a tense relationship since the time she was about eleven years of age. But it seems that in the revelation of your existence after her dad's passing, she transferred all of that and more on to you, even though it was not warranted.

Simon and Hannah's relationship had been quite strained while he was married to his second wife, who was a real nutter by the way, but after that divorce, when she was fourteen, things were much better between them. They were back to being close, and he was very involved in all of her activities and sports.

She simply idolised Simon, so to know that he was not exactly who she thought, and that he kept secrets from her—and all of us, really—was too much for her to take. However, I fully underestimated her capability for something like this.

No one deserves what happened to you. I hope you know that.

I'm sure Detective Mendoza explained the entire story to you, but just so you know, Simon had a short amount of time to get his affairs in order. He updated his will, moved some finances around and began gathering personal items that he wanted to leave to his closest friends and family. One of those people was you.

We were to have a barrister friend of ours handle the dispersing of these effects after his death, but Hannah took it upon herself to do so, perhaps in an effort to do one last thing for her beloved dad. When she found the package meant for you, she was surprised, since she recognised all of the other names in the group. Out of curiosity, she simply googled your name to try and understand the connection. I believe it was all fairly innocent until she saw that you were young and beautiful.

Confused as to why Simon would be so close to a woman in Los Angeles whom she had never heard of, she opened and read a sealed letter he had written you while he was undergoing treatment. She kept it to herself for years. I had no idea of its existence until now.

For two years after his death, she went a bit off the rails, hanging with the wrong crowd and dabbling in horrible things like cutting and drinking too much with her friends. Somehow she always made excellent marks in school. She is incredibly bright and had begged me to let her go back to the States, where she still had childhood friends and citizenship. I think she thought going back to L.A., which she always saw as her real home, would make things better, and that she wouldn't have to deal with the reality of Simon being gone.

I told her that she could go for university if she lived with family friends of ours in Rancho Park. She agreed, and everyone was thrilled when she was accepted into UCLA a year later. She wrote an incredible admissions essay about losing her dad. Eventually she convinced me to have her stay in the dorms on campus.

At some point before leaving, she found those photos and kept her own copies. I cannot explain why, and she hasn't really been able to articulate it either. The word fixation is what comes to mind. I blame Simon for keeping them somewhere so easily accessible. Apparently they were on an old external hard drive in his home office, and Hannah was determined to find any correspondence or proof that he'd indeed had an extramarital affair.

Over the years she kept tabs on you online. She knew you were a successful writer who lived in Los Angeles, and I think when she realised that you were both at UCLA, a sheer coincidence, something snapped inside of her. She said she initially just wanted to see you in person, to see who you were and what you were like, but that wasn't enough to satiate her growing obsession with you and her father and whatever had happened in the past. In her mind, *this affair went on for years, not months, and was the reason for the divorce. If she had just asked me, I could have assured her that this was not the case.*

I think she hoped to confront you or have a discussion about it, but being eighteen and highly emotional, that just wasn't a reality. I know she had questions for you, but I suppose she had no idea how to go about it. Her brother, Michael, now knows of the situation as well, but was not devastated the way Hannah was. Being four years older, and finding out at a more advanced age, he was able to process the news, but he hasn't said much about it. He is finishing a degree in environmental studies at University of Melbourne. We all feel tremendous guilt about what transpired and I hope one day you can forgive her, but I also understand if you cannot.

I'm sure you want to know more about what happened to Simon as well. In early 2010, he was diagnosed with acute myelogenous leukemia (called AML), which is a type of cancer that causes the body to make a huge number of white blood cells. But these cells do not fight infection very well, the way our normal white blood cells do. When the leukemia cells build up in the blood and bone marrow, there's less room for healthy ones, so infections, bleeding and anemia become commonplace.

I remember noticing that he was losing weight; in fact he was bragging that he was down ten kilos one afternoon at Michael's rugby match. But he was very ill soon after. It seemed he was often tired after doing the simplest of tasks. There's no explanation or reason as to why it happened.

I got involved when our son told me that Simon was having night sweats and a feeling of fullness in his abdomen. The health reporter at my network arranged a visit to the top oncologist in Sydney, and he was diagnosed after some blood work. It was heartbreaking for everyone, as he was so loved by many of us, not to mention the Australian public, who always held him in such high regard.

Normally a bone marrow or stem cell transplant (if you can find a match, that is) has a 50 percent chance of curing the disease, but Simon's was so advanced that there was no hope of that. He endured chemo and other treatments to try and prolong his life, but in the end he only had a few short months. It was devastating for us all, and heartbreaking to tell his eighty-two-year-old mother, who simply adored him.

He died peacefully in hospital and was able to say goodbye to the people he loved most. That included you; you just didn't know at the time.

I'm sure you never imagined all of this when you first met Simon more than a decade ago. I never could have either, but I appreciate your care in handling the situation with Hannah. You protected her from serious, warranted punishment and a digital trail that would have never been erased. You didn't have to. I know you did it for Simon, and I know he would have been pleased.

Hannah has transferred to the University of Sydney and is getting the help she obviously needs in the form of regular counseling. She is incredibly sorry and ashamed, but respects your wish to not have any communication at this time.

I also just want you to know that I do not blame you for anything, Georgina. As much as I loved Simon, we were living a bit like brother and sister in those years. Perhaps "the one" at age twenty-five is not "the one" later in life. He tried many times to spark the romance in our relationship, and I resisted each time. I don't know why. He was a lovely man, but I don't think he was meant to be mine.

Sometimes people fall out of love and there is no real explanation. Work and kids get in the way of making yourself, let alone your partner, a priority. Even though we weren't successful in marriage, we always remained friends until the end. I do wish you the best.

Sincerely,
Clare

I'm surprised she is letting me off the hook so easily. There is no attack or cruel dig, even though I slept with her husband and helped cause a chain of events that ended with her daughter nearly jailed for solicitation of rape. But more than that, I am hit with a wave of sadness, knowing the details about Simon's leukemia symptoms and treatment. Of course I've obsessed on the scenario a million times in my head and researched the disease online, but seeing it in black and white is particularly heartrending.

"Bec."

"Coming."

"Read it," I say, stepping out for a moment to grab a tissue.

After she finishes, she lies back in my office chair and exhales deeply. "Unreal," she says. "It's amazing how calm she sounds about it all. I suppose it's been a long time since she was in love with Simon. I guess it's not a fresh wound for her."

"I'm honestly not sure if they ever had a great love, but of course they had something huge—a family. Their kids are them, you know?"

"Are you going to write her back?"

"Not right now," I say. "I need to process, as Barbara would say."

"Please don't go all New Age on me."

"I'm going to consult my crystals first," I tease. "Then I may read some tea leaves before coming up with a response."

"Are you okay?" she asks, turning more serious.

"Yes. Grief is just one of those things that can take over at any minute. It's hard hearing details about Simon's death, but it's better than not knowing."

"It hasn't been all that long since you first found out," she encourages. "And what's happened since certainly hasn't helped."

"I feel terrible that the affair caused so much pain for Hannah. She probably doesn't trust anyone. I even feel guilty about you and Scott. Like I'm part of some larger conspiracy of women who mess up marriages, even if it wasn't my intention."

"Don't be ridiculous," she says. "You are you and Scott is Scott. And let's not forget that married TA I slept with in college. For all I know, he told his wife and she could have left him because of it. At the end of the day the blame falls on Simon, but he's the only one not here to receive punishment."

"Well, you could say that he suffered the most," I say quietly.

"I just mean he was the one who was married, not you, and he was older, wiser and knew better," she says. "I still blame him for what happened to Hannah, and eventually to you."

"I blame all of us."

■ ■ ■

The following evening, Rebecca passes out on my sofa after a marathon of uninterrupted TV watching ("You have no idea what it feels like to be able to watch something that isn't Nickelodeon," she said gratefully), and I go to my office.

From: *Georgina Park*
To: *Clare Morrow*
Date: *September 5, 2013 at 10:37 PM*
Subject: Re: *Thank you*

Hi Clare,

Thank you so much for your email. I never wanted you to know of my existence and I am so sorry for the way my relationship with Simon revealed itself. You don't know much about me, but I can assure you that I am truly mortified at the idea of Hannah discovering those images, especially as she was a teenager in the midst of grieving for her father. It's not okay for a child, or anyone for that matter, to learn of such a thing so explicitly. The thought of her keeping it a secret, and having to formulate opinions of her father and his past, and your marriage, is so upsetting. Of course we all wish she had handled it differently. We were just minutes away from our lives being forever changed. I hope she is getting the help she needs so that she can go on to live the wonderful life she deserves.

I also want to apologize to you for any harm or stress I have caused you personally. I was 22 when I met Simon at a work event. I never thought about dating a married man, but it is indeed what happened, and oftentimes I couldn't believe that I was taking part in an affair. And while I was *mature for my age, I had no real concept of the seriousness and meaning of marriage back then. I was able to rationalize my behavior while it went on, but in the end I knew it was wrong and potentially dangerous.*

I regret the deep pain our affair caused to Hannah (and probably Michael too, even if he hasn't yet said so), but I can't regret knowing Simon. He helped shape the person I am today. Forgive me if this is overstepping, but I thought you should know that he desperately wanted to keep his family together, even if he went about it the wrong way.

If you have any questions that need answering, please don't hesitate to ask. Everything is in the open now, for better or worse.

Best wishes,
Georgina

EPILOGUE

OCTOBER 2013

I'm all packed and expect the movers any minute now. After everything that's transpired, I've decided to sell my house and move on. It's hard to continue living here, even though I know I'm as safe as I was before Will turned up. Just as my realtor predicted, my little bungalow on Ocean Park was on the market for less than twenty-four hours before we were fielding multiple cash offers from hopeful couples who pled their case via sweet letters and home-baked cookies. I went with the fastest closing—a newly married pair of lawyers, who met in court as opposing counsel on a divorce case—and didn't look back.

I don't mean to run away; it's just time for a fresh start. I've been in this city for thirteen years, far longer than I'd ever anticipated.

After giving away boxes of stuff and selling some furniture to Eli at a huge discount, I arranged to put some of my possessions in storage for a few months while I figure things out. The small group of friends I've told about my departure continue to pepper me with questions:

"Where will you go?"

"What will you do?"

"Won't you miss having a byline?"

"When are you coming back?"

It's the first time in my life that I don't know my next move.

I'm going to stay with my parents in Carlsbad for a couple of weeks, which makes them very happy, and then I'll buy a plane ticket to someplace far away, where no one knows me or what happened on Ocean Park. After paying the mortgage, realtor commission and escrow fees, I have a surplus of around $176,000 sitting in my checking account. It's a comforting feeling, and a lot of responsibility. Of course I'll save most of it, but it's nice to not have to worry about chasing Eric Garcetti around all week so I can write an 800-word article on his personal style in order to pay the week's bills. After more than a decade, I've grown a bit tired of telling everyone else's stories.

As I take a box to my car, I notice a small package near a pool of water created by the sprinklers. Even on my last day here, the mail carrier can't bother to ring the bell or set it on the doormat. I can tell it's an international delivery by the stamped customs form affixed to the box, and immediately I know what it is. Just in time. I bring it inside and use my car key to slice the shipping tape. The padded envelope inside it reads, "This belongs to you. I'm sorry it took so long," in pretty blue cursive. I wonder what Simon would think of his ex-wife and his ex-mistress corresponding with each other.

There's another envelope inside. It reads "From the Estate of Simon Grant" and contains a stately black Montblanc pen in a lined case that I remember him using when we were together at that bed and breakfast in Laguna Beach so many years ago. Along with the pen is a letter written on elegant monogrammed stationery. I unfurl the ecru-colored pages and see his handwriting for the very first time, three years too late, and the little hairs on the back of my neck stand at attention. It feels strange to be holding something that he touched. Just seeing his name brings tears to my eyes.

I take a deep breath before reading the first line.

> *Georgina,*
>
> *By now you know what has been too difficult for me to tell you. Selfishly, I suppose I always wanted you to remember me in a certain way. I know we've emailed here and there over the years, but we haven't properly caught up in so long that I don't even know where to start.*
>
> *Overall I am happy with my life, and the regrets really are just a few: working too much when the children were young, getting married for a second time, and losing touch with you, Georgina. Even if we could have had one last day together, it would have been worth everything. Remember you once suggested that I join you in Fiji for a press trip you were going on for that new hotel? I was so busy*

with the kids and work, but why didn't I just say yes? I reckon that anyone who would say no to five days with you in paradise is an absolute fool.

I often wonder why I'm still thinking of you so many years later. Lovers and partners and wives have come and gone, but you are still very much here with me. Does that please you? I hope so. I think the sexiest thing about you was your mind. You were always thinking, always curious and always ready to give an opinion. This is not to say that your full lips and the slope of your lower back are not things I think about on a regular basis, but I just wanted you to know that your brain was what kept me interested.

You are such an unusual person. Do you finally realise that? Surely you must see what all the fuss is about by now. I can only imagine how much more dynamic, interesting and engaging you are today. Even at 22, you already knew who you were. For some, this takes decades, or a lifetime. I should have come back to make a bold gesture, to prove to you that I was serious. But I wanted to respect your wishes, so instead I fondly remember our time together.

I loved that you were always up for an adventure, and I imagine you have had many of them since we last met. Lucky for me, I remember so many of our days together as though they were yesterday. And I'm never jealous when I think of you with someone else, Georgina. I just hope the lucky bastard knows that you are as good as it will ever be for him.

Sometimes, when I am feeling all soppy, I google you. I love reading your stories because there's always a piece of you in them. I picture you coming up with your list of questions and unnerving your subject with your charm and confidence (not to mention that face). One flash of that smile and it's over for them. Of course they'll tell you anything you want to know.

I recently watched a video of you moderating a panel at a writing conference at Stanford. You were very funny, and I see you haven't aged at all since we were last together. How is that possible? I'm afraid you may not recognise me at the moment.

Hooked up to machines that don't allow more than a few hours of uninterrupted sleep, I often dream of you and me together. We are living near the ocean, somewhere outside of the city, where the trees are lush and the sounds of nature envelop the house. Is it Los Angeles or Sydney? Does it matter?

It always starts with you lying on your side, facing me, asleep. I run my hand along the deep curve of your waist and down to your hip and see you begin to stir. The summer morning light is streaming in our bedroom through a big window, making your skin an even deeper shade of gold. I already know the first thing you are going to say when you awake.

I watch as you open your eyes and wonder how I got so lucky to be next to such a gorgeous creature. When you look at me and smile, with your long hair still splayed over the pillow and without a stitch of makeup on, you are the most beautiful you could ever be.

Hi, you say. Did you sleep okay?

Yes darling, with you, I did.

I grab the newspaper, start the coffee and come back to bed to read a few stories before heading into work. I feel your big brown eyes peering over to get a glimpse of the headlines as you stroke the back of my arm.

That's when I always wake up. I so wish I could know what happens next, Georgina.

I'm unsure how to say goodbye to you, as it was hard enough the first time, but I thought you could at least have something to remember me by. Life isn't always fair, is it? I don't know why we met when we did. I guess sometimes you find each other at the wrong time in life. But I'm grateful for the days we had together. Thank you for saying yes that night in the French restaurant. Your uncharacteristic moment of spontaneity just might have been the best thing that could have happened to me.

Always,
Simon

P.S. I know your busy mind is wondering, so I'll just say it. Yes, it was love. Of that I am certain. By now I hope you are, too. I don't know who is sleeping next to you now, but I hope he is as happy to watch you wake up as I am in my dreams.

I fold the letter back into its envelope and place it and the pen in my bag. The moving truck pulls up as I wipe a messy stream of tears from my face. I don't have time to fully absorb what I've just read, so I look up to the sky to attempt to counteract gravity before putting on a welcoming smile for the muscular man who is knocking at the door, clipboard in hand.

"Hi, Miss Park," he says. "I'm Darnell."

"Please just call me Georgina," I say, shaking his hand. "Come in."

"Damn girl, you are really organized, aren't you?" he marvels, looking at the stacks of color-coordinated plastic bins I'm using for the move.

"The green ones are going to the storage unit, I'm taking the clear ones myself, and the rest are going to the Carlsbad address," I explain.

"Okay, got it," he says, then starts counting each stack.

"Once you're done loading, you can follow me to the storage place."

Darnell notices my pink nose and wet cheeks. "You're sad to move?" he asks me.

"Yeah," I say quietly. "I guess I am."

"Well, we'll take good care of your things, so don't worry," he says, motioning to his partner in the truck. "We do this all day, every day. We're the best in the business."

"That's what I hear."

"I just need you to sign here so we can start." He hands me the paperwork on a plastic clipboard. "Do you need a pen?"

"No, it's okay," I say. "I have one right here."

■ ■ ■

ONE MONTH LATER

"Remember that guy, Phillip, I worked with in the pub when I was nineteen?" I ask Rebecca over Skype from the diminutive flat in London I'm renting for a few months.

"He was hilarious," she says. "I remember having so much fun with him when I visited you there."

"He owns a pub now. In Shoreditch."

"Are you going to get in touch with him?"

"I don't know. I'm not sure."

"Why the hell else would you be looking for him online?"

I laugh; I still can't get anything past her. "You're right. I may stop in for a drink one night and see if he remembers me."

"Of course he will, G," she says. "How many Asian girls from California do you think he's worked with over the years? You're kind of hard to forget, in case you hadn't noticed."

I know she's referring to Simon's letter, which I read to her over the phone before tucking it away in the fireproof safe that's currently sitting in my parents' garage. The little wombat he gave me in Century City and the pen are there, too.

"I feel like I owe it to him to at least say hello, but he could be married, for all we know."

"If that's the case, then you know what to do, right?" Rebecca sounds like she's speaking to one of her kids. "You just say hi and then leave. You do not laugh over drinks. You do not go to a hotel. You do not have an affair."

I roll my eyes. "Yeah, yeah, I got it. Sex is honestly the last thing on my mind right now. I'm not ready to date yet. I just thought it would be nice to see a familiar face. He was kind to me, and the least I can do is patronize his pub."

"Well, I'd better go," she says. "I have to get breakfast ready for the kids before I head out."

"Where are you shooting today?"

"The National Portrait Gallery," she says, unable to crack another joke this time, as we both know it's a big deal.

"I'm so proud of you."

"Thanks." She's blushing. "I'm proud of you, too."

After staying with my parents for a full month, I decided to come to London on an open-ended ticket. I needed a break from Los Angeles, and that's exactly what I got. I'm freelancing for *The Telegraph*, doing similar profiles to the ones I did at home except with more serious subjects, and I love it. I'm doing the kind of work I used to dream of. In my spare time I take the Tube to flea markets, though I rarely buy anything, and have managed to stay out until two in the morning carousing in pubs with my twenty-something cousins Katie and Hayden. They make me feel young and carefree again.

My parents are visiting next month, which I'm really looking forward to, and after that, Rebecca and Scott are going to stay for a night or two on their way to a romantic Italian vacation, sans kids. It will be their first trip alone since their honeymoon. Eventually I'll go back home; I'm American, after all. But I'm in no real rush. Skype, email and Gchat make living abroad much easier this time around, and aside from missing the sunshine and the beach, I've adjusted quite well.

Even though I'm in a country Simon and I were never in together, I still find myself thinking of him. Not every day, but when something reminds me of him: hearing "California Dreamin'" in a restaurant when it's raining sheets of gray, anytime I pass a Thomas Pink shop, and mostly when I'm visiting Parliament for work. Sometimes, after interviewing an MP, I grab a sandwich from Pret A Manger and sit near the Thames, watching groups of tourists and schoolchildren pass by. I know he'd be pleased that I came here, and that makes me happy.

I feel more like myself, maybe an even better version, now that a few months have passed since the Hannah incident. She and I both went through trauma as teens, pushing our grief down, but hers boiled over first. I sometimes feel sorry for my old self, the girl who needed to be so fiercely independent and couldn't open up to people without feeling weak or pathetic. Today I happily lean on whatever and whomever I need so I can keep putting one foot in front of the other. I even stay in touch with Barbara over email and find myself missing our chats.

I'm sleeping better here and have found an excellent yoga studio in my neighborhood (for the record, I no longer cry in class). I've already made three friends: two expats like me, and one lifelong Londoner also named Georgina, funnily enough. They don't know about everything yet, but I will tell them if we become close, because it's part of me and that's okay. Most days I walk for ages, something I could never really do in Los Angeles. I get lost in neighborhoods I've never heard of and read books in cafés I don't remember the names of. I see my auntie and uncle on Sunday evenings for home-cooked dinners and feel safe in their cozy little flat. I feel safe in my own, too. Life is pretty good. I can't complain.

One day I may even find someone who would be excited to watch me wake up in the morning. That would be lovely.

ACKNOWLEDGEMENTS

First and foremost, I want to thank my parents, who never once questioned my desire to be a writer and encouraged me every step of the way. Thank you, Chelsea and Brian, for your love and support of everything that I do. My sweet and funny cheerleaders, Emily Brandwin and Nancy McNamara, read the earliest pages I wrote and gave me the confidence to continue. Special thanks to Jill Hooven (who read the first draft on her iPhone while we were in Mexico), Karyn Millet, Regina Huston, Tara Kristick, Jodi Cohen and Jessica Ramakrishnan, for being enthusiastic early readers.

Margaret Sutherland Brown, Michael Gleeson and Catherine Lowe made invaluable contributions to the manuscript for which I am grateful. Detective Lissa Redmond aided me with my procedural questions about police work and charmed me during our phone and email conversations. Tiffany Hawk, Dianne Namkung, Kimberly Brooks, Matt Hooven and Topher Hopkins also provided me with assistance.

Much appreciation to the editors who gave me my start in journalism many years ago: Kean Wong, Eric Mercado, Glynis Costin, Alice Short and Christina Dalton. And to Kip Fulbeck, for helping me find my voice at age 19, when I thought I had nothing to say. Thank you, Anjali Parker, for always being there.

And most of all, to my husband, Tim, who is better than any character I could ever invent.

ABOUT THE AUTHOR

Victoria Namkung has written for the *Los Angeles Times*, *InStyle*, *USA Today*, The Huffington Post, *Los Angeles* and style.com, among other publications. She received her undergraduate degree from UC Santa Barbara and her master's degree from UCLA. She lives in Los Angeles.

VictoriaNamkung.com
Facebook.com/VictoriaNamkung
@VictoriaNamkung

44071212R00207

Made in the USA
Charleston, SC
17 July 2015